...rea H. Japp

...in 1957, Andrea H. Japp trained as a toxicologist and is the ...r of twenty novels. She is the French translator of Patricia ...well and has also written for television.

...za Garcia

...za Garcia translates from French and Spanish. Her two ...recent translations are *The Père-Lachaise Mystery* by ...le Izner, which she co-translated with Isabel Reid, and ...*le in My Head* by Mathilde Monaque.

1

L...
are...
a...

THE SEASON OF THE BEAST

THE SEASON OF THE BEAST

ANDREA H. JAPP

Translated by Lorenza Garcia

GALLIC BOOKS
LONDON

This book is published with support from the French Ministry of
Culture/Centre National du Livre.

A Gallic Book

First published in France as *La Dame Sans Terre 1: Les Chemins de la Bête*
Calmann-Lévy

First published in Great Britain in 2008 by Gallic Books,
134 Lots Road, London, SW10 0RJ

A CIP record for this book is available from the British Library

ISBN 978-1-906040-10-9

Typeset in Fournier MT by SX Composing DTP, Rayleigh, Essex
Printed and bound by Creative Print and Design, Wales

Mr Feng,
Tender and serious little soul,
Friendly wind,
This tale from far ago is for you.

CONTENTS

AUTHOR'S NOTE

Words marked with an asterisk are explained in the Historical References and Glossary starting on page 334.

Manoir de Souarcy-en-Perche, Winter 1294

AGNÈS de Souarcy stood before the hearth in her chamber calmly contemplating the last dying embers. During the past weeks both man and beast had been beset by a deadly cold that seemed intent on putting an end to all living things. So many had already succumbed that there was barely enough wood to make coffins, and those left alive preferred to use what little there was to warm themselves. The people shivered with cold, their insides ravaged by straw-alcohol, their hunger only briefly kept at bay with pellets of suet and sawdust or the last slices of famine bread made from straw, clay, bark or acorn flour. They crowded into the rooms they shared with the animals, lying down beside them and curling up beneath their thick, steamy breath.

Agnès had given her serfs permission to hunt on her land for seventeen days, or until the next new moon, on condition they distribute half the game they killed among the rest of the community, beginning with widows, expectant mothers, the young and the elderly. A quarter of what remained would go to her and the members of her household and the rest to the hunter and his family. Two men had already flouted Agnès de Souarcy's orders, and at her behest the bailiffs had given them a public beating in the village square. Everybody had praised the lady's leniency, but some expressed private disapproval; surely the perpetrators of such a heinous crime deserved execution or the excision of hands or noses – the customary sentences for poaching. Game was their last chance of survival.

Souarcy-en-Perche had buried a third of its peasants in a communal grave, hastily dug at a distance from the hamlet for fear that an epidemic of cholera might infect those wraiths still walking. They had been sprinkled with quicklime like animal carcasses or plague victims.

In the icy chapel next to the manor house the survivors prayed day and night for an improbable miracle, blaming their ill luck on the recent death of their master, Hugues, Seigneur de Souarcy, who had been gored by an injured stag the previous autumn, leaving Agnès widowed, and no male offspring to inherit his title and estate.

They had prayed to heaven until one evening a woman collapsed, knocking over the altar she had been clinging to, and taking with her the ornamental hanging. Dead. Finished off by hunger, fever and cold. Since that day the chapel had remained empty.

Agnès studied the cinders in the grate. The charred wood was coated in places with a silvery film. That was all, no red glow that would have enabled her to postpone any longer the ultimatum she had given herself that morning. It was the last of the wood, the last night. She sighed impatiently at the self-pity she felt. Agnès de Souarcy had turned sixteen three days before, on Christmas Day.

It was strange how afraid she had been to visit the mad old crone; so much so that she had all but slapped her lady's maid, Sybille, in an attempt to oblige the girl to go with her. The hovel that served as a lair for this evil spirit reeked of rancid mutton fat. Agnès had reeled at the stench of filth and perspiration emanating from the soothsayer's rags as she approached to snatch the basket of meagre offerings: a loaf of bread, a bottle of fresh cider, a scrap of bacon and a boiling fowl.

'What use is this to me, pretty one?' the woman had hissed. 'Why, the humblest peasant could offer me more. It's silver I want, or jewels – you must surely have some of those. Or why not that handsome fur-lined cloak of yours?' she added, reaching out to touch the long cape lined with otter skin, Agnès's protection.

The young girl had fought against her impulse to draw back, and had held the gaze of this creature they said was a formidable witch.

She had been so afraid up until the woman had reached out and touched her, scrutinised her. A look of spiteful glee had flashed across the soothsayer's face, and she had spat out her words like poison.

Hugues de Souarcy would have no posthumous heir. Nothing could save her now.

Agnès had stood motionless, incredulous. Incredulous because the terror that had gripped her those past months had suddenly faded into the distance. There was nothing more to do, nothing more to say.

And then, as the young girl pulled the fur-lined hood up over her head, preparing to leave the hovel, something curious happened.

The soothsayer's mouth froze in a grimace and she turned away, crying out:

'Leave here! Leave here at once, and take your basket with you. I want nothing of yours. Be off with you, I say!'

The evil crone's triumphant hatred had been replaced by a bizarre panic which Agnès was at a loss to understand. She had tried reasoning with her:

'I have walked a long way, witch, and . . .'

The woman had wailed like a fury, lifting her apron up over her bonnet to hide her eyes.

'Be off with you, you have no business here. Out of my sight! Out of my hut! And don't come back, don't ever come back, do you hear?'

If the fear consuming Agnès for many moons had not been replaced by deep despair, she would certainly have told the crone to calm down and explain herself. The extraordinary outburst would have certainly intrigued, not to say alarmed her. But as it was, she had walked away, a sudden, intense weariness weighing down her every step. She had struggled with the urge to surrender, right there in the mud soiled with pig excrement, to sleep, to die perhaps.

The icy cold, which had been pushed out towards the bare stone walls when there had been a fire in the enormous hearth, now enveloped her, claiming its revenge. She pulled her fur-lined cloak tightly round her and removed her slippers of boiled wool. Mathilde, her one-and-a-half-year-old daughter, would be wearing these in a few years' time if God saw fit to spare her life.

Agnès walked barefoot down the spiral staircase leading from the vestibule beside her bedchamber into the main hall. She crossed the black flagstones. Only the dull echo of her feet seemed real, the rest of the world had died away, leaving her with no other course of action, no other purpose than the moments that were about to follow. She smiled at the pale skin on her hands turning blue, at her heels sticking to the frost on the granite floor. Soon the biting cold would stop. Soon something else would replace this pointless waiting. Soon.

The chapel. It seemed as though a wave of ice had stopped time within those sombre walls. A frail shadow stood out against one of its wall. Sybille. She walked towards Agnès, her cheeks bloodless from the cold, from hardship and also from fear. She wore a long thin tunic that stretched over her belly, revealing the life that had grown big inside her and would soon be clamouring to see the light. She stretched out her bony hands towards the Dame de Souarcy and her face broke into an ecstatic smile:

'Death will be sweet, Madame. We shall enter the light. My body is weighed down, so impure. It was already unclean before I soiled it even more.'

'Hush,' Agnès commanded.

She obeyed, bowing her head. She was overwhelmed by a perfect peace, like a longing. All that mattered to her now was the infinite gratitude she felt towards Agnès, her angel, with whom she was about to leave this world, this corrupted flesh, saving herself from the worst fate and saving, too, this beautiful, kind woman who had seen fit to take her in, to protect her from the evil hordes. They would die a thousand deaths and weep tears of blood when they realised their terrible mistake, but at least she would have saved Agnès's dove-like soul, at least she would be saved, she and this child she could feel moving with such force below her breast. Thanks to her, her lady would enter the infinite and eternal joy of Christ. Thanks to her, this child she did not want would never be born. It would become light before ever having to suffer the unbearable burden of the flesh.

'Come along,' Agnès continued in a whisper.

'Are you afraid, Madame?'

'Hush, Sybille.'

They approached the altar that had been hurriedly set straight. Agnès untied her cloak, which dragged behind her for a moment like a ghostly train before falling to the floor. As she walked, she unfastened the fine leather thong around her waist and stepped out of her robe. At first she felt almost numb. Then her naked skin began to prickle, burning her almost. The unrelenting cold brought tears to her eyes. She gritted her teeth, fixing her gaze on the painted wooden crucifix, no longer conscious of her thoughts, and slumped to her knees. As though in a dream, she watched the tremors shaking Sybille's deathly-pale little body. The young woman rolled herself up in a ball below the altar and began repeating the same incessant prayer: *Adoramus te, Christe. Adoramus te, Christe. Adoramus te, Christe.*[1]

Sybille's body went into a spasm. She stumbled over the words of the prayer, seemingly unable to breathe, then repeated it once more:

'*Ado . . . ramus te . . . Christe.*'

There was a gasp, followed by a cry and a long-drawn-out sigh, and the emaciated legs of her lady's maid went limp.

Was that death? Was it so simple?

It seemed as though an eternity had passed before Agnès felt her body fall forwards. The icy stone floor received her without mercy. The flesh on her belly protested, but she silenced it, stretching her arms out to form a cross, and waiting. There was nowhere else for her to surrender.

How long did she spend praying for Mathilde's life, how long accepting that she was sinning against her body and soul and deserved no mercy? And yet one was granted her as she gradually lost consciousness. She no longer felt the relentless cold of the stone floor biting into her. The blood no longer pulsed through the veins in her neck. She would soon be asleep, with no fear of ever waking up.

'Stand up! Stand up this instant.'

Agnès smiled at the voice whose words she did not understand. A hand roughly grasped her hair, which spread out in a silky wave across the stone floor.

'Stand up. It is a crime. You will be damned and your child will suffer for your sins.'

Agnès turned her head the other way; perhaps then the voice would stop.

A heavy layer of warmth covered her back. A rush of hot air burned her neck and two hands burrowed under her belly in order to turn her over. It was the weight of another body lying on top of hers in order to warm her.

The nursemaid, Gisèle, struggled with the young girl's rigid body. She wrapped her coat around her and tried to pull her to her feet. Agnès fought with every last fibre of her frail body against being saved. Tears of rage and exhaustion rolled down her cheeks, turning to ice on her lips.

She murmured:

'Sybille?'

'She will soon be dead. And she's better off that way. You will stand up if I have to thrash you. It is a sin, and unworthy of one of your lineage.'

'And the child?'

'Presently.'

Manoir de Souarcy-en-Perche, May 1304

ELEVEN-YEAR-OLD Mathilde was circling the honey spice-cake which Mabile had just removed from the stone oven. She shifted restlessly about the room, eager for the arrival of her uncle who so captivated her. Clément, the ill-fated child Sybille had pushed from her womb before finally expiring, and who was nearly ten now, was quiet as usual, his big blue-green eyes fixed on Agnès. Gisèle had taken the new-born baby and, after cutting the umbilical cord, had wrapped him in her cloak to keep him from freezing to death. Agnès and the nursemaid had feared the child would not survive his terrible birth, but life already held him firmly in its grip. It had, however, released Gisèle the previous winter, despite the care Agnès had lavished on her and the ministrations of her half-brother Eudes de Larnay's physic, whom Agnès had implored him to send; the practitioner's celery decoctions and leeches had not been enough to cure the old woman of the fevers of pleuro-pneumonia, and she had succumbed at dawn, her head resting in the lap of her mistress who had lain beside her to provide extra warmth.

To begin with, the passing of this formidable pillar of strength, who had protected and ordered Agnès's life for so long, grieved her to the point where she lost all desire to eat.

However, her grief was soon replaced by a feeling of relief – so soon, in fact, that the young woman had a sense of shame. She was alone now and in danger, but for the first time there was nothing to link her to the past besides her daughter, who was still so young. Gisèle, the last remaining witness to that night of horror in the icy chapel long ago, had gone to her grave.

Agnès sat bolt upright at the end of the long kitchen table, trying to control the anxiety she had been feeling since she learned of Eudes's visit. Mabile, sent as a gift by her half-brother following Gisèle's death, cast occasional glances at her. She was obedient and hard-working, but the Dame de Souarcy disliked the girl, whose presence was a constant, niggling reminder of Eudes. She suspected that the gentle Clément, despite his extreme youth, shared her misgivings. Had he not said to her one day in a mischievous voice, which his serious expression belied:

'Mabile is in your room, Madame. She is tidying your things – again, taking them out and carefully examining them before replacing them. But how can she rearrange your registers if, as she claims, she cannot read?'

Agnès needed no clarification in order to grasp the child's meaning: Mabile had been sent by her former master to spy on her. Not that this came as any surprise – indeed, it explained rather better than compassion her brother's persistent generosity.

Clément's extraordinary precocity astounded Agnès. His keen intelligence, his relentless powers of observation and his remarkable ability to learn and memorise caused her on occasion to forget how young he was in years. Scarcely had Agnès finished teaching him the rudiments of the alphabet than he knew how to read and write. In contrast, her daughter Mathilde's indifference to the advantages of knowledge meant she was at pains to recite even the simplest prayer. Mathilde possessed the grace and delicacy of a butterfly and the complexities of life quickly bored her. Perhaps the explanation lay in Clément's strange birth. Mathilde was still a child, whereas it seemed to Agnès sometimes that Clément was becoming more and more like a companion upon whom she could depend. To what extent had the child understood Eudes's wicked scheming? How conscious was he of the threat hanging over the three of them? Did he know the cruel fate that awaited him if his true origin were ever brought to light? The bastard progeny of a violated servant girl, the orphan of a suicide seduced by the fables of heresy, who had escaped torture and burning at the stake thanks to Agnès's unwitting collusion. And what if someone were to suspect what the child knew he must conceal? She shuddered at the thought. How could she have been so oblivious to Sybille's asceticism that she attributed her compulsive behaviour to the pregnancy forced on her by a common brute? Had she been blind? And yet in all honesty, what would she have done had she known? Nothing, to be sure. She would certainly not have turned the poor wretched girl out. As for denouncing her – that was a vile, wicked act to which Agnès would never have stooped.

'Will my good master, the Baron de Larnay, be passing the night here, Madame? If so I should send Adeline to prepare his quarters,' Mabile observed, lowering her gaze.

'I know not whether he intends to honour us with his presence tonight.'

'The journey is nearly seven or eight leagues.* He and his steed will doubtless be weary. I don't suppose they will arrive here until after none, *or even vespers,'* she lamented.

What a relief it would be if he lost his way in the forest and never came out! Agnès thought, and declared:

'Indeed, what a tiring journey, and how kind of him to undertake it in order to pay us a visit.'

Mabile gave a little nod of approval at her new mistress's observation, adding:

'How true. You have an admirable brother, Madame.'

Agnès's eyes met Clément's and the boy quickly turned away, concentrating his gaze on the glowing embers in the huge hearth. Whole stags had been roasted there when Hugues was still of this world.

Agnès had never loved her husband while he was alive; the idea of forming an emotional bond with this man to whom she was being given in matrimony had never crossed her mind. At just thirteen, she was of age,[2] and was obliged to wed the pious, courteous gentleman. He showed her the same respect as he would if her true mother had been the Baroness de Larnay rather than her lady-in-waiting. In any event, he had been gracious enough never to remind her that she was the last illegitimate child of noble birth sired by Eudes's father Robert, the late Baron de Larnay. Robert, in a fit of remorse that coincided with a tardy devoutness, had demanded that his daughter be recognised, and even Eudes, who would not gain from such an official recognition of parenthood, had complied. And so the old Baron Robert de Larnay had quickly married the adolescent girl off to his old drinking, feasting and fighting companion, Hugues de Souarcy, a childless widower, but, above all, his most loyal vassal. He had settled a small dowry on Agnès, but her astonishing beauty and extreme youth had been enough to conquer the heart of her future spouse. For her part she had accepted with good grace this marriage that conferred upon her a certain status, but more importantly placed her beyond her half-brother's reach. But Hugues had died without producing a son and now, at twenty-five, the position in which she found herself was hardly better than when she had lived in her father's house. Naturally, she received a dower[3] from her husband's estate, though it was barely enough for her to run her household. It represented only a third of the few remaining properties Hugues had not squandered, comprising the Manoir de Souarcy and its adjoining land, as well as an expanse of arid grey terrain known as La Haute-Gravière where only thistles and nettles grew. However, her dower was far from safe, for if, as she feared, Eudes was able to show that her conduct as a widow was inappropriate, she would be dispossessed in accordance with an old Normandy custom stipulating: 'A loose-living woman forfeits her dower.' At the cost of interminable wars, the province of Normandy had remained in the realm for the past hundred years, but it conserved its customs and fiercely asserted the right to a 'Norman Charter' that enshrined its traditional privileges. These did not favour women, and if Agnès's half-brother achieved his ends there would be only three ways for her to escape destitution: the convent – which would mean leaving her daughter in Eudes's predatory hands; remarriage, if he gave his consent – which he could withhold. And death. For she would never yield to him.

Mabile's sighs brought her back to reality.

'What a pity it is Wednesday, a fast day.[4] Were my master to stay until tomorrow he could enjoy our fine pheasants. Tonight he will have to make do with plain vegetable soup, no pork, spiced mushrooms and a dried fruit pudding.'

'There is no place for regrets of this kind in my house, Mabile. As for my brother, I am sure that, like the rest of us, he finds great solace in penitence,' Agnès retorted, her thoughts elsewhere.

'Oh yes, like the rest of us, Madame,' repeated the other woman, fearful her remark might be deemed sacrilegious.

A loud commotion emanating from the main courtyard put an end to Mabile's discomposure. Eudes had arrived. She hurried over to fetch the whip hanging behind the door that was used to calm the dogs, and rushed out squeaking with joy. The thought occurred to Agnès that her half-brother might enjoy in this lady's maid something more than a loyal servant. Perhaps the poor girl hoped Eudes would leave her with child, and deceived herself into thinking her bastard progeny would enjoy the same fate as Agnès and be recognised. She was mistaken. Eudes was not his father, Robert. Far from it, and yet the Baron had been no saint or even a man of honour. No, his son would sooner cast her out without a penny than suffer the slightest inconvenience. She would join the legions of dishonoured women who ended up in houses of ill repute, or worked on farms as day labourers in exchange for a meal and a tiny room in which to carry out their thankless chores.

*

Mathilde leapt up, scampering after Mabile to greet her uncle, who as a rule arrived bearing armfuls of rare and precious gifts. The Larnay wealth was among the most coveted in the Perche region. The family had had the good fortune to discover iron ore on their lands, which they exploited in the form of an opencast mine. The monarchy valued the ore – which was the envy of the English – and this manna had earned the feudal Baron a measure of royal patronage since King Philip IV the Fair* was eager to avoid any temptation on the part of the Larnay family to form an alliance with the age-old enemy. The kingdom of France had reached a partial accord with the English, but it was a volatile alliance on both sides, despite the planned union between Philip's daughter Isabelle and Edward II Plantagenet.[5]

Eudes, while not renowned for his intelligence, was no fool. Philip the Fair's limitless need for funds made him a difficult, even a dangerous sovereign. The Baron's approach was simple and had borne fruit: he would grovel and pledge his loyalty to the King by alluding indirectly to the demands and the offers of the English; in brief, he would show his allegiance, reassure him, while at the same time encouraging his generosity. It did not pay, however, to go too far; Philip and his counsellors had not hesitated to imprison Gui de Dampierre in order to rob him of Flanders, to confiscate the property of the Lombards and the Jews or even to order the abduction of Pope Boniface VIII* during his visit to Anagni.* Eudes was well aware that if he opposed the King or displeased him in the smallest way, it would not be long before he was discovered at the bottom of a ditch or stabbed to death by some providential vagabond.

*

Agnès stood up with a sigh, adjusting her belt and veil. A quiet voice made her jump:

'Take heart, Madame. He is no match for you.'

It was Clément. He was so good at making himself inconspicuous, invisible almost, that she had all but forgotten he was there.

'Do you believe that?'

'I know it. After all, he is only a dangerous fool.'

'Dangerous, indeed – dangerous and powerful.'

'More powerful than you, but less so than others.'

And with these words he slipped through a small postern door leading to the servants' garderobe.[6]

What a strange child, she thought, making her way towards the hubbub outside. Was he capable of reading her thoughts?

Eudes's voice boomed out. He was shouting orders, bullying this person and showering abuse on that. The moment Agnès appeared in the courtyard, the expression of loathing and irritation on her brother's face was replaced by a smile. He walked over to her with open arms and cried out:

'Madame, you grow more radiant every day! Those mastiffs of yours are wild animals. You must set aside a pair of males for me from the next litter.'

'What a pleasure to see you, brother. Indeed, they are fierce towards strangers, but loyal and gentle with their masters and the herds. I trust your household is thriving. And how is your good lady wife, my sister Apolline?'

'Big with child, as is her custom. If only she could manage to produce a son! And how she stinks of garlic, sweet Jesus! She pollutes the air from dawn till dusk. Her physic maintains that taking brews and baths made from the revolting bulb will produce a male. So she swallows it, stews in it, spews it – in short, she makes my days a living hell, and as for my nights . . .'

'Let us pray that she will soon bear you a sturdy son, and me a handsome nephew,' interrupted Agnès.

She, too, opened her arms in order to seize the hands that threatened to close around her body. And then she quickly moved away under the pretext of giving orders to the farm hand, who was struggling to control Eudes's exhausted, nervous mount.

'Why don't you get off that horse!' Eudes barked at the page, who was nodding off astride his broad-chested gelding.

The young lad, barely twelve years old, leapt from the saddle as if he had been kicked.

'Good. Now get a move on! A pox on your sluggishness,' Eudes roared.

The terrified boy began seeing to the load weighing down his packhorse.

Acting the suzerain, Eudes led his sister into the vast dining hall – so cool even the worst heat wave could barely warm its walls. Mabile had laid the table and was leaning against the wall awaiting her orders, her head bowed and her hands clasped in front of her apron. Agnès noticed that she had taken the trouble to change her bonnet.

'Fetch me a ewer so I may rinse my hands,' Eudes ordered, without so much as a glance in her direction.

As soon as the girl had gone, he asked Agnès:

'Does she please you, my lamb?'

'Indeed, brother, she is obedient and hard-working. Although I suspect she misses serving in your household.'

'What of it! Her opinion doesn't interest me. Good God, I'm ravenous! Well, my beauty. What news from your part of the world?'

'Not a great deal, to be sure, brother. We had four new piglets this spring, and so far the rye and barley crops are flourishing. We expect a good yield, if the continual rain of the past few years stays away. When I think that less than fifteen years ago they were harvesting strawberries in Alsace in January! But I mustn't bore you with my farmer's complaints. Your niece,' she pointed to Mathilde, 'has been bursting with eagerness to see you again.'

He turned towards the little girl, who had been vainly attempting to attract his attention with smiles and sighs.

'How pretty she is, with that little face and those honey-blonde curls. And those big dreamy eyes! What passions you will soon provoke, my beloved.'

The overjoyed girl gave a polite curtsey. Her uncle continued:

'She is made in your image, Agnès.'

'On the contrary, I think she resembles you when you were a child – much to my pleasure. Although you and I, it is true, might have been mistaken for twins had it not been for your superior strength.'

She was lying deliberately. They had never borne the slightest resemblance to one another – except for the colour of their coppery golden hair. Eudes was stocky, with heavy features, a square jaw, an overly pointed nose, and his skinny lips resembled a gash when they were not uttering some bawdy word or insult.

All of a sudden his face grew sullen, and she wondered if she had gone too far. His eyes still riveted on his half-sister, he said to the girl in a soft voice:

'How would you like to do me a good turn, my angel?'

'Nothing would please me more, uncle.'

'Run and find out what has become of that good-for-nothing page. He's taking a long time to unload his horse and bring me what I requested.'

Mathilde turned and hurried out to the courtyard. Eudes continued solemnly:

'Were it not for your goodness, Agnès, I would have resented the distress your arrival into this world caused my mother. What a slight, what an insult for such a pious, irre-proachable woman.'

Agnès was glad of the remark, for she feared he had seen through her charade. Indeed, at every visit he managed to recall in the most obvious way his generosity as a boy, forgetting how he had snubbed and mistreated her until Baron Robert demanded that she be regarded as a young lady. Strangely, after her mother had died, when Agnès was barely three years old, Baroness Clémence had grown tremendously attached to this child of an adulterous union. It had amused her to show the girl how to read and write, to teach her Latin and the rudiments of arithmetic and philosophy, as well as her own two great passions: sewing and astronomy.

'Your mother was my good angel, Eudes. I can never thank her enough in my prayers for the kindness she showed me. Her memory is alive in my heart and a constant comfort.'

Tears welled up in her eyes, spontaneous tears for once that were a sign of true affection and grief.

'Forgive my brutishness, my beauty! I am well aware of your devotion to my mother. At times I behave like an oaf, pray forgive me.'

She forced a smile:

'No, brother. You are always good.'

Persuaded of her gratitude and respect for him, he changed the subject:

'And what of that little rascal who is always hiding behind your skirts. What is his name? He has not made an appearance yet.'

Agnès knew instantly that he was referring to Clément, but pretended she was racking her brains in order to give herself time to decide what attitude she should adopt.

'A little rascal, you say?'

'You know. The orphan whom your kindness compelled to take into your household.'

'Do you mean Clément?'

'Indeed. What a shame he isn't a girl then we could have given him to the sisters at Clairets Abbey* as an offering to God[7] and spared you the extra mouth to feed.'

As overlord, Eudes had the authority to do this if he wished, and Agnès would have no say in the matter.

'Clément is no trouble to me, brother. He is content with little and has a gentle, quiet nature. I rarely see him, but at times his presence amuses me.' Convinced that her brother's aim was to gratify her at little cost to himself, she added, 'I confess that I would miss him. He accompanies me on my rounds of the estate and its neighbouring communes.'

'Indeed, too gentle and too puny to make a soldier out of him. He could become a friar, perhaps, in a few years' time.'

She must on no account openly oppose Eudes. He was one of those fools who dug in their heels at the slightest resistance, immediately manoeuvring others into a position of defeat. It was their customary way of convincing themselves of their power. Agnès continued in the same measured tone with a hint of feigned uncertainty:

'If he proves competent enough my intention is to make him my apothecary or physic. I shall be much in need of one. Learning fascinates him, and he already knows all about the medicinal herbs. But he is young yet. We shall discuss it when the time comes, brother, for I know you to be an able judge where people are concerned.'

Children are credited with an infallible instinct. Mathilde was worrying proof of the contrary. Having first tasted the fruits and sweetmeats, she sat at her uncle's feet chattering away, delighted each time he kissed her hair or slipped his fingers down the collar of her tunic to caress the nape of her neck. Her uncle's accounts of his hunting exploits and his travels fascinated her. She devoured him with her eyes, an enchanted smile spreading across her pretty face. Agnès thought that she must soon explain her uncle's shameful nature to her. But how? Mathilde adored Eudes. She regarded him as so powerful, so radiant; in short, so wonderful. He brought within the thick cold grey walls of the Manoir de Souarcy the promise of a life of easy grandeur that intoxicated her daughter to the point of clouding her judgement. Agnès could not blame her. What did she know of the ways of the world, this little girl who in less than a year would become a woman? She had only ever known the pressures of farm life: the mud of stables and sties, the worry of the harvests, the coarse clothing and the fear of famine and illness.

An unbearable thought struck Agnès with full force. Eudes would repeat with his niece what he had attempted with his half-sister when she was barely eight, given half the chance. The extent to which he was in thrall to his incestuous passion terrified Agnès. There were plenty of peasants and maids for him to mount, some of whom were flattered by the interest their master showed in their charms, while others – the majority – simply resigned themselves. After all, they had already suffered the father and grandfather before him.

Pleading the lateness of the hour, Agnès ordered her daughter to be put to bed. Where was Clément? She had not seen him since Eudes de Larnay's arrival.

Clairets Forest, May 1304

THE massive torso bore down on him. A solid wall of rage. It seemed to the novice as though he had been standing for an eternity contemplating the perfect musculature rippling beneath the silky black skin slick with sweat. And yet the horse had only advanced a few paces towards him. The voice rang out again:

'The letter. Where is the letter? Give it to me and I will spare your life.'

The hand holding the reins tapered off into a set of long gleaming metal talons. The novice was able to make out a pair of straps attaching the lethal glove to the wrist. He thought he saw blood on the metal tips.

His panting breath resounded in his ears. The clawed hand moved upwards, perhaps in a gesture of conciliation. The novice watched each infinitesimal movement as though it were fractured through a prism. The action had been swift and yet the hand appeared to be endlessly repeating the same gesture. He closed his eyes for a split second, hoping to drive away the image. His head was reeling, and a terrible thirst caused his tongue to stick to the roof of his mouth.

'Give me the letter. You will live.'

From what dark depths did this voice emanate? It belonged to no ordinary mortal.

The novice turned his head, weighing up his chances of escape. Nearby, a thick clump of trees and shrubs shimmered in the setting sun. Their swaying branches were too tight for a horse to pass through. He made a dash for it. Careering like a madman, he nearly fell over twice and had to clutch the overhead branches to steady himself. His wheezing breath rose from his throat in loud gasps. He resisted the urge to collapse on the forest floor and lie there sobbing, waiting for his pursuer to catch up with him. Further to his right, the shrill echo of a magpie's startled chatter pierced the young man's eardrums. He ran on. A few more yards. Up ahead in a clearing, a tall bramble patch had colonised every inch of space. If he managed to hide there his pursuer might lose his trail. He leapt into the middle of the hellish undergrowth.

He clasped his hand over his mouth to stifle the cry that threatened to choke him. The blood throbbed in his throat, his ears and his temples.

There, motionless, silent, barely breathing. The brambles snagged his arms and legs and clung to his face. He watched their hooked claws creeping towards him. They quivered, stretching out and slackening, poised to tear into his flesh. They dug into his skin, twisting in order to snare their prey.

He tried hard to convince himself brambles were inanimate, yet they moved.

The night was crimson red when it fell. Even the trees turned crimson. The grass, the moss further off, the brambles, the mist, everything was tinged with crimson.

A terrible pain pulsed through his limbs as though he were being scorched by a flameless fire.

A faint noise. A noise like swirling water. If only he could put his hands over his ears to stop the rushing sound in his head. But he could not. The brambles clung to him with redoubled spite. The sound of approaching hooves.

The letter. It must not be found. He had promised to guard it with his life.

He tried to pray but stumbled over the words of his entreaty. They ran through his mind again and again like some meaningless litany. He clenched his jaw and pulled his right arm free of the spines that were crucifying him. He felt his skin ripping under the plant's stubborn barbs. His whole hand had turned black. His fingers would barely move, and felt so numb all of a sudden that he found it difficult to push them inside his cape to seize the parchment.

The missive was brief. The hooves were drawing near. In a matter of seconds they would be upon him. He ripped up the small piece of paper and crammed the fragments into his mouth, chewing frantically in order to ingest what was written before the hooves appeared. When the novice finally managed to swallow and the ball moistened with saliva disappeared inside him, he had the impression that those few magnificent lines were ripping his throat apart.

Flat against the forest floor which was thick with blackberry bushes, all he could see at first were the black horse's front legs. And yet it seemed to him they were multiplying, that suddenly there were four, six, eight animal's legs.

He tried to stop his breathing – so loud it must be echoing through the forest.

'The letter. Give me the letter.'

The voice was cavernous, distorted, as though it were coming from the depths of the earth. Could it be the devil?

The throbbing pain from the remorseless brambles disappeared as if by magic. God had heard his prayer at last. The young man rose up, emerging from the barbed snarl, indifferent to the scratches and gashes lacerating his skin. Blood was pouring down his face and from his hands, which he held out before him, red against the crimson night. Beads of it formed along the veins of his forearms as far as his elbows then vanished as quickly as they had come.

'The letter!' ordered the booming voice, resounding in his head.

He gazed down at his feet clad in sandals. They were so swollen he could no longer see the leather straps beneath the black blistered flesh.

He had sworn to guard the letter with his life. Was it not a crime then to have eaten it? He had given his word. Now he must give his life. He looked back at the ocean of brambles he had foolishly believed would be his salvation, and tried to judge its height. It stirred with a curious breathing motion, the blackberry branches rising, falling, rising again. Making the most of a long exhalation, he leapt over the hostile mass and ran in a straight line.

It felt as if he had been running for hours, or a few seconds, when the sound of galloping hooves caught up with him. He opened his lips wide and gulped a mouthful of air. The blood rushed to his throat and he burst into laughter. He was laughing so hard that he had to stop to catch his breath. He bent over and only then did he notice the long spike sticking out of his chest.

How did the broad spear come to be there? Who had run him through?

The young man slumped to his knees. A river of red flowed down his stomach and thighs and was soaked up by the crimson grass.

The horse pulled up a yard in front of the novice, and its rider, dressed in a long, hooded cape, dismounted. The spectre removed the lance swiftly and wiped its bloody shaft on the grass. He knelt down and searched the friar, cursing angrily as he did so.

Where was the letter?

The figure leapt up furiously and aimed a violent kick at the dying man. He was seized by a murderous rage just as the dried, shrivelled lips of the young man opened one last time to breathe:

'Amen.'

His head fell back.

Five long shiny metal claws approached the dead man's face and the spectre regretted only one thing: that his victim could no longer feel the pitiless destruction they were about to unleash upon his flesh.

Manoir de Souarcy-en-Perche, May 1304

SUPPER was a lengthy affair. The table manners of Agnès's half-brother revolted her. Had he never heard of the eminent Parisian theologian Hugues de Saint-Victor, who over half a century before had explained the rules of table etiquette? In his work he specified that one should not 'eat with one's fingers but with a spoon, nor wipe one's hands on one's clothes, nor place half-eaten food or detritus from between one's teeth on one's plate'. Eudes gorged himself noisily, chewed with his mouth open and used his sleeve to wipe away the flecks of soup on his face. He belched profusely as he finished off the last crumbs of the fruit pudding. Sated by the supper Mabile had managed to make delicious despite the lack of meat – forbidden on this fast day – Eudes said all of a sudden:

'And now . . . Gifts for my lamb and her little beloved. Send for Mathilde.'

'She is surely sleeping, brother.'

'Then let her be woken. I wish to perceive her joy.'

Agnès obeyed, curbing her irritation.

A few moments later, the girl, her clothes thrown on in haste, came into the vast hall, her eyes glassy with sleep and with desire.

Eudes walked over to the big wooden box covered with

hessian, which the page had carried in earlier. He relished carefully untying the ropes as his niece's expectancy mounted. At last he pulled out an earthenware flask, declaring enticingly:

'Naturally, for your toilet I have brought vinegar from Modena, ladies. They say its dark hue turns the skin pale and silky as a dew-covered petal. The finest Italian ladies use it in abundance.'

'You spoil us, brother.'

'And what of it? This is a mere trifle. Let us move on to more serious matters. Ah! What do I see next in my box . . . five ells* of Genovese silk . . .'

It was a gift worthy of a princess. Agnès had to remind herself what lay behind her half-brother's extravagance in order not to run over and feel the saffron-coloured fabric. But she could not stop herself from crying out:

'What finery! My God! Whatever shall we use it for? Why, I would be afraid to spoil it with some clumsy gesture.'

'Just imagine, Madame, that the dream of all silk is to caress your skin.'

The intensity of the look he gave her made her lower her eyes. He continued, however, in the same playful tone:

'And what might this heavy crimson velvet pouch contain? What could give off such a heady fragrance? Do you know what it is, Mademoiselle?' he teased, leaning towards his gaping niece.

'I admit I do not, uncle.'

'Well, let us open it then.'

He walked over to the table and spread out the blend of aniseed, coriander, fennel, ginger, juniper, almond, walnut and hazelnut, which the wealthy liked to sample before going to bed to freshen their breath and aid their digestion.

'*Épices de chambre*,' breathed the girl in an admiring, mesmerised voice.

'Correct. And for my beloved what have we in our treasure trove? For I do believe your birthday is fast approaching, is it not, pretty young lady?'

Choked with emotion, the excited Mathilde pranced around her uncle, twittering:

'In a few weeks' time, uncle.'

'Perfect! Then I shall be the first to congratulate you, and you'll not object to my haste, will you?'

'Oh no, uncle!'

'Now then, what have we here that might make a birthday gift worthy of a young princess? Ah! A silver and turquoise filigree brooch fashioned by Flemish silversmiths. And from Constantinople a mother-of-pearl comb that will make her even prettier and the moon grow green with envy . . .'

The ecstatic child hardly dared touch the piece of jewellery shaped like a long pin. Her lower lip trembled as if she were about to burst into tears before such beauty, and Agnès thought again how the simplicity of their lives would soon become a burden to her daughter. But how would she explain to this girl, who was still a child, that in a few years' time her charming uncle would see in his half-niece a new source of pleasure. Agnès knew that she would stop at nothing to avoid it. He would never touch her daughter's soft skin with his filthy paws. Fortunately, as a boy, Clément was safe from such desires – and a lot more besides. Rumours concerning the strange tastes of other lords had reached Souarcy, but Eudes only liked girls, very young girls.

'And lastly, this!' he declaimed histrionically, as he pulled from the saddlebag a sack made of hide and fashioned in the shape of a long finger. He undid the thin piece of cord and took out a greyish phial.

Mathilde let out a cry of joy:

'Oh my lady mother! Sweet salt! Oh, how wonderful! I have never seen any before. May I taste it?'

'Presently. Show a little restraint, now, Mathilde! Take my daughter back to her room, will you, Mabile? It is late and she has already stayed up far too long.'

Before reluctantly following the servant, the little girl politely took her leave, first of her uncle, who kissed her hair, and then of her mother.

'Well, brother, I admit to being no less impressed than my daughter. They say that Mahaut d'Artois, Comtesse de Bourgogne, is so partial to the stuff that she recently purchased fifteen bars of it at the Lagny fair.'

'It is true.'

'Yet I thought her poor. Sweet salt is said to be worth more than gold.'

'The woman pleads poverty loudly while possessing great wealth. At two gold crowns and five pennies the pound, fifteen bars, each weighing twenty pounds, represents a small fortune. Have you ever tasted sweet salt, Agnès? The Arabs call it saccharon.'[8]

'No. I only know that it is sap collected from a bamboo cane.'

'Then let us rectify the situation at once. Here, lick this, my dear. You will be amazed by the spice. It is so smooth and combines well with pastries and beverages.'

He lifted a long grey finger up to her lips and a wave of revulsion that was difficult to control caused the young woman's eyelids to close.

The evening stretched on. The stiff posture Agnès had obliged herself to maintain since her half-brother's arrival, in order to discourage any familiarity on his part, was taking its toll on her shoulders. Her head was spinning from listening to Eudes's endless stories, the sole aim of which was to show him in a good light. Without warning he exclaimed:

'Is it true what they tell me, Madame, that you have built bee yards[9] for the wild swarms where your land borders Souarcy Forest?'

For a while she had only been half listening to him, and his deceptively casual question almost threw her:

'You have been correctly informed, brother. In accordance with common practice we hollowed out some old tree stumps with a red-hot iron, installing crossed sticks before depositing the wild colonies.'

'But raising bees and harvesting honey is a man's work!'

'I have someone to assist me.'

Eudes's eyes burned with curiosity.

'Have you seen the king of the colony yet?'[10]

'I confess I have not. The other bees guard him bravely and fiercely. Indeed, the idea of producing honey came to me when one of my farm hands was badly stung while helping himself to a free meal in the forest.'

'Such petty theft is considered to be poaching and is punishable by death. I know that you are a sensitive soul, and it is a charming attribute of womanhood. All the same, you could at least have ordered his hands to be cut off.'

'What use would I have for a farm hand with no hands?'

He responded to her remark with a hollow-sounding laugh, and she had the impression that he was trying to catch her out. Vassals were obliged to hand over two-thirds of their honey and a third of their wax to their lord – a levy Agnès had neglected to pay since she set up her bee yards two years before.

'Let me sample this nectar, then, my beauty.'

'Sadly, brother, we are still novices. Our very first harvest, last year, was a great disappointment. The continual rains turned the honey, making it unfit to eat. That is why I sent you none – for fear of making you and your servants ill. We fed it to our pigs, who tolerated it. On top of which I managed clumsily to spill one of the two pails. This year's harvest only yielded three pounds of poor quality – barely good enough to flavour the wine dregs. Let us hope that the harvest will be better this summer, and that I shall have the pleasure of sharing it with you and your household,' she said, feigning a sigh of despair before continuing, 'Oh, my sweet brother Eudes, I do not know how we would survive without your continued goodwill. The soil at Souarcy is poor. Imagine, I have only been able to replace half our draught animals with plough horses – oxen being so slow and clumsy. These bee yards should allow us to supplement our meagre everyday fare. Hugues, my dear departed husband, didn't . . . Well, he wasn't . . .'

'He was just a senile old man.'

'As you will soon be,' she muttered under her breath, and lowered her head as though out of embarrassment.

'That was an unwise decision of my father's if ever there was one. Marrying you to an old man of fifty, whose only claim to glory was a rash of battle scars! War does not make a man, it betrays his true nature – striking down the coward who hitherto employed a wealth of cunning to escape the slightest wound.'

'My father believed he was acting in my interests, Eudes.'

Since the beginning of their exchange she had attempted to adjust her speech, to emphasise their blood relationship – which he was at great pains to keep out of his own discourse, always addressing her as 'my beauty', 'my Agnès', 'my lamb', and occasionally as 'Madame'.

Nonetheless, Eudes's hesitation was palpable. Agnès cultivated it as best she could, in the knowledge that her only salvation lay in this final reticence. As long as he doubted his half-sister's awareness, he would continue to paw at the ground without daring to take the last guilty leap. On the other hand, the day he discovered she was wise to his deplorable lechery . . . Well, she did not know how else she could try to stop him.

She stood up from the bench and with a smile offered him her hand.

'Let us pray together to the Holy Virgin, brother. Nothing would give me greater pleasure, besides your presence here tonight. It would make Brother Bernard, my new chaplain, so happy to see us kneeling side by side. And afterwards you must rest. I regret being the motive for your undertaking such a long journey.'

He did not notice that she was taking leave of him, and was obliged reluctantly to do as she said.

When at last the following morning after terce* she watched Eudes and his page disappear across a field, Agnès felt exhausted and her head was spinning. She decided to make an inspection of the outlying buildings, more as a way of dispelling her continual unrest than out of any real necessity. Mabile, who was staring mournfully down the empty track, mistook Agnès's mood and remarked in a sorrowful voice:

'Such a short visit!'

Her face was pale and drawn, and Agnès reflected that for Eudes and his servant the night must have seemed even shorter.

'Yes indeed, Mabile, and yet how pleasant while it lasted,' she lied with such ease that she felt an almost superstitious fear creeping through her.

Was lying and cheating really that simple despite all the Gospel's teachings? Undoubtedly – or at least when it was the only existing form of self-defence.

'How right you are, Madame.'

Only then did Agnès notice the strip of dark-purple muslin draped over the girl's shoulders. She had not seen it before. Was it payment for services rendered or for favours granted?

'Let Mathilde sleep. She was up so late. Clément will accompany me – if and when he reappears.'

She hadn't seen the child since the previous evening. Was

this coincidence or guile? Whatever the case, he was wise to keep away from Eudes's prying eyes.

'I am right behind you, Madame.'

She turned towards the soft voice, amused and at the same time intrigued. She had not heard him arrive. Clément would come and go, disappearing for days at a time without anyone knowing where he was, only to reappear suddenly as if by magic. She really should order him to stay by her side, for the surrounding forest was an unsafe place, especially for one so young, and indeed Agnès was constantly afraid that someone might come upon him bathing in a pond or a river. On the other hand, Clément was cautious, and his independence inspired Agnès – perhaps because she herself felt spied upon, trapped.

He followed noiselessly a few steps behind her, flanked by the two guard dogs, and only drew closer when Agnès, confident that they were out of earshot of the inquisitive Mabile, enquired gently:

'Where do your roamings take you?'

'I do not roam, Madame, I watch, I learn.'

'Whom do you watch? What do you learn?'

'You. Many things – thanks to the sisters at Clairets Abbey. And thanks to you,' he added.

She looked down at him. His strange blue-green almond-shaped eyes stared back at her gravely, and with a flicker of suspicion. She said in a hushed voice:

'Clairets Abbey is so far from here. Oh, I don't know whether it was right of me to insist that you attend lessons there. It is almost a league away – too far for a child.'

'Half that if you go through the forest.'

'I don't like to think of you in that forest.'

'The forest is my friend. It teaches me many things.'

'Clairets Forest is . . . Well, they say it is sometimes visited by creatures, evil creatures.'

'By fairies and werewolves? Tall stories, Madame.'

'You mean you don't believe in werewolves?'

'No more than I believe in fairies.'

'And why not?'

'Because if they existed and were so powerful, Madame, at worst they would have already killed or eaten us and at best made our daily lives a hell.'

He smiled, and for the first time it occurred to Agnès that he only ever allowed himself to express amusement or joy with her. Clément and Mathilde's relationship was restricted to a good-natured selflessness on his part and an ill-tempered arrogance on hers. It was true that her daughter considered him a sort of privileged servant, and on no account would she have lowered herself by treating him as an equal.

'Upon my word, you have quite convinced me. And I am greatly relieved for I would have hated to come face to face with a werewolf,' she exclaimed jovially and then, growing serious again, she added in a worried voice, 'Will you be careful about what we have discussed, Clément? No one must know. Your life, and mine, depends on it.'

'I know that, Madame. I have known it for a long time. You need have no fear.'

They continued their dialogue in silence.

The village of Souarcy was built on a small hill. The alleyways leading up to the manor were lined with dwellings that twisted and turned, making it difficult for the hay-carts to manoeuvre without damaging the roofs of the houses. The positioning of the higgledy-piggledy buildings was entirely random, and yet they appeared to be huddled together as though seeking warmth. Souarcy, like a good many other manors, had no right to hold weaponry. At the time it was built, the English threat weighed heavily over the region and defence was the only option – hence its raised position in the middle of a forest. Indeed, the thick outer walls, within which peasants, serfs and craftsmen dwelled, had resisted many an attack with calm impudence.

Agnès replied with a perfunctory smile to the greetings, bows and curtseys of those she encountered as she made her way up to the manor via the muddy pathways, slippery with yellow clay after the recent rains. She stopped at the dovecote, but did not draw any of her usual pleasure from it. Eudes and his possible machinations were constantly on her mind. Even so, the magnificent birds welcomed her with a torrent of gently excited warbling. She glanced at the large, puffed-up male whose proud strutting always brought a smile to her lips. Not today. She had baptised him Vigil – the Watchful One – because at first light he liked to perch on the ridge beam of the manor house, cooing and watching the day break. He was the only bird who had a name. Yet another gift from her half-brother, who had brought the animal from Normandy the year before to inject new blood into her dovecote. He stretched out his muscular dark-pink neck, flecked with mauve, and she favoured him with a brief caress before leaving.

It was only after she had returned to the great hall at the manor that she realised Clément had cleverly avoided answering her question. It was too late now. The boy had disappeared again, and she would have to wait to ask him to explain the nature of what was increasingly keeping him away from the manor.

Eudes, too, was exhausted. He had only slept for an hour between Mabile's thighs. The strumpet was unstinting when it came to taking her pleasure. Happily – since her engagement in Agnès's household had yielded precious little else of any interest to her master. Unable to trap the mistress, he had tupped the servant. Scant compensation for the handsome piece of silk and the morsel of sweet salt, which alone had cost a small fortune, but it would have to do for the time being.

God, how his half-sister detested him! In Agnès's eyes he was insufferably conceited, boorish and depraved. He had come to realise that she loathed him some years before when she believed herself finally rid of him thanks to her marriage. The passion, the corrupt desire he had conceived for her when she was just eight and he ten had changed into a consuming hatred. He would break her and she would grovel at his feet. She would submit to his incestuous desire – so repugnant to her that sometimes it made the colour drain from her face. He had once hoped to conquer her love and that it would be strong enough to make her commit the unpardonable sin, but this was no longer the case. Now he wanted her to submit, to beg him.

He took out his vicious ill humour on his page, who had fallen asleep and was threatening to topple forward onto his gelding's neck.

'Wake up! Why, anyone would think you were a maid! And if indeed you are a maid I know how to make a woman of you.'

The threat had the desired effect. The young boy sat bolt upright as if he had been whipped.

Yes, he would break her. Soon. At twenty-five she had lost none of her beauty, although she was no longer a girl. And anyway, she had given birth, and it was well known that pregnancy spoiled a woman's body, in particular her breasts – and he preferred them pert, as was the fashion at the time, like little rounded apples, their skin pale and translucent. Who was to say that Agnès's had not been ruined by purple stretch marks? Perhaps even her belly was withered. In contrast, Mathilde was so pretty, so slim and graceful, just like her mother had been at her age. And Mathilde adored her extravagant uncle. In a year's time she would come of age and be ripe for the taking.

The thought cheered him no end, and he gave a loud guffaw: two birds with one stone. The worst revenge he could imagine taking on Agnès was called Mathilde. He would caress the daughter and destroy the mother. Of course, she would not leave the way clear for him. Despite his general lack of respect towards the fairer sex, Eudes was forced to acknowledge his half-sister's intelligence. She would strike him with all her might. A pox on females! All the same, the challenge could be exciting.

Upon further reflection, this particular stone would kill not two birds but three, since the Larnay mine, which assured his wealth and relative political safety, would soon be exhausted. Certainly, the earth's depths contained more hidden riches, but to get at them would require deep mining and neither his finances nor the geological conditions were favourable. The clay soil would give way at the first attempt to dig.

'Agnès, my lamb,' he murmured through his clenched jaw, 'your end is near. Tears of blood, my precious beauty, tears of blood will run down your sweet cheeks.'

Yes, he had been worrying about the mine for some time now. He decided to go there and check the progress of the iron-ore extraction.

Baron de Larnay's mining works, Perche, May 1304

'BRING him to me! Drag him here on his backside if you have to! He won't be needing it much longer,' bellowed Eudes de Larnay as he glowered at the tiny pile of iron ore at his feet, the meagre result of a whole week's mining.

The two serfs, heads bowed, had stepped back a few yards. The Baron's angry outbursts were well known, and could end in vicious blows, or worse.

They did not wait to be asked twice, and were only too glad to have such an excellent excuse to put the greatest possible distance between them and their master's fists. And in any case, that half-wit Jules, who was no better than they were, had done his fair share of swaggering since being promoted to overseer. He had become too big for his boots and now the boot was on the other foot.

The two men, exhausted by overwork and lack of sleep and nourishment, hurled themselves across the tiny arid plain towards the oak grove that stretched for leagues – almost as far as Authon-du-Perche.

Once they had reached the relative safety of the trees, they slowed down, stopping for a moment to catch their breath.

'Why have we come to the forest, Anguille? This isn't where

Jules ran off when the master arrived,' said the older of the two men.

'I don't know, damn it. What does it matter? We had to run somewhere or we'd be the ones taking the beating.'

'Do you know where Jules went?'

'No, and I don't care,' snapped Anguille, 'but it makes no odds, he won't get far. The master's mad as a drunken lord, and a nasty piece of work to boot.'

'What is it with that cursed mine? It's not for lack of digging. My legs and arms are well nigh dropping off.'

Anguille shrugged his shoulders before replying:

'His cursed mine's dried up, hasn't it? Jules told him, but it's no good, he won't listen. It's about as useless as a dead rat and not worth all the fuss. He can cry all he likes, he'll get nothing but dust from it now.'

'And to think it gave them bags of lovely gold for nigh on three generations. What a deadly blow for the master. He must be taking it hard!'

'Oh yes? Well, he'll be over it before it ever bothers me. Because, you see, that cursed mine might have given him bags of gold, but what has it ever given me, or us, except aching limbs, floggings and an empty belly? Come on, let's go deeper into the forest and have a little snooze. We'll tell him we couldn't find Jules.'

'But that's a lie.'

Anguille looked at him, flabbergasted by his naivety, and said reassuringly:

'Yes, but if you don't tell him, he won't know.'

Cyprus, May 1304

THE confused nightmare. Francesco de Leone sat up with a start on his straw mattress, his shirt drenched in sweat. He concentrated on breathing slowly to try to calm his wildly beating heart. Above all he wanted to avoid going back to sleep for fear the dream would continue.

And yet the Knight Hospitaller of Justice and Grace[11] had lived so long with this fear that he often wondered if he would ever be rid of it. The nightmare was more like a bad dream that had no end and always began with the echo of footsteps – his footsteps – on a stone floor. He was walking along the ambulatory of a church, brushing the rood screen shielding the chancel, trying by the weak light filtering through the dome to study the shadows massed behind the columns. What church was this? The rotunda suggested the Holy Sepulchre in Jerusalem or even the bravura architecture of the dome of the Hagia Sophia in Constantinople. Or could it be the Santa Costanza in Rome, the church which he believed opened onto the Light? What did it matter? In his dream, he knew exactly what he was looking for within those colossal walls of pinkish stone. He tried to catch up with the silently moving figure, betrayed only by the slight rustle of fabric. It was the figure of a woman, a woman hiding. It was at this point in the dream that he realised he was chasing her and that the design of the church, centred on the chancel, was hindering him. The figure circled as he circled, always a few steps ahead of him as though anticipating his movements, staying on the outside of the ambulatory while he moved along on the inside.

Francesco de Leone's hand reached slowly for the pommel of his sword, even as an overwhelming love made his eyes fill with tears. Why was he chasing this woman? Who was she? Was she real?

He gave a loud sigh, exhausted but tense at the same time. Only old women believed dreams were premonitions. And yet he had dreamt of the deaths of his sister and his mother only to discover their corpses soon afterwards.

He looked up at the tiny arrow slit opening onto the sky. The fragrant Cypriot night had no calming effect on him. He had been to so many places, known so many people that he could barely remember the town where he was born. He was from nowhere and felt like a stranger in this vast citadel, reconquered, following the siege of Acre in 1291, after a fierce battle led by the Knights Templar* and the Hospitallers. Guillaume de Beaujeu, the Grand-Master of the Knights Templar, had lost his life and Jean de Villiers, Grand-Master of the Knights Hospitallers, had been a hair's breadth from succumbing to his wounds. Only seven Hospitallers and ten Templars had survived the siege and the ensuing battle that signalled the end of Christendom in the Orient.

Most of the Knights Templar had returned to the West. As for the Knights Hospitaller, their hurried retreat to Cyprus had taken place with the mild opposition of the ruler of the island,

King Henri II of Lusignan, who had reluctantly allowed them to settle in the town of Limassol on the southern coast. The monarch was worried about what might soon become a state within a state – both orders being exempt from all authority save that of the Pope. Lusignan had imposed on them boundless restrictions. Thus, to a man, their number on the island must never exceed seventy knights plus their entourages. It was a clever way of curbing their expansion and above all their influence. The Holy Knights were forced to submit while they waited for more auspicious times. It mattered little. Cyprus was a mere step, a brief respite that would allow them to recover their strength and regroup before reconquering the Holy Land. For the birthplace of Our Lord must not remain in the hands of the infidels. Guillaume de Villaret, who in 1296 succeeded his brother as Grand-Master, had had a premonition, and his attention was now turned to Rhodes, a fresh refuge for his order.

Francesco de Leone experienced a frisson of elation and joy when he imagined advancing towards the Holy Sepulchre, raised on the site where Joseph of Arimathea's garden had once stood. It was in the crypt beneath the church that Constantine's mother had discovered the cross.

He would fall to his knees on the flagstones, warm from the fierce desert sun outside. He envisaged the tip of his outstretched hand brushing the strap of the sandal. He was ready to lay down his life with devotion and infinite humility for this deed; it was the Knight's supreme sacrifice.

The time had not yet arrived. Hours, days, months, even years, lay ahead. So many things must come to pass before then. Had he lost his way? Was his faith no longer entirely pure? Was he not beginning to enjoy the scheming of the powerful, which he was supposed to thwart?

He stood up. Despite his relative youth he felt as if he were a thousand years old. The human heart held few mysteries for him; it had afforded him some rare but dazzling moments of wonder and a great many more of despair, even disgust. To love man in Christ's image seemed to him at times an impossible ideal. And yet he would do well to conceal this chink in his faith. All the more so as man was not his mission; his mission, his many missions were Him. It was the indescribable joy of sacrifice that sustained Francesco de Leone during his darkest hours.

He moved noiselessly through the wing containing the cells and dormitory. Reaching the outside, he slipped on his sandals before crossing to the centre of a vast courtyard where the building housing the hospital was located.

He briskly descended the steps leading to the morgue beneath the infirmary. It was in this cramped cellar that bodies were laid out awaiting burial, their decomposition accelerated by the sweltering heat. On that particular morning, it was empty – not that the Knight would have been disturbed by the sight of a corpse. He had seen so many dead bodies, had advanced among them, stepping over them and occasionally turning one to search for a familiar face, blood up to his ankles. At the far end of the cellar a small postern door led to the carp pond chiselled out of the granite rock. This fish farm, inspired by a thousand-year-old Chinese tradition, provided additional food for the residents of the citadel and represented an economy since the carp lived on chicken excrement. His ablutions in the icy water of the deep pond, and the carp – rendered blind by years of darkness – brushing against his calves, did nothing to dislodge the profound unease he had felt since he awoke that morning.

By the time he entered the chapel to join the prior, who also occupied the position of Grand-Commander, dawn was just breaking.

Arnaud de Viancourt, a small slim man with light-grey hair and an ageless face, turned to him smiling, and folded his hands across his black monk's habit.

'Let us go outside, brother, and make the most of these few hours of relative coolness,' he suggested.

Francesco de Leone nodded, certain that the early-morning air was not the reason for the frail man's proposition. He was afraid of the spies Lusignan had placed everywhere, perhaps even within their order.

The two men walked for a while, their heads bowed and the hoods of their cloaks raised. Leone followed Arnaud de Viancourt to the great stone wall. His relationship with Guillaume de Villaret, their current Grand-Master, was founded upon the loyalty that bound the two men, as well as their intellectual complementarity. And yet the prior was unaware that this mutual trust had its limits; Guillaume de Villaret was well acquainted with the fears, hopes and motives of his Grand-Commander – as was his nephew and likely successor, Foulques de Villaret – but the reverse was not true.

Arnaud de Viancourt stopped walking and looked around carefully to make sure they were alone.

'Listen to the cicadas, brother. Like us they wake at dawn.

What wonderful stubbornness they possess, do they not? But are they aware of why they sing? Surely not. Cicadas do not question their lot.'

'Then I am a cicada.'

'Like all of us here.'

Francesco waited. The prior was given to these preambles, to speaking in metaphors. Arnaud de Viancourt's mind made him think of a gigantic universal chessboard whose pieces were constantly moving and never obeyed the same rules. He wove such a complex web and it was easy to lose sight of the individual threads. Then suddenly each element would fall into place to form a perfect whole.

The prior said in an almost detached voice, as though he were thinking aloud:

'Our late lamented Holy Father Boniface VIII* had the makings of an emperor. He dreamed of installing a papal theocracy, a Christian empire united under one sole power . . .'

The veiled criticism was not lost on Francesco. Boniface had ruled with a rod of iron and been little disposed to dialogue, and his intransigence had won him many critics even within the Church.

'. . . His successor Nicolas Boccasini, our Pope Benoît XI,* is quite unlike him. No doubt his election surprised him more than anyone. Should I confess, brother, that we fear for his life? He wisely pardoned Philip the Fair for attempting to murder his predecessor.'

The idea that Benoît's life might be threatened filled the Knight with silent dread. The new Pope's purity of vision, his spiritualism even, was a cornerstone of the century-old combat which Leone had devoted himself to. He waited, however, for the other man to continue. The prior proceeded with customary caution:

'It . . . It has been brought to our attention that Benoît intended to excommunicate Guillaume de Nogaret,* the monarch's ubiquitous shadow, who only played an accidental part in that abomination, although rumour has it Nogaret insulted Boniface. Be that as it may, Benoît must be seen to respond, to hold somebody to account. Complete absolution would undermine the Pope's already wavering authority.' He sighed before continuing. 'King Philip is no fool and he won't stop there. He needs a compliant pope and will have him elected if necessary. He will no longer tolerate any forces of opposition that might interfere with his plans. If our fears are justified and the Pope's succession is imminent we could find ourselves on very uncertain, not to say dangerous ground. We are no less in the firing line than the Knights Templar. I need not go on – you know as well as I.'

Francesco de Leone gazed up at the sky. The last stars were fading. Was the newly elected Pope's life really in danger? The prior digressed:

'Are they not miraculous? We might fear they will fade forever, and yet each evening they return to us, piercing the blackest night.'

Arnaud de Viancourt glanced at the taciturn Knight. The man never ceased to amaze him. Leone could have become one of the pillars of the Italian-speaking world – as admiral of the Hospitaller fleet or even a Grand-Master of their order. The noble blood that flowed in his veins, his bravery and his intelligence predisposed him to it. And yet he had refused these honours, these burdensome responsibilities. Why? Certainly not for fear of not measuring up to the task, even less so out of immaturity. Perhaps it was simply pride, a gentle pure sort of pride that made him long to give his life for his faith. An implacable, terrible pride that convinced him that he alone was capable of following his mission through to the end.

The old man observed his fellow Knight once more. He was tall, his features delicate but well defined. His honey-blond hair and dark blue eyes betrayed his northern Italian origins. The shapely sensuality of his lips might have suggested a carnal nature, and yet the prior was in no doubt as to his complete chastity – imperative in their order. What most astonished him was the extraordinary versatility of his brilliant mind, a strength that sometimes frightened him. Locked behind that lofty, pale brow was a world to which no one possessed the keys.

Leone was filled with foreboding. What would become of his quest without the private, not to say secret, backing of the Pope? He sensed that the drawn-out silence of his superior required a response.

'Are your suspicions about this . . . threat to our Holy Father related to the names Nogaret or Philip?'

'It is hard to tell the difference between the two. The critics abound: no one knows who governs France, Philip or his counsellors Nogaret, Pons d'Aumelas, Enguerran de Marigny, to name but a few. Do not be misled by my words. Philip is a stubborn, hard-hearted man and well known for his ruthless-ness. Even so, to answer your question: no, King Philip is too convinced of his legitimacy to stoop to commit murder against

God's representative on earth. We believe he will do as he did with Boniface and demand his removal from office. As for Nogaret – I doubt it. He is a man of faith and of the law. Moreover, were he to conceive such a plot without the endorsement of his monarch, he would be forced to commit – or have someone commit – a devious abhorrent form of murder, and I do not see him as a poisoner. However . . .' Arnaud de Viancourt accentuated his pause with a slight nervous gesture of his hand '. . . a zealous follower might interpret and carry out their desires.'

'It wouldn't be the first time,' avowed Leone, feeling a frisson of horror at the idea.

'Hmm . . .'

'Should we stay close to the Pope, then, in order to safeguard his life? I would willingly defend it with my own.'

As he spoke, the Knight was certain that the prior had been leading up to something else. The palpable sorrow in the man's eyes as he stared at Leone told him he had not been mistaken.

'My friend, my brother, you must know how difficult, nay, impossible it is to prevent this horror, and do we still have time? Of course Benoît's life is our first priority. As we speak, two of our brave brothers are at his side, protecting him with their constant vigilance, tracking the would-be poisoners. However, if . . . If he were to pass away . . . In our grief we must not forget the future . . .'

Leone finished the sentence for him, pronouncing the painful words he knew nevertheless to be true:

'. . . which we must already begin forging if we are to prevent the destruction of Christendom.'

These words applied equally to the sacred mission to which he had committed himself body and soul, and about which Arnaud de Viancourt knew nothing. About which no one must know.

'The future, indeed. Benoît's succession – if our desperate attempts of the last few weeks to prevent it fail.'

'Are we hoping that an intervention on our part might influence events?'

'Hope? There is always hope, brother. Hope is our main strength. But hope is not enough in this instance. We must be certain that King Philip IV's plan fails. If his counsellors succeed, as I fear they will, in electing a puppet pope to the Vatican, they will be free to attack those whom they cannot control as they would wish – that is to say, the Order of the Knights Templar and our own, since we are considered to be the Pope's personal guard, a wealthy guard – and you know as well as I do of the King's need for money.'

'In which case the Templars are first in the line of fire,' observed Leone. 'Their extreme power has become their failing. The wealth that passes through their hands incites greed in others. Their system of depositing and transferring funds from one side of the world to the other has greatly facilitated this. Crusaders and pilgrims to the Holy Land need no longer live in fear of being robbed. Additionally, they receive a stream of donations and alms from all over Christendom.'

'We benefit from it as much as they, and I must remind you that we are almost certainly as wealthy,' corrected Arnaud de Viancourt.

'True, but the Templars are censured for their arrogance,

their privileges, their wealth, even for being idle and uncharitable, whereas we are spared such criticism. There is no better way to fuel a fire than with jealousy and envy.'

'That is no reason to think, or more precisely to make others think, that this money has yielded such profits that they are now sitting on a veritable fortune. Have you ever asked yourself, Francesco, why Philip the Fair withdrew the administration of the royal finances from the Paris Templars in 1295 and entrusted it to the Italian moneylenders?'

'It was simpler for him to cancel his debt to the moneylenders by arresting them and confiscating their assets. The same strategy would have proved more risky if used against the Templars.'

'Precisely. And yet strangely enough two years ago the King granted the same Templars the right to collect taxes. Is it not a contradiction?'

'A measure which, when added to the rumours already circulating about the Templars, provoked the anger of the people.' The scattered elements of the prior's discourse had come together in Leone's mind, and he continued, 'So this is part of a long-term strategy thought up by the King in order to discredit the Templars permanently.'

'Stoking the fire as you said just now.'

The prior's words trailed off in a sigh. The prospect of the fate that awaited them had troubled him for so long now. Francesco de Leone finished his train of thought for him:

'And so the fire is already blazing. A conflagration would suit the King of France's purposes very well, and the other monarchs of Europe will not be displeased by the prospect of strengthening their power with regard to the Church. The defeat at Acre will only serve to kindle the flames. Their reasoning will be simple: why so much wealth and power for these military orders that lose us the Holy Land? In other words we cannot expect any help from outside. None will be forthcoming unless the other monarchs smell Philip the Fair's possible defeat, in which case they would flock to the Pope's side.'

'What a curious monologue-for-two our discussion is turning out to be, brother,' observed the prior. 'Is it possible that we have foreseen the future since we refer to it in the same terms?' A sudden sadness caused his pale features to stiffen. 'I am old, Francesco. Every day I count the tasks I am no longer able to undertake. All the years of war, crusades, death and blood . . . All the years of obedience and self-denial. To what end?'

'Do you doubt your commitment, the sincerity of our order, of our mission, or worse still of your faith?'

'Nay, brother, certainly I do not doubt our order or my faith. I doubt only myself, my failing strength and ability. At times I feel like a frightened old woman whose only recourse is to tears.'

'Self-doubt, when mastered, is a friend to all men except fools and simpletons. Self-doubt is the resounding proof that we are but an infinitesimal, troubled part of the divine understanding. We are aware of our failings, yet we progress.'

'You are still young.'

'Not so young any more. I shall be twenty-six this coming March.'

'I am fifty-seven and nearing my end. It will be a glorious

reward, I believe. I shall at last enter the Light. Until then my task is to continue to fight with you as my magnificent warrior, Francesco. Our enemies will use any means, including ignoble ones. It is a secret war, but a merciless one. And it has already begun.'

Leone sensed the prior's hesitation. What was he holding back? Knowing that a direct question would be awkward, he tried to curb his impatience.

'Are we to prevent Benoît's murder and the election of a pope favourable to Philip?'

Arnaud de Viancourt looked down, as though searching for the right words, before replying:

'What you do not yet know, brother, is that the old idea advocated twelve years ago by Pope Nicholas IV in his encyclical *Dura nimis*, of uniting the military orders, primarily those of the Templars and Hospitallers, is still alive.'

'Yet our relations with the Templars are . . . strained,' Leone argued.

Viancourt hesitated before deciding to keep quiet about the pace of negotiations between their Grand-Master, the Pope and the King of France. The union would benefit the Hospitallers who would take control of the other orders. A confrontation with the Templars, who would not willingly give up their autonomy, was imminent, all the more so as Jacques de Molay, the Templars' Grand-Master, was a traditionalist. An outstanding soldier and man of faith, he was weakened by his political naivety and blinkered by pride.

'Strained . . . That is putting it mildly. Philip the Fair is a fervent advocate of this union.'

Leone raised his eyebrows.

'His position is most surprising. A single order under the Pope's authority would represent an even greater threat to him.'

'That is true. However, the situation would be reversed if the union took place under his authority. Philip plans to name one of his sons Grand-Master of the newly constituted order.'

'The Pope will never agree to it.'

'The question is whether he will be in a position to refuse,' the prior clarified.

'And so we return to the problem of preventing the election of a pope favourable to Philip,' murmured Leone.

'Indeed. But do we have the right to influence the history of Christendom? The question plagues me.'

'Do we have the choice?' the Knight corrected gently.

'I am afraid the coming years will provide us with little room for manoeuvre. Therefore, no, we do not have the choice.'

The prior became engrossed in the study of a tuft of wild grass that had pushed its roots between two large blocks of stone. He murmured softly:

'The sheer tenacity of life. What a supreme miracle.'

He continued in a firmer voice:

'How should I put this? A fortuitous and unwitting intermediary will . . . assist us against his will.'

The prior cleared his throat. Leone looked enquiringly at Arnaud de Viancourt, sensing that what he was about to say vexed him. He was not mistaken.

'Good God, even his name is . . . difficult for me to pronounce.' He sighed before confessing, 'This intermediary is none other than Giotto Capella, one of the best-known Lombardy moneylenders of the Place de Paris.'

Leone grew faint and his eyes closed. He tried to protest but Viancourt interrupted:

'No. There is nothing you can say that I do not already know. I also know that time cannot heal all wounds. I spent days searching for another solution, in vain. Capella will never escape his tainted past. It is our trump card.'

Leone propped himself against the wall of broad, rough-hewn stones. He was overwhelmed by his emotions and struggling with his hatred. In truth he had been fighting it for so long now it had become like an unwanted companion he had learnt over the years to silence and control. And yet he knew if he freed himself, if he rid his soul of the loathing he felt for Capella he would be one step closer to the Light. In a faltering voice he said:

'Blackmail? What if Capella is a reformed man, what if he simply acted out of cowardice . . . ? One needs to have experienced terrible fear in order to forgive a coward. I was so young then, but now . . .'

Arnaud de Viancourt replied in a despondent voice:

'Brother, what purity of soul you possess. Many men would have been incapable . . .' He stopped himself, deeming it unacceptable to add to the pain Leone was clearly already suffering. 'Why should Capella help us in return for nothing when we have so little that interests him, and the King so much? I doubt it and it grieves me. Do men change unless they are compelled to? You may judge for yourself, brother. I know you to be a formidable judge of men's souls. You will soon perceive how much he has changed, or simply how willing he is to oblige. I hope for our sake – and for his too – that you will deem the letter we have prepared for him superfluous. I sincerely hope you find the solace of forgiveness – forgetting is human, forgiving is divine. If such is the case you may destroy the missive. Otherwise . . . I regret inflicting this ordeal on you but you must leave for France straight away. I have prepared letters of introduction as well as a leave of absence[12] of unspecified duration. You will stay in our commanderies as and when required. You will find all the comfort and spiritual succour you need there. Giotto Capella should enable you to come within reach of our most redoubtable enemy, Guillaume de Nogaret. If we are right and Nogaret is already looking for a replacement pope, he will need money, a great deal of money. We suspect that the French cardinals are among the candidates of the King's Counsellor. They are licentious and extravagant and will not pass up this opportunity to fill their purses. To begin with your task will consist in identifying the most likely candidate, for there are already several lining up. At best a name, or at worst two, Francesco. It is our only chance of intervening before it is too late.'

So everything had long been decided. The prior's uncertainty and regrets were doubtless sincere, but he and the Grand-Master had already woven their web.

A clamour of contrasting emotions raged inside Francesco de Leone. An incredible feeling of hope overlaid his hatred for Capella.

Arville-en-Perche, France, site of one of the Templars' most important commanderies. The place where for months he had despaired of arriving, the place where another door, surely the decisive one, would open for him. His throat was dry, and he limited himself to a brief remark:

'They say Guillaume de Nogaret is a dangerous man.'

'He is. And all the more so as he possesses one of the most brilliant minds I have ever known. Remember, he is the worthy successor of Pierre Flote and, like him, a jurist and staunch advocate of the supremacy of the monarchy's power over that of the French clergy. We must under no circumstances allow a schism to occur in the Church, or any part of it to break away from the authority of the Pope. If this religious and political controversy were to assume greater proportions the result would be catastrophic.'

'For the monarchy's power would become a divine right. Philip would rule directly through God, making him the highest authority in the realm.'

The prior nodded. He had spent entire nights devising strategies to defend against the coming avalanche, only at dawn to reject every last one as hopeless. The only remaining solution was to anticipate and prevent Philip from putting an end to the supreme authority of the Church over all the monarchs of Christendom.

Leone had regained some of his composure. He felt far away from the island sanctuary. He was already there, in the one place where his quest could continue.

'What practical information can you provide that will help me to . . .' he began, when Arnaud de Viancourt interrupted him:

'We are groping in the dark, brother. Any conjecture on my part would be a dangerous imprudence.'

'And my weapons, my powers?'

The prior appeared to hesitate and then, in a clipped tone that left the Knight unperturbed, he replied:

'The choice is yours, provided they serve Christ, the Pope and . . . our order.'

Had he been in any doubt this declaration would have made it clear. Like the other orders, the Knights Hospitaller were strictly hierarchical and individual initiatives were strongly discouraged. The free rein given him was easy to interpret: the order was facing the most ruinous crisis it had known since its formation almost two centuries earlier.

'Will my mission be recorded?'

'You are not afraid, are you, Francesco? I cannot believe it. No. You know how suspicious we are of written records. That is why we only recently felt the need to have one of our own, Guillaume de Saint-Estène, copy out our founding texts. Few written transcripts of our rules exist and they must never find their way outside the order or be copied, as you know. You are not afraid, are you?' the prior repeated.

'No,' murmured Francesco de Leone and smiled. His first smile that early morning.

He knew that true fear would come later. What he felt now was an intense pressure crushing him, and he had to stop himself from slumping to his knees on the dust-covered ground to pray or perhaps even to cry out.

The last hours of daylight lingered in the west. Francesco de Leone had worked like a slave the whole day long, missing both meals as part of a private fast. He had helped care for 'our lords the sick' – one of the duties of the Order of the Hospitallers that distinguished it from the other military orders – as well as providing training in the use of arms for some of the recently admitted novices. The heat and physical exhaustion had offered him a vague respite.

Might Benoît die? Might everything fall into place now? After four long years of a quest that had been as discreet and unrelenting as it had been fruitless, might a political threat lead him to a doorway hitherto hidden? The reason for his journey was admittedly this difficult mission. And yet the coincidence seemed too great for it to be entirely accidental. A sign. He had waited so long for the Sign. He was going to France, to the country where the Ineffable Trace had re-emerged and with full powers granted to him by the prior and consequently by the Grand-Master himself. He was going to discover there at last, perhaps, the meaning of the Light that had immersed him for a fleeting and divine moment at the heart of the Santa Costanza in Rome.

A ripple of anxiety coursed through him like a fever. What if it were only another illusion, another deadly disappointment? Would he have the strength to go on?

That choice was not his to make either.

Hoc quicumque stolam sanguine proluit, absergit maculas; et roseum decus, quo fiat similis protinus Angelis.[13]

Chartres, May 1304

NIGHT was slowly falling. The clamour in the streets had gradually died down. It was almost supper time. The cloaked figure stepped over a pile of debris blocking the central drain and turned right into Rue du Cygne.

The foul acrid smell drifting on the breeze gave a better indication of the tavern's location than any sign. It was one of those establishments where workers and craftsmen from the guilds gathered in the evenings – in this case the tanners' and leatherworkers' guild. While some fiery preachers described them as 'dens of iniquity' that encouraged sinful behaviour, the truth was far more benign. They were drinking places with a family atmosphere: people settled most of their deals and differences there and stopped for a welcome rest surrounded by a friendly din.

The cloaked figure paused in front of the door. Laughter and cries echoed from inside. He had deliberately arrived late so that the customers' curiosity would not be roused by seeing a solitary figure seated at a table. The person he was meeting would then already be waiting inside. He drew his hood down over his forehead and, clasping the sides of his heavy cloak, which was far too warm for such a sultry evening, he pushed open the door.

Two steps. Two steps were all it took. An ocean; a universe. A gulf separating innocence from almost certain damnation. And yet innocence can be a burden and above all rarely profitable. Innocence affords private satisfaction; money and power simple recompense.

The cloaked figure descended the first step and then the second.

Except perhaps for a welcoming smile from one woman sitting at a table, his entrance elicited little response from the tavern's regular customers.

Calmly crossing the trodden earth floor strewn with straw, the cloaked figure approached a table towards the back of the room, which was plunged into darkness. The man he was meeting had snuffed out the oil lamp in front of him.

The figure sat down. The hubbub of conversation around them was in full swing and would conveniently drown out the transaction that was about to take place.

The man was plump and jovial. He filled a second glass with wine and said in a hushed voice:

'I ordered the best. Since her husband passed away, the landlady has developed the regrettable habit of watering down the drink. It's only natural. She buys it for a few pennies a barrel from one of her nieces, a nun at Épernon. They say the abbey possesses some fine presses.'

Did he really believe that such harmless banter would detract from the enormity of the matter that had brought them there? And yet, the cloaked figure betrayed no irritation but remained silent, bolt upright, awaiting his next move.

At last, the man, a former barber-surgeon if what he said was true – that is a butcher[14] of beards and of human flesh – vexed by the silence of the person opposite, slid his fleshy hand across the table. Clasped in his palm between his hairy thumb and fingers was a phial wrapped in a thin strip of paper. A second hand wearing a thick brown leather glove reached out from under the cloak to take it, and at the same time set down a bulging purse, which the barber quickly pocketed. He explained in an almost piqued, slightly menacing voice:

'I've brought the instructions. It requires somewhat delicate handling. The aconite enters through the skin. It's slower but every bit as lethal as if it's swallowed.'

The cloaked figure stood up, not having uttered a single word, nor tasted a single drop of wine, which would have meant pulling back the hood of the cloak.

Two steps. Only two steps to climb. Back in that dimly lit room buzzing with relaxed conversation lay the past. It no longer bore any relation to the future.

The past had been inflicted, had imposed itself with all its cruel injustices. The future would be freely chosen. But first it must be fashioned.

Clairets Abbey, Perche, May 1304

THE abbey of the Order of Bernadine Cistercians was generously patronised and exempt from duties, as well as enjoying the privilege of low, middle and high justice, borne out by the gibbet erected on the gallows site. The abbey had permission to harvest timber for fuel and building from the forests owned by the Comte de Chartres. In addition to these charitable contributions, the abbey owned land at Masle and Theil that brought in a sizeable annual income, not to mention the numerous donations from local burghers or nobles or even from the more affluent peasants that had been pouring in steadily for years. The abbey's dedication service[15] had been witnessed by a certain Guillaume, commander of the Knights Templar at Arville.

Éleusie de Beaufort, Abbess of Clairets since the advent of her widowhood five years earlier, set down the letter written on Italian paper,[16] which she had received only moments before in the strictest secrecy. Had she not been convinced by the seals protecting the letter, she would certainly have burnt it or else dismissed it as a blasphemous fraud.

She looked up at the exhausted messenger who stood in silence awaiting her reply. She could tell by the man's despondent expression that he knew the contents of the missive. She played for time:

'My brother in Christ, you must rest a few hours. Your journey will be a long one.'

'Time is running out, Abbess. I have no desire to rest and as for my needs, well, they must wait.'

She smiled at him sadly and corrected herself:

'Then let us say I request the favour of a few moments' reflection and contemplation.'

'I consent, but do not forget that time is running out.'

Éleusie de Beaufort walked over to a doorway concealed behind a hanging. She led the man up a carved stone staircase to a heavy padlocked door that hid from the eyes of the world, and her fellow nuns, her private library – one of the most prestigious and the most dangerous in all Christendom. The counts and bishops of Chartres, various scholars, not to mention a few kings, princes and even some knights, had for decades deposited there the works they brought back from all four corners of the world, some of them in languages the Abbess, despite her great learning, was unable to decipher. She was the secret guardian of this science, of these books – most of them forgotten by the heirs and descendants of their original donors – and at times she experienced a frisson of uneasiness when she touched their covers. For she knew, she had read in Latin, in French and in the little she was able to decipher of English, that some of these volumes contained unrepeatable secrets. The mysteries of the universe were explained in three or four of them – possibly more for she read no Greek (a language that was little known and even looked down upon at the time), Arabic or Egyptian, and even less Aramaic. These secrets must remain beyond the reach of men, and no higher authority, save that of the Holy

Father, would convince her otherwise. Why, then, did she not simply destroy them, reduce them to ashes? She had lain awake many a night asking herself that question. She had even got up to go to the great hearth in the library with the intention of fuelling a sacrilegious fire, only to make her way back to bed incapable of carrying out her plan. Why? Because they contained knowledge, and knowledge, however unbelievable, was sacred.

The Abbess made the messenger as comfortable as she could before unbolting another door opening onto the corridor. Cautiously poking her head out to check that the coast was clear, she walked through and closed it behind her. She made her way swiftly towards the kitchen to fetch a ewer of water, some bread and cheese and perhaps a few slices of smoked bacon – enough to replenish the traveller after his exhausting journey. She hurried along the corridor, like a thief, hugging the walls, listening out for the slightest sound for fear of being surprised.

A jovial voice rang out behind her. She swung round, summoning up all her strength in order to greet Yolande de Fleury's words with a smile. The young sister worked in the granary and was accompanied by the granary's custodian, Sister Adèle de Vigneux. Yolande de Fleury was a small, plump woman whose perpetual good humour, it appeared, nothing could dampen. She enquired:

'Abbess, where are you going in such a hurry? Might we assist you in some task?'

'No, my dear children. I felt a sudden but persistent thirst – a result of my bookkeeping no doubt. A walk to the kitchens will stretch my legs.'

Éleusie watched the two women disappear round the corner at the end of the corridor. Naturally she trusted her nuns, even her novices, as well as the majority of the lay servants, who were offerings to God. She could no doubt have shared the burden of her secret with some of them: Jeanne d'Amblin, for example, the most loyal of all, intelligent and, despite having no great illusions about the world, an optimist. These qualities, coupled with her tenacity, had encouraged Éleusie to confer on her the challenging task of Extern Sister.[17] Adélaïde Condeau was no less of an ally. She had been baptised thus after a cooper discovered her at the edge of a forest of that name. She was only a few weeks old, two or three at the most. The man was not glad of his discovery and took the infant to the abbey. He had no need of a baby girl but the famished new-born infant's cries had moved him. Despite her youth and impressionability, Adélaïde, too, was already showing evidence of great perseverance coupled with an unwavering faith. Blanche de Blinot, the most senior nun and her prioress and second in command, had long been her confidante. Blanche's advanced age was her greatest asset, for she forgot most of what she was told. Even Annelette Beaupré, the apothecary nun, for all her tetchiness and arrogance was someone upon whom she knew she could rely. On the other hand, she did not entirely trust Berthe de Marchiennes, the cellarer nun,[18] who already occupied that demanding post before Éleusie's arrival at the abbey. Berthe's resentment was palpable beneath the façade of her devoutness. Her lack of physical beauty and a dowry had left her no other option but the monastic life, although she would certainly have preferred the secular one.

No, absolutely not. A secret is best kept when it is shared with no one. And in any case what right had she to burden these good women with dangerous revelations that were difficult to bear? It would be selfish of her. No, none of the sisters must know of this man's presence. He would leave as he had arrived, like a troubling enigma.

In order to reach the kitchen, Éleusie decided to cut through the guest house[19] that was squeezed in between the hot-room and the storeroom. With the exception of Thibaude de Gartempe, the guest mistress, and possibly of Jeanne d'Amblin, neither of whom were cloistered, she ran little risk of bumping into anyone at that hour. She hadn't noticed the small figure pressed behind one of the pillars beside the schoolroom door. Clément paused, ashamed at having hidden instinctively. He was disconcerted by the Abbess's behaviour. Why such caution, such furtiveness in her own convent?

Back in her study Éleusie de Beaufort sat down behind her heavy oak table. She touched the letter with the tip of her finger. It still bore the two crease marks where it had been folded, and looked inoffensive lying there among the registers to whose pages the Abbess carefully consigned the details of their daily lives: the donations, the harvests, the number and quality of wine barrels in the cellar, the amount of timber felled, received or donated, the births and deaths in the pigeon-house, plus the weight of droppings, which were used as fertiliser, the visits to the sick, the deaths, the levies imposed, the ingredients of the nuns' meals or their new linen. Half an hour ago, the task had bored her; she had baulked at it and wondered what possible use the endless lists, over which she nevertheless took great care, might one day have. Half an hour ago, she was still unaware how much she would soon mourn the thankless task. In the insignificant space of that half-hour, her world had collapsed, and she had not even sensed the approaching cataclysm that would silently ravage the calm of her study.

She was choked by a terrible grief. She stood by helplessly as the sanctuary that had been her home for five years was devastated. All those images she had managed to suppress, or rather to eradicate. All those hideous waking nightmares. Would they come back to haunt her now? The incomprehensible, bloody, violent and terrifying scenes she was powerless to stop that pulsed through her imagination. At one point, she had thought she was losing her mind, or that a demon was tormenting her with visions of hell. She never knew when she might be visited by the terrifying hallucinations. For nights on end she had prayed to the Holy Virgin for some reprieve. Her prayer had been answered the moment she arrived at the convent. She had almost managed to rid herself even of the memory of them. Were they going to come back? She would rather die than endure them again.

A woman lay face down on the rack, the blood from the gashes on her back oozing to the floor. The woman was moaning. Her long fair hair was sticky with sweat and blood. A hand brushed against her martyred flesh, pouring a grey powder onto her wounds. The woman arched her back and went limp, fainting. Suddenly Éleusie could make out the pale face. It was she. Éleusie.

*

This vision in particular had haunted her all those years ago, night after night for months on end. Éleusie had decided to take her religious vows.

She had to keep telling herself that it was only a horrible memory, nothing more. She could feel her heart pounding against her chest. Reluctantly she picked up the letter and forced herself to calm down. She proceeded to read it for the tenth time:

Hoc quicumque stolam sanguine proluit, absergit maculas; et roseum decus, quo fiat similis protinus Angelis.

The thing she had been dreading for years had caught up with her that day.

How should she reply to this demand? Could she pretend not to know, not to understand? What foolishness! What did her own blood matter compared to the divine blood that cleansed all sins? Little or nothing.

She began to trace the curved letters of her reply, which she knew by heart. She had repeated them for hours on end like an exorcism, thinking, hoping she would never need to write them:

Amen. Miserere nostri. Dies illa, solvet saeclum in favilla.[20]

A cold sweat drenched the hem of her veil, making her shiver suddenly and drop her quill.

She picked it up again and continued writing:

Statim autem post tribulationem dierum illorum sol

obscurabitur et luna non dabit lumen suum et stellae cadent de caelo et virtutes caelorum commovebuntur.[21]

Amen.

He was blinking from exhaustion. The filthy rags he wore made him feel nauseated. And yet the messenger was accustomed to this endless journeying, these arduous missions under various guises. Occasionally, he would sleep for leagues at a time face down on his horse's neck, allowing the animal's legs to decide his fate and his path. However, this time he had been obliged to travel incognito and in this impoverished countryside a horse would have been too conspicuous.

A surge of joy lifted his spirits. He was the go-between, the necessary tool, the link between the powerful of this earth, those who shaped the world for future generations. Without him their decisions would remain as mere wishes, mere hopes. He gave them life, shape and substance. He was the humble artisan of the future.

He was only a hundred yards outside the abbey enclosure when the soft sound of racing feet made him swing round. A figure in a white tunic was running towards him, a wicker basket joggling back and forth on one arm.

'Oh dear God!' she gasped. 'I should not be here, but you are a brother monk. Our Abbess . . . Well, I came here on my own initiative. You are so exhausted. Why did you not spend the night in our guest house? We often receive visitors. Oh here I am chattering away like a jackdaw . . . You see, I feel so ashamed. Take these . . .'

She handed him the provisions she had prepared and, blushing, explained:

'I thought to myself, if our Reverend Mother received you, it was because she trusted you and you were a friend. I know her well. She has much work and many responsibilities. I knew she would have thought to feed you, but not to supply you with food for your journey.'

He smiled. She had been right. She looked rather frail and yet a remarkable strength radiated from her every gesture. The kindly sister gazing up at him had broken the rule of the cloister for his sake, and she was glowing proof that his exhaustion was deserving and that Christ lived in them both.

'Thank you, sister.'

'Adélaïde . . . I am Sister Adélaïde, in charge of the kitchens and of meals. Hush! Do not thank me. You know I should not be here, and I wasn't told to come – it was a simple oversight. I wished to make amends, that is all. I deserve no thanks. And yet I am happy to offer you these humble provisions – this rye bread, black but very nourishing, a bottle of our own cider – you'll find it delicious – a goat's cheese, some fruit and a big slice of spice cake, which I made myself. They say it's very flavourful.' She laughed, before confessing awkwardly, 'I love to feed people, no doubt it is a failing. I don't know why, it just gives me pleasure.' Suddenly guilty, she stammered, 'Oh dear, I should not say such things . . .'

'Indeed you should. It is good to feed people, above all the needy. Thank you for your precious offerings, Sister Adélaïde.' Suddenly glad of this brief exchange, which had lightened his spirits before his gruelling journey, he added, 'And you have my word, this will remain strictly between us – like a little secret that unites us over distance.'

Overjoyed, she bit her bottom lip and then, frightened, said hastily:

'I must go back. I sense your path will be a long one, brother. Let it be safe from harm. My prayers will follow you. No, they will accompany you. Make a little place for me in yours.'

He leant towards her, planted a fraternal kiss on her anxious brow, and murmured:

'Amen.'

CLÉMENT felt confident. All was quiet. The nuns had retired to their cells after supper and compline.* Outside, a chorus of frogs croaked and the jays' raucous complaints ricocheted from nest to nest. Further to his right, the tireless garden dormice tunnelled furiously between the stones with their claws. They were such cautious creatures that it was rare to catch a glimpse of their little black masked faces. The slightest unfamiliar presence would silence them. Clément delighted in the treasure trail nature left for those who knew how to watch and listen. He had uncovered most of its secrets, and its dangers too.

Cautiously, he stretched a numb leg out of his hiding place in the large hollowed stone the herbalist used for soaking the leaves, rhizomes, and berries she collected. The air was rank with the smell of rotten foliage. It would be dark within an hour. He had time to eat something and to reflect.

What was to become of them? The two of them that was, for Mathilde's fate was of little concern to him. She was far too vain and foolish to worry about anything except her little breasts that were not budding as fast as she would like, her ribbons and hair combs. What would become of Agnès and him? A feeling of joy made his eyes brim with tears, for there were two of them, he was not alone. The Dame de Souarcy would never forsake him, even at risk to her own life. The certain knowledge that it was true wrenched his heart.

Crouching unseen behind the door to the main hall, he had witnessed the gruelling evening to which her half-brother had subjected her the day before. As usual she had outwitted him. And yet the following day, just after the scoundrel had left, while they were doing their round of the outbuildings, he had sensed her uncertainty and understood her fears: how far was Eudes prepared to go? What would he stop at?

The answer to the second question was obvious and Agnès knew it as well as Clément. He would stop at fear, when he came face to face with a beast more ferocious than he.

They were so alone, so vulnerable. They had no beast to champion them, to come to their aid. For months now the child had struggled with his despair. He must find a way out, a solution. He cursed his youth and his physical frailty. He cursed the truth of his origins, which he was forced to conceal for both their sakes. Agnès had explained this to him as soon as she could, and he knew her fears were well founded.

Knowledge was a weapon, Agnès had explained, especially when confronted with an ignorant boor like Eudes. Knowledge. It was passed on, to some extent, by the schoolmistresses at Clairets. And so, two years earlier, his lady had allowed him to attend the few classes open to children of all ages from the rich burgher families and gentry from the surrounding countryside. These offered him scant intellectual nourishment since, thanks to Agnès, he had long ago learnt to read and write in French and Latin. He had vainly hoped he might learn about the sciences, about life in distant lands. In reality, most of the time was spent on the study of the Gospels and learning by rote the words of worthy Latin scholars such as Cicero, Suetonius and Seneca. Added to these limitations was the terror the schoolmistress,[22] Emma de Pathus, inspired in them all. Her permanent sullenness and readiness to raise her hand was enough to strike fear into the hearts of her young charges.

In the end, it mattered little. The goodly Bernardines were unstinting in their efforts, zealously caring for some, educating others, settling discords, calming hostilities, accompanying the dying. Unlike some of the other orders, they could not be accused of indifference towards the world outside the abbey, or of profiting from the misfortunes of humble folk. It mattered little because Clément had learnt so many things. Each seed of knowledge sprouted another. Each new key to understanding he forged unlocked a bigger door than the last. He had also learnt not to ask questions the sisters were unable to answer, for he realised that his curiosity, which initially rewarded their pains, ended by perplexing and then troubling them. In truth it mattered little because he had become convinced that the abbey contained an intriguing mystery.

Why had he slipped behind the pillar? He had been waiting for the Latin mistress. Was it instinct? Or was it the strange behaviour of the figure in white? The Abbess had looked around furtively before hurriedly locking the small postern door she had just emerged from, and then darted down the corridor, like a thief.

A quick, discreet enquiry left him none the wiser. No one seemed to know where that door led. What was in the room on the other side? Was it a secret cell for some important prisoner? Perhaps it was a torture chamber? The child's fertile imagination ran away with him until he decided to solve the mystery himself. A roughly drawn map of the central part of the abbey helped him to determine that if there were a secret chamber it must be quite small, unless it contained a window – one of the ones that gave onto the interior garden that ran alongside the scriptorium and the dormitories. And if his modest topographical plan was at all accurate it must be in the middle of the Abbess's chambers and study.

He had been burning with curiosity and impatience ever since. He had given a great deal of thought to the problem of how to remain within the abbey enclosure in order to pursue his secret inquiry and test his theories. In the end one solution imposed itself: the herbarium adjacent to the medicinal garden would give him shelter for a few hours while he waited for nightfall.

The full moon that night was Clément's unwitting accomplice. He left the herbarium, moving silent as a ghost and blending in to the outer wall of the dormitory. He passed beneath the scriptorium windows, taller and broader than the rest in order to allow the copyists as much light as possible. He continued alongside the smaller windows of the steam room, the only part of the abbey that was heated in winter, and the place where the sick were tended and the ink stored overnight so it wouldn't freeze. Only a couple more yards to go. The young boy was breathless with anxiety, wondering what explanation he might give for being there in the middle of the night if he were discovered, hardly daring to imagine the ensuing punishment. He slipped below the two small windows in the Abbess's study and below the two air vents cut into the stone wall of the circular room in her chamber containing the garderobe. The mystery chamber should be located somewhere between these two rooms. Clément retraced his steps and measured the distance in paces between Éleusie de Beaufort's chamber and her study. He estimated about twelve yards. Abbess or not, a nun's cell could not be that wide or spacious. The secret chamber, then, though much bigger than he had first calculated, must be windowless. The thought sent a shiver of fear and excitement down his spine. What if the room was an inquisitorial chamber? What if he discovered signs of torture there? No. There was no such thing as a female Inquisitor. He went back over the same patch, this time on his hands and knees, his nose to the ground. A cellar window, measuring approximately two yards long and a foot high, opened onto the ornamental flowerbeds at the base of the wall. Thick bars protected the window against intruders. Full-grown intruders, he supposed correctly, for they were widely enough spaced to allow a slim child to pass through. Relief gave way to panic. What should he do now? Curiosity prevailed over the many excellent reasons he could think of for turning back and leaving the abbey enclosure as quickly and, above all, as quietly as possible.

How far was the cellar window from the floor? A piece of gravel from the pathway bordering the flowerbeds served as a sounding device. Clément calculated from the clear and almost instantaneous impact it made on the ground that five feet at the very most lay between him and his objective. He was wrong.

Stretched out on his side, he struggled through the bars that dug into his flesh, holding his stomach in and exhaling as deeply as he could to make himself as thin as possible. Finally his chest squeezed through and he let himself fall to the floor. The length of time he was suspended in the void startled him. He landed like a dead weight and a searing pain almost made him cry out. His suffering soon gave way to panic. What if he had broken something? How would he find his way out of there? He gripped his rapidly swelling ankle, rotating it this way and that and forcing back the tears that pricked his eyes. It was a sprain, only a bad sprain. It would hurt but he would be able to walk.

He was encircled by thick blackness. A humid darkness in which wafts of dank air combined with a lingering sweet smell reminiscent of animal glue. The cool gloom of a cellar. He began to tremble with rage at himself. How could he have been so stupid, he who was so proud of his quick wits? How was he going to get out of there? He hadn't given it a thought. What a fool!

He waited a few moments for his eyes to become accustomed to that indoor gloom, denser than the darkness that had camouflaged him in the garden. A long table, like a work bench, covered in uneven heaps was the first thing he was able to make out. He limped towards it, his arms outstretched. Books. Piles of books on a table. Then, out of the gloom, the shape of a ladder. No. More like a small stepladder leaning against some shelves containing more books. A library. He was in a library. Over in the corner stretching up to the ceiling, a large indistinct shape loomed. He walked over to it, wincing from the pain in his ankle. It was a spiral staircase leading to another room, and below the steps were pinned pieces of fine leather, no doubt intended to repair the book bindings. He carefully climbed the stairs. The darkness seemed to grow less opaque the further up he went. Emerging on all fours into the room at the top, he slowly rose to his feet. He froze with astonishment. It was a vast library with a soaring ceiling and books covering every wall. Moonlight filtered through the horizontal arrow slits, ingeniously positioned more than four yards above ground level, which was why he had failed to notice them earlier. Their function was to allow both light and air to filter discreetly into the room. As though in a trance, he walked over to one of the bookcases and with reverential awe pulled out a few of the weighty volumes. The good condition they were in was proof of the care they received. Choked with emotion, Clément managed to read some of the titles. He sensed the world was opening up just for him. Everything he had always longed to discover, to learn, to know was here, within his grasp. Overcome, he murmured:

'My God! Could it be that the entire works of Claudius Galen* are here? *De sanitate tuenda* . . . And *De anatomicis administrationibus* . . . And even *De usu partium corporis* . . .'

The child's breathless voice trailed off.

He found a translation from the Latin by a certain Farag ben Salem of a book by Abu-Bakr-Mohammed-ibn-Zakariya al-Razi,* a name he had never heard of before. The work, *Al-Hawi*, or, in Latin, *Continens*, appeared to be on pharmacology but the feeble light of the moon hampered his ability to read.

Other books remained inaccessible to Clément, their strange-looking titles in foreign tongues guarding their secrets.

Was it Arabic, Greek or Hebrew? He did not know.

So the room he had gone through to reach there was only a storeroom, or possibly a workshop. That would explain the smell of glue and the pieces of leather.

Exhilarated, he studied the books for hours, losing all notion of time. The night sky filtering through the arrow slits became tinged with milky blue, finally alerting him that day was approaching.

With the help of the stepladder, Clément managed with great difficulty to climb back out through the cellar window. He could feel his ankle pounding – an immense throbbing pulse.

Porte Bucy, Paris, June 1304

THE oppressive afternoon heat did not bother Francesco de Leone any more than the stench emanating from the mounds of refuse at the corner of every alleyway. On the other hand, the ceaseless activity of the human ant hill made his head spin.

The city numbered over sixty thousand hearths, meaning a population of close on two hundred thousand souls. This buzzing populace was distributed on both sides of the river Seine, spanned by only two wooden bridges: the Grand Pont and the Petit Pont, which were recklessly over-constructed – the larger of the two accommodating a hundred and forty dwellings and a hundred shops, as well as the added weight of watermills. As a result, it was not unknown for flood waters to wash the bridges away as if they were clumps of straw.

The Knight slowly climbed Rue de Bucy, benignly refusing the advances of a famished-looking young woman with dark shadows under her eyes. He thought she must have come out of one of the steam rooms. It was common knowledge that the mixed public baths were also used for assignations of an amorous nature, whether of the clandestine or the remunerated variety. Sex was for sale all over Paris and there was no lack of customers. Carnal love was considered a minor sin so long as it had a price on it. It allowed men whose poverty inhibited them from marrying to satisfy their urgent needs, their desires. It also allowed starving girls, cast into the street because of an untimely pregnancy or by penniless parents, to survive, while at the same time saving married women from the lechery of the powerful. At least these were a few of the glib arguments that acted as a balm for the consciences of some and the guilt of others. They did not persuade Francesco de Leone, and he was filled with a strange sadness. The oldest profession in the world, practised by women who were increasingly excluded from any others, was spreading in the city. At this rate they would soon be able to count their options on one hand: born to wealth, married, nuns or prostitutes. In the latter case they would end up eaten away by tuberculosis or intestinal diseases, or even slashed to ribbons by some casual client. Who cared what became of these spectres? Not the powers that be, not the Church, certainly not their families.

The girl kept her eyes fixed on him. She was intimidated by his appearance yet driven by hunger and fear of destitution. He paused to study her.

He was chasing that woman, always the same one, in the ambulatory of that church, always the same place. Did he want to kill her or was he trying to save her from some unseen enemy? He had prayed for the second theory to be the true one. And yet he remained unable to convince himself that it was.

The eternal misery of women, their astonishing frailty. His mother and infant sister, their throats slit like lambs, left to rot in the blazing sun, their wounds crawling with flies. He closed his eyes for a moment. When he opened them again the girl was smiling at him, the pathetic smile of a poor unwanted creature looking for money for her supper and a bed for the night. There was nothing seductive or alluring about those sickly-looking lips. And yet, though powerless to seduce, she still attempted to persuade him.

He took five silver pennies from his purse, a fortune for a pauper, and walked over to her:

'Eat and rest a while, sister.'

She stared at the coins he had placed in the palm of her hand and shook her head.

When she looked up at him her pale cheeks were streaked.

'I . . . Come, I'm sweet and gentle, and I'm not sick, I promise . . . I . . .'

'Hush, rest.'

'But . . . How may I . . .'

'Pray for me.'

He turned on his heel and walked away quickly, leaving her weeping, overcome with relief and despair.

For her and for his mother and sister, for all women who had no man to protect them, for Christ and his immense love for women, a love that had so long been scorned by miserable buffoons. Sinners, sinners disguised as practitioners of the faith.

Giotto Capella. Long ago in a land where the sun scorched the earth, the Knight would have given his life to slay this man. Arnaud de Viancourt knew nearly all there was to know of Francesco de Leone's childhood and had hesitated before pronouncing the name of their 'unwitting intermediary'. When he had finally uttered it and awaited his brother's response, he had evoked the threat that was hanging over them in order to justify imposing on him such a difficult task.

The handsome white stone house, completed only months before, dominated Rue de Bucy. It belonged to Giotto Capella, a native of Crema, a small Lombard village to the south-east of Milan. His third-floor windows gave onto the Seine and the Louvre. It was the reason he had chosen the location: to be close to the heart of power and thus to the biggest borrowers, but also to Paris's natural frontier. For the disposition of the powerful towards moneylenders was a fickle one. A fact that the Lombards – the name given to Italian and Jewish moneylenders alike regardless of whether they were natives of that province – had had the recent misfortune to discover. In reality, the inconsistencies of the new century with regard to usury should have amused Giotto, who was not an uncultivated man but one for whom money was a means and above all an end and a passion. How could they as merchants be expected to lend money to strangers without making a profit? Nonsense! There was a good reason why usury had been outlawed. It allowed kings and noblemen to borrow money and then banish the usurers, confiscating their assets and brandishing religion as a justification. How many times had they had to listen to that convenient verse from the Gospel encouraging the lender to expect nothing in return? Thus the debtors rid themselves of creditors, interest and debt. What fools they were. For someone who knew how to negotiate, a debt was always repayable, whether against cash or against less obvious forms of payment.

*

Giotto Capella set down his glass of mulled wine, a rare treat he permitted himself regardless of the gout that seared his foot and was progressively immobilising him. The Knight Hospitaller had been waiting outside in his anteroom for some minutes. What did he want? The moneylender had felt uneasy the moment he agreed to the meeting. The Leones were one of the most eminent Italian families and had been in the service of the papacy for centuries. They were exceedingly wealthy, notwithstanding the vows of poverty taken by a number of their male offspring, which included Francesco. The Templars and Hospitallers were the type of complex and powerful entity it was preferable not to associate with. No prince, king or bishop could make them yield so what chance had a moneylender! Even less so, as Leone was not there to ask for money. On this Giotto Capella would have staked his life. A pity, since money was so simple: it retained, restrained, and subjugated. What did he want, then? A favour, a mediator, the means with which to blackmail somebody? If Giotto Capella had had the courage, he would have turned the Knight of Christ away. But that was a luxury he could ill afford. Conflict with a military order would hamper his long-held ambition: to hold the post of Captain General of the Lombards of France by adroitly forcing out the current holder, Giorgio Zuccari – if necessary into his grave. For years he had been unable to abide Zuccari. A man given to preaching and impossible to catch at his own game, such was the loathsome integrity he showed towards his peers and, worse still, towards his debtors. Thus he applied to the letter Saint Louis's recommendation that interest should not exceed 33 per cent. Why, if there were people crazy or desperate enough to pay 45 per cent? After all, Capella did not force potential borrowers onto his premises!

This line of reasoning repeated a hundred times worked like a charm. It had the power to lift his spirits. His light-heartedness, however, was short-lived. What the devil did Leone want from him? Why hadn't he gone directly to Zuccari? His name and the fact that he was a Hospitaller permitted it, and the old moneylender would have welcomed him with open arms. A pox on inscrutable people!

His unease combined with a feeling of displeasure the moment Francesco de Leone walked into his study – a veritable Ali Baba's cave jam-packed with paintings, carved wooden boxes, furs and valuable pieces of porcelain from his latest seizures. God, the man was handsome, while he resembled an ugly toad, wizened and yellow-looking from the constant privations decreed by his physic in a clipped voice. Even his wife closed her eyes in disgust now, the rare times he stroked her thighs.

He stood up, holding out his hands, forcing himself to be gracious.

'Knight, you honour my humble dwelling.'

Leone immediately sensed Capella's hostility. He moved forward a few paces, responding to the perfunctory greeting only with a slight raising of his eyebrows. It occurred to Giotto that the man belonged to that select few before whom others knelt without them even noticing. His resentment mounted. He checked it, however, by enquiring:

'Would you accept a goblet of my best wine?'

'With pleasure. I do not doubt that it is excellent.'

The moneylender considered for a moment whether the seemingly anodyne remark contained a hidden reproach. What he really wanted was for the Knight to show that he was as greedy as his fellow man, but shielded by his name, his order, his piety. Then he could despise him freely, dismiss him with feigned indignation. He could already hear himself saying:

'What! And you a Knight Hospitaller, Monsieur! What a disgrace!'

All those nobles and prelates, those so-called dignitaries who had filed before him and whom he had flattered, reassured and encouraged in their vices, which were the source of his livelihood – the never-ending source. Most had abandoned themselves to the deadly sins of cupidity and covetousness, which had corrupted their souls, their hearts, even their speech. But the man before him possessed the calm confidence of the pure, and they were the worst – especially when they were intelligent and no longer knew fear.

The two men sat in deceptively companionable silence while a maidservant fetched the wine. Leone took the measure of the man opposite him. A few seconds were sufficient for him to know that Capella remained what he had always been: an avaricious swindler who only refrained sometimes from committing the vilest acts out of cowardice. An image flashed through his mind of a repulsive, carnivorous beast lying in wait uneasily, ready to pounce on his enemy's throat at the slightest sign of weakness. The possibility of redemption was not distributed equally among men, for there were those who did not wish it.

Francesco took a sip of wine and set down the goblet, made

ugly by an excess of chasing and inlaid precious stones. He reached beneath his heavy linen surcoat[23] for the Grand-Master's letter and handed it to Capella. After the Lombard had broken the seal and read the first few lines, everything around him started spinning. He murmured:

'My God . . .'

He shot a glance at Leone, who signalled to him to continue reading.

It had never occurred to Capella that this blood-soaked memory from nearly fifteen years ago might one day come back to haunt him. He had paid dearly enough for it in every sense of the word.

A warm tear fell on his hand, followed by another. He let the sheet of vellum fall to the marble floor he had had brought over from his native Carrara at great expense.

Was he aware that he was crying? Leone could not be sure.

Francesco de Leone waited. He knew the contents of the letter, of the blackmail note more precisely: any weapon, the prior had specified, himself having recourse to this strategy of extremes.

What did he care about the usurer's tears, or his memories? So many people had died because of him.

The other man whispered breathlessly:

'This is monstrous.'

'Why? Because it is the truth?'

Giotto Capella gave the Knight the look of a drowning man and spluttered:

'Why? Because it was so long ago . . . Because I have suffered the torment of guilt, and of the worst kind: that which we inflict on ourselves. And because I have tried so hard to be worthy of forgiveness . . .'

'You mean, to be forgotten. We have never forgotten and we have not forgiven. And as for the torments of guilt, why, I would laugh if I were a mere soldier. Who let the Mamelukes invade Acre more than a month into the siege? Sultan Al-Ashraf Khalil was champing at the bit outside the city walls with his seventy thousand men on horseback and his hundred and fifty foot soldiers from Egypt and Syria. The defence of the citadel of Saint-Jean was heroic: there were only fifteen thousand Christian soldiers inside the city walls. They fought like lions, out-numbered by fifteen to one. The Sultan's men identified the weak points in the enclosure and in groups of a thousand tunnelled into the sewers and the butchers' pit with remarkable precision.'

Leone paused to study the breathless man, who was gripping the edges of his writing table with both hands.

Capella made an attempt to justify himself in a barely audible voice:

'The negotiations had been successful. Al-Ashraf had agreed to the citadel being evacuated if the defenders left behind all their possessions.'

'Come now. King Henri would never have accepted such a complete, such a dishonourable surrender. What is more, the defenders of the citadel were soon able to judge for themselves how far they could trust the Sultan's word,' retorted Leone in a calm voice, fixing the usurer with his deep-blue eyes. 'On 15 May, the New Tower, donated by the Comtesse de Blois, collapsed, having been undermined by sappers. Al-Ashraf then promised to allow the conquered to evacuate, above all their women and children. But the Mamelukes were already in the central square desecrating the chapel and raping the women. What followed was a bloodbath. The Dominicans, Franciscans, Clarisses were massacred and the women and children were taken away to be sold as slaves. That was only the beginning of the destruction. Almost everyone was slain: my brother Hospitallers, the Knights Templar of Saint-Lazare and Saint-Thomas. Only a handful of cripples were left alive.'

'But it was inevitable,' Capella whined. 'Two years before — in the month of August, I believe — some peasants and Muslim merchants were attacked by Hugues de Sully's Italian crusaders in a marketplace. The merchants were forced to seek refuge in their inn, and . . .'

'And who came to their aid?' Leone interrupted in a voice that was now openly contemptuous. 'The Knights Templar and Hospitaller!'

'It was a war. Wars are . . .'

'No. It was an ambush. An ambush that was admirably thought out and therefore worth its weight in gold. Was it not, moneylender? As for that skirmish at the marketplace, it was nothing but a poor excuse. Anyone starting a war must always provide some kind of justification. But that is neither here nor there. Had the Mamelukes not known the precise location of the New Tower and the sewers, the work of the sappers would have been useless, or at least slowed down. We could have waited for reinforcements or, at worst, negotiated the evacuation of most of the people. How much did they pay, Giotto Capella, for the slaughter of fifteen thousand men and almost as many women and children?'

'They . . . they beat me. They . . . they threatened to castrate me. They were going to . . . They were laughing . . .' he stammered.

The usurer's eyes swept the room, as if he were expecting some miraculous intervention. Leone stared at him. The sly rat was using his last defence: pity.

Early June 1291. The centre of the battle had moved. The Sidon Fort was now under siege and would not hold out much longer. A young boy of twelve struggled against the hand clutching his shoulder, that of his Uncle Henri, and, freeing himself from the iron grip, ran towards the ruins of Acre. He tripped and fell then leapt to his feet, his hands sticky with blood.

The broad white steps were bathed in sunlight. The broad white steps of the chapel defiled by streaks of dried blood and a morass of human flesh. The broad steps swarming with bloated, feasting flies.

Some of the women had attempted to seek refuge in the chapel, to hide their children there. Underneath one of them, whose head, almost severed from the neck, was facing the sky, the young boy recognised a mass of flaxen hair. Flaxen hair congealed with blood. His sister's hair.

'How much, Capella? How much for my mother and seven-year-old sister, defiled, their throats slit, left to rot in the sun, ravaged by dogs so that I could no longer recognise them? How much for your soul?'

The other man's gaze settled at last on the Knight. The gaze of a dead man, a gaze from the past. In a voice he no longer recognised as his own, and suspecting he might never recover from this confession, he said:

'Five hundred gold pieces.'

'You are lying. I can always detect your feeble lies. It was a smaller sum, wasn't it?'

Faced with the other man's silence, the Knight persisted:

'Wasn't it? What did you think? That doubling or tripling the amount in gold would absolve you? That by multiplying the price of your treachery and greed they would somehow be legitimised? That everything in this world has a price? How much do you imagine a thousand pounds, or a hundred thousand, or ten million is worth in the eyes of God? Why, the same as a single penny.'

'Three hundred . . . And I only saw half of it. They broke their word. They spat in my face when I went to claim the balance.'

'The rascals!' said the Knight, mockingly.

He closed his eyes, tilted back his head, and, as though speaking to himself, repeated:

'A hundred and fifty gold pieces for all those corpses, for those two women . . . A hundred and fifty gold pieces, which allowed you to become a usurer. A tidy sum for a . . . what were you when you still had a soul?'

'A meat merchant.'

'Oh yes . . . That would explain your perfect knowledge of the sewers at Acre and of the butchers' pit.' Leone sighed, before continuing in a hushed voice, 'I know you and your kind so well that I sometimes feel I am enveloped by a rotten stench. It follows me everywhere, sticks to my skin, makes my stomach heave. I can sense you before I see you, before I hear you. I can smell you. The stale odour of your dead decaying souls suffocates me. Do you know the stench of a rotting soul? It is worse than any stinking carcass.'

The other man leapt up, suddenly oblivious to the stabbing pain in his foot. His face drained of blood, he moved towards the Hospitaller's armchair, and fell to his knees, wailing:

'Mercy, I beg you, mercy!'

'That is beyond me, and I regret it. For my own sake.'

Some minutes passed, punctuated by the kneeling man's sobs. A violent sadness shook Leone. How could a simple act of forgiveness cause his infinite love for Him to waver? What had he lost, what had he destroyed of his faith? He pulled himself up with the thought that he had not yet become the Light, that he was still drawing near, with such difficulty, so much effort, like a desperate ant, deranged and sickened by darkness.

One day. One day he would reach out and touch it at last, the Light he had only been able to glimpse in the nave at Santa Costanza. One day he would embrace it, he would breathe it in, be immersed in it and all his sins would be cleansed. He was drawing near, he could feel it. For so long the tireless ant he had become had crossed oceans, climbed mountains, braved every obstacle, nearly died a hundred deaths, seared by the desert sun, wasted by fever, swept away by storms. And yet each time he had picked himself up and continued towards the Light. He longed one day to die inside the Light, to dissolve and at last to be at peace.

The Ineffable Trace, the Unutterable Secret was within his reach, all that was necessary to attain it was to shed blood, his own blood.

Leone stood up, gently pushing aside the broken man.

'I await this meeting with Guillaume de Nogaret. You are after all an official moneylender to the kingdom of France, and I am sure you will find an excellent reason to explain my presence here. And remember: at the slightest sign of treachery Philip the Fair will learn who was responsible for the slaughter at Acre. I shall remain in your house for the duration of this enterprise. Do not speak to me, usurer, about any other matter. I shall take my meals alone in the room you will provide for me in your residence. I want it ready within the hour. I am going outside to breathe the putrid smell of the streets. It must be more tolerable than the one you mask with incense in your chambers.'

He paused in the doorway without turning and addressed the shell of a man:

'Never lie to me. I know so much about you, Capella, so much that you do not know. Should you be tempted to betray me for a fat sum or simply out of fear, I swear before God that I shall punish your days and nights with torments such as you have only touched upon in your wildest imaginings.'

Clairets Abbey, Perche, June 1304

EVERY night for weeks Clément had been coming back, drawn almost in spite of himself by the treasures in the secret library that were hidden from the eyes of the world. After a few uneasy forays he had gradually gained in confidence. He would enter at nightfall and occasionally felt bold enough to stay for the whole of the following day. He lived on the provisions he pilfered from the kitchens at Souarcy – for he was becoming more and more distrustful of Mabile. Indeed, his initial, rather dormant mistrust had grown keener since Eudes de Larnay's last visit. Up until then, he had been content to spy upon the spy in order to protect Agnès, but now he was on the lookout for any suspicious activity. He had soon seen through the folly of his first plan: catching Mabile red-handed in order to give the Dame de Souarcy a legitimate excuse to turn her out was too obvious – too obvious but, above all, of little or no use. Why not instead catch the spy out at her own game? Why not plant a few harmless secrets for her to find? Then if Eudes tried to use them against his half-sister it would be easy to discredit him in spite of his lineage and wealth, which gave him nevertheless a significant advantage. All Clément needed to do now was convince his mistress to agree to this subterfuge. He knew that his lady was beginning to glimpse an unpleasant truth.

Noble victories or dignified defeats are only possible when confronting a noble enemy. The weak can fight a powerful villain only with cunning and deceit. He was certain Agnès had understood this even though she had still not accepted it completely. Still, in one sense Eudes's villainy had done the Dame de Souarcy a good turn; it had silenced her remaining scruples and remorse. Eudes was an evil beast and in order to defeat him any line of attack was permissible.

His nightly forays into the secret library at Clairets Abbey were part of this. To begin with, Clément had comforted himself with the idea that if the Abbess had a sudden wish to go in there, he could simply hide under the spiral staircase, behind the pieces of leather that formed an improvised curtain. His fears soon proved groundless. The Abbess rarely entered the library, to which she alone possessed the keys, and of whose existence only she was aware. The fact that it held so little appeal for Éleusie de Beaufort, who was renowned for her learning, had at first surprised the child. But he had gradually begun to understand why. A number of these works contained such revelations, such shocking secrets – some so upsetting they had reduced Clément to tears. To begin with he had doubted the veracity of the words that expressed them. But the evidence was so overwhelming it had finally convinced him. Thus the earth was not surrounded by a void, but by some intangible fluid within which coexisted elements and organisms so microscopic as to be invisible to the human eye. Thus the stone in toads' brains that protected against poison was a mere fable, as were unicorns. Thus comas, convulsions, trembling and headaches were not symptoms of demonic possession but of a malfunction in the brain – if one were to believe Abu Marwan Abd Al-Malik Ibn Zuhr, called Avenzoar in the West, one of the twelfth century's most eminent Arab doctors of Jewish origin. Thus it was not enough to spit three times in a toad's mouth in order not to conceive for a year. Thus, thus, thus . . .

Was Éleusie de Beaufort trying to hold back this tidal wave? Had she grown pale at the thought of the threat this science posed to all the stale dogmas and, more importantly, the power it gave to those who wielded it?

A single slim volume had absorbed him for almost a whole month. It was a Greek primer for Latinists. He had even been bold enough to borrow it for a few days in order to further his learning of that strange language, which seemed to him more and more essential to an understanding of the world.

He had then scoured the library's interminable shelves for a similar work that would allow him to penetrate the mysteries of Hebrew and Aramaic; for during his feverish research a sort of logic had soon become apparent, an indefinable conducting thread that led him from one work to another.

He was stunned upon carefully opening a small collection of aphorisms bound in a kind of coarse red silk. That same name. That same name written in ink at the top of the first page in the last three books he had deciphered. He had discovered the connecting thread. Eustache de Rioux, Knight Hospitaller. Was the man dead? Had he bequeathed his books directly to Clairets Abbey or through a legatee? What was it that had drawn Clément to the works in his collection those past few days?

A sudden impulse made him go back to the shelf where he had found the book. One by one he pulled out the adjacent volumes, glancing inside them before replacing them. At last he found what he had been looking for. The large book was bound in roughly tanned leather of an unpleasant dark-purple hue that still gave off the sour smell of suint. There was no sign of any title, even on the title page, only the name of its former owner, like a code: Eustache de Rioux. From the diagrams that filled the first few pages Clément supposed it was a textbook on astronomy or astrology. The subsequent pages astonished him: in them appeared the signs of the zodiac, some accompanied by a profusion of arrows pointing to complicated calculations and annotations penned by two distinct hands. One set of writing was even and graceful, though rushed, the other more squat. It was not so much a book as a personal notebook. Did it belong to the Knight de Rioux, and to another whose name did not appear in its pages? A sentence written in italics caught his attention:

Et tunc parabit signum Filii hominis.[24]

Another arrow pointed from this proclamation to the following page. What he discovered there left him utterly bewildered.

An ecliptic circle featuring only three of the zodiac signs – Capricorn, Aries and Virgo – was covered in the jottings and crossings-out of someone searching for answers. Comments ending in question marks bore out the impression of uncertainty. Others seemed only to be reminders for the author, or authors.

The Moon will eclipse the Sun on the day of his birth. The

place of his birth is still unknown. Revisit the words of the
Viking, a bondi, a trader in walrus tusks, amber and furs
chanced upon in Constantinople.

Five women and at the centre a sixth.

Capricorn in the first decan and Virgo in the third being
variable and the consanguinity of Aries in any decan too
great.

The initial calculations were incorrect, failing to take into
account the error relating to the year of birth of the Saviour.
It is a fortunate blunder for it gives us a little more time.

These comments had been penned by the more graceful hand –
visibly at ease with a quill pen. But to whom did they refer?
This *Filii hominis,* the Son of Man, Christ? If so, then the first
sentence made no sense at all, and the third even less so. More
time to do what? And who was meant by 'we'? The two
authors? As for the astrological reference, it was too abstruse.
What was the 'consanguinity' of a sign? Who were the women
referred to?

Clément raised his head towards the arrow slits. Outside, the
sun was setting. He had not shown his face at the manor since
the previous day, and Agnès would be worried. It was almost
vespers. He could slip away while they were holding the service
and go back.

He paused. He had a strong urge to take the notebook he had
found back to Souarcy and study it at his leisure. But his good
sense quickly dissuaded him, all the more so as the volume was
unwieldy. So be it, he would return to the library after matins*
and pick up where he had left off.

He stood up and snuffed out his little oil lamp, the benefits of which were that it smoked less than a torch and there were enough of them at the manor for one missing to go unnoticed, unlike the tallow lamps or candles, which were costly and therefore included in the kitchen inventory. He walked down to the storeroom.

Vatican Palace, Rome, June 1304

CARDINAL Honorius Benedetti marvelled at the relief provided by the magnificent fan made of fine strips of mother-of-pearl. It had been given to him one morning, following a long and wakeful night, by a rosy-cheeked young lady from Jumièges – a pleasant souvenir over twenty years old. One of the few remaining from his brief secular life before it was touched by grace, leaving him changed and at the same time disoriented. The only son of a wealthy burgher from Verona, he had been companionable and a lover of the fair sex. Few of his qualities predisposed him to the cloth, least of all his penchant for the material things in life, at any rate when these proved pleasurable. Nevertheless, his rise through the religious hierarchy had been vertiginous. He had been helped by a towering intellect, a vast knowledge and, as he freely admitted, by simple cunning. And, no less, by a certain appetite for power – or rather for the possibilities it offered to those who knew how to manipulate it.

The sweat was streaming down Honorius Benedetti's face. For days now the city had been in the grip of an unbearable heat wave that seemed determined never to loosen its hold. The young Dominican sitting opposite him was surprised by his visible discomfort. Archbishop Benedetti was a small, slender, almost frail man, and it was difficult to imagine where he stored all the fluid that was drenching his silky grey hair and rolling down his forehead.

The prelate cast his eye over the nervous young friar whose hands trembled slightly as they lay stretched out on his knees. This was not the first accusation of cruelty and physical abuse involving an Inquisitor to be brought before him. Not long ago, Robert le Bougre* had caused them a good deal of trouble and disgrace. The then Pope, Gregory IX, had lost sleep over the horrors uncovered during the investigation ordered by the Church. Naturally he recalled only too well his own error of judgement, for he had seen in that repentant former Cathar* a valuable 'rooter-out' of heretics.

'Brother Bartolomeo,' continued the Cardinal, 'what you have told me about the young Inquisitor Nicolas Florin puts me in a very awkward position.'

'Believe me, Your Eminence, I regret it deeply,' the novice apologised.

'If the Church, drawing on our late lamented Gregory IX's constitution *Excommunicamus*, decided to recruit her Inquisitors from the Dominican and, to a lesser extent, from the Franciscan orders, it is undoubtedly owing to their excellent knowledge of theology, but also to their humility and compassion. We have always viewed torture as the very last means of obtaining a confession and thus saving the soul of the accused. To have recourse to it from the outset of a trial is . . . The expression "unacceptable" that you used just now will do. For indeed, there exists a – how should I say? – a scale of penalties and punishments which can, which must be applied beforehand, whether in the form of a pilgrimage – with or without the burden of the Cross – a public beating or a fine.'

Brother Bartolomeo stifled a sigh of relief. So he had not been mistaken. The prelate measured up to his reputation for wisdom and intelligence. And yet, having finally been ushered into the study of the Pope's private secretary, after a three-hour-long wait in the stuffy atmosphere of the anteroom, he had felt suddenly apprehensive. How would the Cardinal respond to his accusations? And was he, Bartolomeo, clear in his heart, and in his conscience, about the true nature of what had motivated his request for this interview? Was it a noble desire for justice or was there something more shameful involved: denunciation of a feared brother? For it was hopeless to try to deceive himself: Brother Nicolas Florin terrified him. It was strange how this angelic-faced young man appeared to take a sinister delight in brutalising, torturing and mutilating. He plunged his hands into the raw, screaming flesh without even a ripple of displeasure creasing his handsome brow or clouding his expression.

'Naturally, Your Eminence, since our only duty is to achieve repentance,' ventured Bartolomeo.

'Hmm . . .'

More than anything Honorius Benedetti feared a disastrous repetition of the Robert le Bougre affair. A silent rage mingled with his political concern. The fools! Innocent III had laid down the rules governing the inquisitorial process in his papal bull *Vergentis in senium*. His aim had not been to exterminate individuals but to eradicate heresies that threatened the foundations of the Church, holding up, among others, the example of Christ's poverty which – judging by the vast landed wealth of nearly all the monasteries – was not held in high esteem. As for Innocent IV, he had removed the final obstacle by permitting, from 1252 onwards, the use of torture in his papal bull *Ad extirpanda*.

Torturers. Inept, base torturers. Honorius Benedetti did not know whether he felt more angry or sad. And yet, if he were honest, he too had accepted the bizarre notion that love of the Saviour could, at times, be imposed by means of coercion or even extreme violence. He had felt absolved by the fact that a pope had opened the way before him. Ultimately, was not the boundless joy of having saved a soul, of having returned it to the bosom of Christ, what counted?

This young Bartolomeo and his love for his fellow man had placed him in a difficult situation, for he could no longer feign ignorance. What a fool to have received him! He should have left him mouldering in the anteroom. He might have ended up leaving, bored or annoyed. No, he was not the type to grow tired or impatient. His little mouth withered from the heat, the courage visible in his demeanour – even as his eyes were full of fear – his faltering but determined voice, all pointed to the doggedness of the pure and, in some way, evoked Archbishop Honorius Benedetti's own distant youth. There was only one way out: punishment or absolution. Absolution would be tantamount to endorsing an unacceptable cruelty and would fuel growing criticism among thinkers throughout Europe. It would provide Philip IV of France with a rod to break their backs, even though the monarch himself had not hesitated to resort to the methods of the Inquisition* in the past. It would be – and here the childishness of this last reasoning almost brought a smile to his lips – to disappoint the young man sitting opposite him, who believed in the possibility of governing without ever being content to compromise one's faith. So what about punishment? The prelate would be only too pleased to fight this Nicolas Florin, to make him choke on the power that had corrupted him, perhaps to demand his excommunication. And yet by sacrificing one diseased member of the flock he risked bringing disgrace upon all the Dominicans and the few Franciscans who had been named Inquisitors, and consequently upon the papacy itself. And the path from disgrace to rebellion was frequently a short one.

These were such troubled, such volatile times. The slightest scandal would be blown out of all proportion by the King of France, and other monarchs, who were just waiting for such an opportunity.

Just then, one of the innumerable chamberlains that haunted the papal palace crept silently into his study and, bending down towards his ear, informed him in a whisper that his next visitor had arrived. He thanked the man more effusively than was his custom. At last, the excuse he had been waiting for to rid himself of the novice.

'Brother Bartolomeo, someone is waiting to see me.'

The other man leapt to his feet, blushing. The Cardinal reassured him with a gesture and continued:

'I am obliged to you, my son. I am unable, you understand, to reach any decision regarding the fate of Nicolas Florin on my own. However, I assure you that His Holiness will no more tolerate such monstrosities than I. They go against our faith and are a discredit to us all. Go in peace. Justice will soon be done.'

Bartolomeo left the vast chamber as though he were floating on air. How foolish he had been to harbour so many doubts and fears! His daily tormentor, the man who hounded, humiliated and tempted him, would soon darken his days, and his nights, no more. The butcher of humble folk would vanish like a bad dream.

He smiled feebly at the hooded figure waiting in the ante-room. It was only once he was outside, striding across the vast square with the euphoria of the triumphant, that it occurred to him that the person must have been very hot wearing all those clothes.

Clairets Forest, Perche, June 1304

THE mist enveloping Clément was so thick and close to the ground that he could barely see where he was putting his feet. Mists were common in that part of the country. Agnès found them poetic. She maintained that the swirls that clung to the wild grasses and bushes softened the too-sharp outlines of things. But today this veil was heavy with the scent of death.

The swarm of frenzied flies crawled over the evil-smelling carcass. A piece of half-torn flesh hanging from the cheek almost touched the ground, and moved to the rhythm of the tiny beetles boring below the cheekbone. The upper thigh and buttocks had been gnawed down to the bone.

The child let the small crossbow Agnès insisted he carry for his protection in the forest fall to his feet. He took another step forward, trying with difficulty to suppress the little gulps that brought an acid saliva into his mouth.

It was a man – a serf no doubt, judging from his filthy rags, stained with viscid fluids and dried blood. He was lying on his side, his face turned up to the sky, his eye sockets staring towards the setting sun. The blackened leathery skin, mostly that on his hands and forearms, looked charred as if it had been exposed to naked flames. Had the man been attacked? Had he defended himself? Had he been set alight and then robbed? Of what? Beggars like him carried nothing of any value. Even so, Clément glanced around at the undergrowth and the bushes. There was no sign of any fire. Another step forward, then another. When he was less than a yard from the man, he forced himself to smell the air. The lingering odour of decaying flesh made his stomach heave. And yet he could detect no smell of burnt wood or smoke. The child recoiled suddenly, clasping his hand to his mouth. He was not afraid. The dead, unlike the living, were without guile and harmless. Moreover, what was spread out before him on the forest floor bore no resemblance to the descriptions he had read of plague victims.

Lying a few yards from the corpse at Clément's feet was a peasant's walking stick. He picked it up and examined it. It looked like the branch of a young ash, and had the pale milky hue of freshly carved wood. It bore no traces of blood. One detail surprised him: the pointed metal tip meant to strengthen it and give it more hold on the ground. What serf would have laboured to add such a feature when he could carve as many walking sticks as he wanted? Clément pointed the metal tip at the corpse and, aiming at the hand, he poked it. The wrist broke away partially and the forefinger dropped to the floor.

How long had the body being lying in this tiny clearing over half a league from the nearest dwelling? It was difficult to tell, especially given the state of the shrivelled brown skin. Then again he saw no sign of any bluebottles, although it was the season for them. He circled the pitiful remains and crouched a few feet away. Through a tear in the linen shirt he glimpsed a large blister covering the small of the back that was filled with a yellowy liquid. Aiming again with the end of the stick, he burst it, and turned his head just in time to avoid vomiting on his breeches. A small sea of maggots tumbled from the wound cavity. The bluebottles had had the time to lay their eggs, and the warm weather had favoured the larvae's development. The man must have been dead for at least three weeks.

Clément rose to his feet – in a sudden hurry to continue on his way. There was nothing more anyone could do for this poor wretch. The child had decided not to tell a living soul about his discovery, hardly eager to have to go all that way back just to show the bailiffs. He was struck by something odd. The man had mid-length hair, almost certainly light chestnut – though it was hard to tell with all the detritus, mud and parasites sticking to it. And yet, the tiny tonsure on his crown was still visible. The hair had grown back, but not enough to hide the trace of the barber's knife. Who might he have been? A cleric? Or perhaps one of those scholars who requested the tonsure as a sign of devotion and repentance?

His curiosity proved stronger than the queasiness he felt from his proximity to the stinking remains. He removed the crusts of bread and the plants from his shoulder bag, and thrust his right hand inside. Using the improvised glove for protection, he pulled aside the evil-smelling rags covering the man's body. Sweat poured down the child's face and ran into his eyes, and yet the nausea of the past few minutes had given way to exhilaration, to the extent that the putrid odour no longer affected him so strongly. He fought off the insects – exasperated by the disruption of their feast – driving them away with his gloved hand, and proceeded to inspect every inch of the corpse. Why would the man be wearing rags if he was a scholar? And if he was a friar, then where was his habit? Had he been travelling on foot? Where had he come from? What had caused his death? Had he perished in the clearing, or had somebody left him there after partially burning him somewhere else? Unfortunately, it was impossible for him to judge from the state of the hands, which were shrivelled up like pieces of old leather, whether the corpse had been a scholar or a peasant. Nothing, no object or any other particular feature, besides the tonsure, gave him any clues. Had he been robbed? If so, was it before or after he died? The obvious thought occurred to him that the hair on the man's head, and the body hair clinging to the flesh on his forearms and on his chest ravaged by vermin, though soiled with putre-faction, was intact. There was no sign of any singeing on the torn clothes hanging in shreds, which meant the man had not been set alight, for they would have caught fire before the skin could be attacked by the searing flames.

Clément struggled to roll the massive corpse onto its back and was almost propelled backwards by its weight. He peeled off the large piece of cloth adhering to the skin on the abdomen. The viscera were heaving with bloodless maggots. It was then that he noticed in the narrow strip of flattened grass where the man had been lying on his side a tiny hole no bigger than the size of a coin in the forest floor. It looked as though somebody had pushed their finger into the ground. Clément scraped care-fully. Hidden beneath an inch or so of loose leaves and earth lay a wax seal. He cleaned the wax medallion and examined it closely. His mouth went dry. It was the ring of the fisherman! The papal seal. He was certain, having already come across it in the secret library at Clairets Abbey. But who was this man? An emissary of the Pope in disguise? Had he tried to bury the seal so that no one would find it? But what had become of the private missive the seal protected? Had he delivered it to Clairets Abbey – the only religious order of any importance in the vicinity? The child cast his gaze over the area immediately surrounding the tiny opening. What was that mark about a foot away? It looked like a letter of the alphabet. He leant closer and blew on the dried earth. There was a curved stroke like the beginning of the letter M or N or even a capital B or D. No. There was a tiny bar lower down – an E perhaps? No. There was no question: it was an A. Without knowing what motivated his gesture, he brushed the earth with his fingers, rubbing out all trace of the letter. He spent a moment longer filling in the hole that had shown him where to find the seal.

What did the A mean? Was it a surname? A Christian name? The name of the man's murderer? Or of a loved one who must be found and warned? Had the dead man left a sign for whoever found him? If this were the case then he had indeed died in the clearing, and his death had been slow enough to enable him to hide the seal and to scratch the letter.

Clément silenced the clamour of questions racing through his mind. He must leave this place, and quickly. If the messenger was really as important as he seemed then they were most likely searching for him already – or at least for the letter he had been carrying. The bailiffs were capable of anything to please their superior and the Comte d'Authon – not to mention the Pope. Anything, even roasting an innocent boy, provided it meant being left in peace.

Clément put the seal into his shoulder bag and hurried away.

I N a flurry of rustling fabric, a figure darted behind the pillars in the little chapel. Brother Bernard was dining with Agnès and there was only a short time between courses.

Mabile was not displeased with herself. Agnès de Souarcy had expressed her wish to thank the good chaplain and the servant had prepared a proper feast – a six-course meal, no less. Following an hors d'oeuvre of fresh fruit, whose acidity was supposed to act as an aid to digestion, there was a broth made of almond milk. For the third course the servant had plumped for roasted quail spiced with a black pepper sauce. That insufferable Agnès de Souarcy was such a stickler for table manners that the baby fowl should keep her busy for a while. Brother Bernard would no doubt follow her example, thus allowing Mabile time to move onto the attack. The chaplain was young and attractive and his tonsure gave him an air of perpetual surprise and joviality. Mabile would gladly have let herself be seduced. Thus far, her judicious attempts in that direction had ended in failure. Was he harbouring shameful feelings towards Agnès de Souarcy? The thought made Mabile's mouth water. Eudes de Larnay would be happy to learn of it; and out of gratitude he would show her a little affection and, above all, generosity. Suddenly the girl became gloomy. Happy? Undoubtedly not.

Satisfied, yes, but incensed with rage. At times he frightened her. Often. His loathing was so great it consumed him. Agnès and everything relating to her was like a knife piercing his entrails. He hounded her yet derived no pleasure from plotting his revenge. Even so, Mabile helped him, or, better still, she anticipated his murderous desires. She did not know exactly why. For love of her master? Certainly not. She yearned for him to lie on her belly, to possess her like he would a strumpet or a lady, according to his whim. And she liked it when occasionally, after their love-making and before drifting off to sleep, he would murmur: 'Agnès, my sweet.' So he was not thinking of her? How wrong he was! For she was his only Agnès and he would have to content himself with her. Mabile blinked back the tears of rage welling up in her eyes. One day. One day she would have obtained enough money from her master to be able to leave him behind without a single regret. She would go to the city and set herself up as a gold embroiderer. She was patient and clever. Ultimately . . . Mabile rather liked the fiction of Agnès's fondness for her chaplain, for not only would it harm Agnès's reputation, it would also wound her master. Mabile's bitterness was instantly replaced by a malicious glee.

The register in which the births and deaths at the manor were recorded would be in the sacristy. Mabile made her way straight there. She was trembling with rage. She enjoyed being the architect of Agnès's doom. It was a salve to the terrible envy that consumed her. In her view as long as the natural order of things required that the serfs laboured while the master under-took to protect them, defectors like Agnès were intolerable. She had escaped her lot through marriage. A bastard. Agnès was nothing but a bastard, the daughter of a lady's maid just like her, Mabile. Why Agnès? If old Comte Robert hadn't begun to fear the wrath of heaven as he neared his end he would never have recognised her. He had sowed enough wild oats in the hovels and farms on his estate. Why Agnès? Why should Mabile, born of a sacred union and into conditions that were enviable to many, seeing as her father was a dyer from Nogent-le-Rotrou, obtain less than a bastard – albeit a noble one? The hatred she felt for the Dame de Souarcy made her head spin at times. Regardless of whether he paid for her daily treachery, she would still have served Eudes de Larnay.

The bulky register was resting on a wooden lectern. Mabile hurriedly leafed through it until she came to the year 1294, the year that little good-for-nothing Clément, who spied on her so brazenly, was born. She searched through the columns filled in by the clumsy hand of the previous chaplain, who, judging from the fine lettering in the remainder of the register, had passed away at midnight on 26 January 1295. Mabile recalled that deadly winter when she had still been just a child. Finally her finger paused beside the entry she had been looking for: Clément, born posthumously to Sybille on the night of 28 December 1294.

She must hurry. The quail would not keep them busy forever. She should be back in the kitchen helping Adeline serve the desserts: a traditional goat's-milk blancmange followed by black nougat made from boiling honey and adding last year's walnuts and spices. To round off the meal she had prepared some hippocras, a mixture of red and white wine sweetened with honey and spiced with cinnamon and ginger.

She closed the register and hurried to the kitchens, declaring to the gaping-mouthed Adeline that the warm evening had made her sleepy and she had felt a sudden need to take the air.

'Only, they finished the third course and I didn't know what to do,' the young girl protested feebly.

'Serve the dessert on a fine trencher and pour the hippocras into the decanter to let it breathe, you fool! And remember Madame Agnès likes everyone to have their own trencher. This isn't a pauper's house, you know. I'm tired of having to tell you the same thing over and over again!' Mabile scolded.

Adeline lowered her head. She was so used to the other woman's reproaches that she barely registered them.

The conversation was flowing easily in the great hall. Mabile studied the distance between her mistress and the chaplain and wondered whether the gap hadn't closed a little. Agnès looked relaxed. And yet during her half-brother's visit her discomfort had been palpable. Mabile listened closely in the hope of overhearing some compromising snatch of conversation, but there was nothing in their exchange that would have been of any interest to Eudes.

'I scarcely see how castration could be a cure for leprosy, hernias and gout,' argued Agnès. 'They are such different afflictions, and it is well known that the wretched patients who were subjected to the operation in the leper hospital at Chartagne in the Mortagne region are none the better for it.'

'I am no expert in medical science, Madame, though I believe it is related to the similarity between the humours of the afflictions.'

Brother Bernard's perpetual good humour disposed him

towards the pleasant things in life and so he turned from the gout and leprosy sufferers to enthuse once more about the quails he had just eaten.

Mabile returned to the kitchens. For some minutes her thoughts had been occupied by a nagging question. Why did the surname of this Sybille, her mistress's lady's maid, not figure in the register? Had she not received a Christian burial? Her grave was marked with a cross and had been dug at the edge of the plot reserved for the servants, which adjoined the cemetery where the lords of the manor, their wives and their descendants were buried. A few Souarcys lay buried beneath the chapel flagstones, but the limited space had necessitated the clearing of three hundred square yards of forest a good hundred yards from the chapel. Irrespective of her hostility towards Agnès, Mabile acknowledged that the Souarcys had always treated their servants' mortal remains with dignity. Not like a lot of others who would dump them in common graves unless a family member came to claim them. In point of fact, Eudes de Larnay showed no such compassion where his servants were concerned. She shook her head in irritation. What use had she for the Dame de Souarcy's kindness? It had nothing to do with her mission. Another thought flashed through her mind. The boundary where Clément's mother's remains lay; was it consecrated ground? She must try to find out. Sybille's having been a mother out of wedlock did not surprise Mabile. It was a common risk for girls in service. They found themselves inopportunely with child and their choice was clear: abortion, frequently followed by the mother's death, or, if the master was decent, a pregnancy carried to full term in secret. However, it did not explain why Clément was only registered under his Christian name? Who were his godparents? Without their presence a baptism would have been unthinkable. Their Christian names and surnames should be recorded in the register beside the child's. This baptism seemed to her altogether too clandestine for it to be completely orthodox.

Clément waited for a few moments, listening out just to make sure. Her snooping in the chapel having been successful, Mabile would not return again tonight. He crawled out of his hiding place in the honeysuckle bush. A cold sweat had drenched his shirt. It did not take a genius to guess what the fiendish woman had been trying to find out. So he was right and she did know how to read. He was annoyed with himself for not having anticipated this new piece of cunning. He should have taken the register of births and deaths even without telling Agnès, for she would doubtless disapprove of any act that deprived Souarcy of its history.

He knew it. Eudes de Larnay was baring his teeth. His jaws were exposed, preparing to snap at their defenceless flesh.

The weather was so beautiful, so mild. From time to time Agnès caught a glimpse of the cloudless blue sky through an opening in the leaves. The boat was bobbing gently downstream. She lay with her head to the stern. She was alone, in sweet solitude. Her right hand caressed the calm surface of the water. A sudden eddy rocked the flimsy vessel. She sat up and looked around at the waves rippling out from the boat. What was it? A surprise current? A vast aquatic beast? Menacing? The shaking grew more violent and the boat jibbed, lurching dangerously from side to side. She wanted to cry out for help but no sound came from her throat. Suddenly she was aware of a small insistent voice whispering in her ear:

'Madame, Madame, I beg you, wake up, but do not make a sound.'

Agnès sat up in bed. Clément was staring at her, his head framed by the canopy curtains. Agnès's relief was short-lived and she demanded in a whisper:

'What are you doing in my chambers? What time is it?'

'It is after matins, Madame, but not yet dawn.'

'What are you doing here?' she repeated.

'I waited until Mabile and the other servants were asleep. While you were dining with Brother Bernard she stole into the chapel in order to look through the register.'

Agnès, wide awake now, concluded:

'So we know for certain that she can read.'

'Enough to perform her misdeeds.'

'What do you suppose? I'll wager she was searching for details about your birth or of Sybille's death.'

'I am convinced of it too.'

'What could she learn from reading those lines?' Agnès reflected out loud.

'I went over them again after she had left to try to imagine where her wickedness might be leading. I am registered under my Christian name only, and there is no mention of my god-father or godmother. As for Sybille, I may remind you,

Madame, that her death is not recorded. She was a heretic and refused the sacraments of our Holy Church.'

'Hush! Do not utter that word. It is over. Gisèle was your godmother, and as for your godfather, it was too much of a risk. The only person we might have trusted was my previous chaplain, but he was dying and passed away shortly afterwards. What is more, it would have meant confessing to him, which was impossible. And so Gisèle and I decided to enter no surname at all since only one would have been more harmful. At the very worst, had an examination of the register been ordered, we could have claimed it was the error of an enfeebled hand and a mind already clouded by death.'

'So my baptism isn't . . . It's as though I had never been baptised, isn't it?' asked Clément in a soft trembling voice.

Her blue-grey eyes gazed into those of the child, and she gestured to him to sit down beside her.

'God is our only true judge, Clément. Men, whoever they may be, are merely His tireless interpreters. What conceited fool can claim to know the sum of His desires, His designs, His truth? They are impenetrable and we can only glimpse them.'

Her own words troubled her. They had been intended to comfort the child. And yet, up until that moment none of her attempts to describe her tentative search for the true path to God had seemed so sincere. Was she seriously mistaken, was this blasphemy?

'Is that what you truly think, Madame?'

She replied unfalteringly:

'It shocks me and yet it is truly what I believe. Your baptism delivered you into the arms of God, Clément. Two women, Gisèle and I, bore you there with open hearts.'

The child sighed and leant against her. A few seconds later he asked:

'What are we going to do about the spy, Madame?'

'How does she plan to warn my brother, for he is the instigator of this sinister scheme? Larnay is far from here. The journey would take her two days on foot. Could Eudes have employed someone else to carry messages to him?'

'I doubt it very much, Madame. Eudes may be a fool but even he must realise that the more accomplices he has the greater the risk of his secret being discovered.'

'You are right. So how does she inform him? He seldom comes to Souarcy, God be praised.'

'I shall find out, I promise. Rest now, Madame, I will return to my lair.'

Clément had made a little place for himself under the eaves. He had chosen the location with great care. He had built a ladder flimsy enough to deter any adult from climbing up. It gave him easy access from the end of the passageway that led to his mistress's anteroom and chamber. In this way he could see anyone approaching. Another advantage was a tiny window that ventilated the eaves, and allowed him, with the aid of a rope, to come and go without the servants seeing him.

Carcassonne, *June 1304

A TALL brown angel. Brother Nicolas Florin paused suddenly. The tonsure had not made this young man ugly; on the contrary it lengthened his pale brow, giving him the appearance of a proud chimera.

Brother Bartolomeo de Florence was standing on his right, his eyes lowered towards his clasped hands.

Nicolas murmured in his strangely soft yet cavernous voice:

'I am at a loss to understand why they are sending me north when I proved so useful to them here in the South during the riots last August that unleashed bloodshed and destruction on our good city. I took part in foiling the devilish plot of that depraved Franciscan, the execrable Bernard Délicieux. Never was a name more ill suited. No, I honestly do not understand, unless they mean to honour me. Yet my instinct tells me the inverse is true.'

With a willowy hand Nicolas raised the resolutely lowered chin of his victim.

'What is your opinion, sweet brother?' he repeated, fixing Bartolomeo's eyes with his soft dark gaze.

The novice's throat was dry. He had prayed night and day for a miracle powerful enough to rid him of his tormentor, and now he dreaded the consequences. However much he reproached himself, repeated to himself *ad nauseam* that he had nothing to be afraid of, that the order for the transfer was signed by Cardinal Benedetti with no more mention of his name than of the true reason for the relocation, he remained uneasy. Nicolas and his insatiable desire for power, his appetite for inflicting pain, everything about this excessively beautiful, cunning creature terrified him.

The naive young Dominican had soon realised that faith was not the driving force behind his cell companion. For certain ambitious offspring of low birth, entry into the orders had always been a useful tool.

Bartolomeo had gathered from Nicolas's circumspect confessions that his father had been a lay illuminator to Charles d'Évreux, the Comte d'Étampes. Although as a child he showed little interest in the task of colouring and lettering, his lively mind had, with the aid of the Comte's splendid library, soaked up a fair amount of knowledge. He had been pampered and spoiled by an ageing mother for whom this late gift of a child was compensation for the years of suspicion about her ability to conceive. Added to the poor woman's humiliation was fear, for she exercised the profession of midwife to the ladies-in-waiting of Madame Marie d'Espagne, daughter of Ferdinand II and wife of the Comte.

One day, when they were praying side by side, Nicolas had whispered in Bartolomeo's ear in a voice that had made him tremble:

'The world is ours if we know how to take it.'

One night, as Bartolomeo lay sleeping in the cool darkness of their cell he thought he heard the words:

'Flesh is not earned, and only the feeble-minded share it. Flesh should be taken, snatched.'

Nicolas's excesses had begun soon after he arrived in the town of the four mendicant convents,* which at the time boasted ten thousand inhabitants. Bartolomeo was convinced that they had contributed to the hatred the populace felt towards them and to their uprising against the royal and religious authorities.

One particular memory wrung the young Dominican's heart. That poor girl Raimonde, who was touched in the head, and claimed to be visited at night by spirits. Encouraged by Nicolas, who preyed on her like a cat preys on a mouse, she attempted to demonstrate her powers, which she professed came from the Virgin. She stubbornly repeated incantations she claimed were capable of piercing rats and field mice. Despite the fact that her efforts ended in failure, Nicolas managed to make her admit responsibility for the death of a neighbour carried off by a mysterious summer fever, as well as for some cows miscarrying. The young Inquisitor's case was weak, and yet he proved her guilt, arguing that the Virgin could not transmit a lethal power, even one used only against harmful rodents. The devil alone could do that in exchange for a soul. The poor mad girl's insides hung from the rack. Her suffering had been interminable. Nicolas stared with satisfaction at the blood flowing from her entrails into the underground chamber's central drain, dug out for the purpose. Bartolomeo had fled the Viscount's Palace, loathing himself for his cowardice.

In reality, the young man was too rational to be able to turn a blind eye. He radiated faith, and love for his fellow man. He might have found the inner strength to rebel and even, why not, to defeat Nicolas. But a sort of evil curse of his own design prevented him. His excitement when Nicolas's hand brushed against his arm. His unpardonable urge to justify what was simple debauchery and cruelty on the part of his cell companion. Bartolomeo loved Nicolas with a love that was anything but fraternal. He loved him and he hated him. He would gladly die and at the same time live for his next smile. Naturally, Bartolomeo was aware that monks practised sodomy, as they did concubinage. Not he. Not he who dreamt of angels as others dream of girls or finery.

The beautiful demon must go, he must vanish for evermore.

'I am talking to you, Bartolomeo. What do you think?'

The novice mustered all his strength to reply in a steady voice:

'I see in it only a sign of approval. Surely it is not a reprimand, much less a punishment.'

'But you will miss me, will you not?' Nicolas taunted him.

'Yes . . .'

He spoke the truth and it made him want to weep with rage, and sorrow too. The firm belief that his morbid fascination for Nicolas would be the only insurmountable ordeal he must endure devastated him.

Clairets Forest and the Manoir de Souarcy-en-Perche, June 1304

THE brambles and the long grass still trapped the early-morning mist. It was as if the earth, jealous of the sky, had formed its own clouds. Gilbert used to be afraid of it. Everybody said it was the breath of spirits, some of whom were so resentful of their fate that they would lure you into their limbo. But his good fairy had told him that was just nonsense and stories to make little children do as they were told. Mist came from the forest floor when it was full of water and the heat made it rise. That was all. Gilbert had found this explanation very reassuring and had felt suddenly superior to all the fools taken in by a lot of tall tales. For his good fairy was always right.

Gilbert chuckled with glee. His shoulder bag was already full to bursting with morels. The autumn rains and forest fires the previous year had been favourable. He would keep one large handful for himself to cook in the embers the way he liked. All the rest would go to his good fairy. For he was certain she was a fairy. One of those fairies who have grown accustomed to human ways and who make their lives more beautiful and sweet.

With the underneath of his sleeve, he wiped away the saliva running down his chin. He was jubilant.

She adored the morels he picked for her each spring. Oh! He

could already imagine her feeling the weight of them in her beautiful pale hands and declaring:

'Why, Gilbert, they look even bigger than last year's crop! Where do you manage to find such marvels?'

He wouldn't tell her. And yet he was prepared to do anything to please her. But he was no fool; if he showed her his secret places for picking morels, ceps and chanterelles, he would have no more lovely gifts to bring her. And that would be sad because then she wouldn't give him that happy smile any more. Just like the magnificent wild trout he caught with his bare hands in the icy waters of the river Huisne. Gilbert swelled with pride: only he knew where to find the tiny creeks that held the biggest fish. What is more, he took great pains when going there to make sure nobody was following him, looking back and listening out. If he stood still where the current was weakest he could almost pluck them from the water like fruit. Every Friday he brought a pair for his good fairy to brighten up her fast days.

His mood changed abruptly, and he became sullen. Of course he would give his life for his good fairy. And yet he was so afraid of death since he had lain in bed with it for two days and three nights. He could have sworn that open-eyed death was staring at him even while he slept. It didn't smell too bad though because of the cold. It was in winter; he forgot which year. A cruel winter when many people died, even at the manor, even the old chaplain and his good fairy's maidservant, the one who was with child. He remembered that the Dame de Souarcy had allowed hunting on her land because he had caught some rabbits. At first, he had lain close to open-eyed death, hoping in vain for some warmth. He had been too young at the time to know that dead people suck up all the heat. When they, the others, finally noticed them, death and him, they dragged open-eyed death away and flung her on top of a pile of other bodies on a cart. One of the others had said:

'What'll we do with the idiot now the old woman's gone? He's just another mouth to feed. I think we should leave him at the edge of the forest to fend for himself.'

A woman who was standing apart from the others protested as a matter of form:

'It's not Christian! He's too young. He'll perish in no time.'

'He has no sense in his head so it's not as bad as if it were one of us.'

'I say it's not Christian,' the woman had insisted before walking away.

The nine-year-old Gilbert had watched them, hardly understanding what they were scheming, only sensing that his chances of survival were waning as his quivering mother, sprawled on top of a pile of other corpses, was drawn away on a rattling ox-cart.

Blanche, the tanner's wife, renowned for her piety and good sense, had declared:

'Mariette's right. It isn't Christian. He's still a child.'

'He's a dirty little cat-killer,' replied the man, who was in a hurry to despatch Gilbert to a better world, preferably one where he wouldn't need feeding.

True, he had skinned a couple of the neighbours' cats. But it wasn't as if they were dogs, and anyway it was so he could line his clogs with their pelts. It was wrong of him to be sure. It was wrong to harm the predators of the field mice that ravaged the grain stocks, except if they were black. He could kill any number of those, for safety, for they were liable to turn into hosts of the devil.

Blanche had shot the man an angry look that had all but made him recoil. She replied in a sharp voice:

'I think I shall bring the subject of our disaccord before our lady. I feel sure that she will see it my way.'

The man had lowered his head. He, too, felt sure.

And so it was. Agnès had ordered the simpleton to be brought before her, and had warned that anyone unjustly beating, harming or punishing the boy in any way would have her to answer to.

Gilbert the simpleton had grown in size and strength under the protection of the manor, but his mind was still that of a child. Like a child he sought his good fairy's affection, growing gentle and meek when she stroked his hair or spoke softly to him. And like a child a wild temper could flare up in him when he feared for his good fairy or for himself. His colossal strength had not only protected the Dame de Souarcy but had also discouraged any attempts on the part of the villagers to taunt or mistreat him.

For some time, the one they so often called the idiot had been alerted by a strange premonition: the season of the beast was drawing near. It would soon be upon them. Occasionally, when night fell, Gilbert would be thrown into a panic, unable to imagine what form this beast would take. And yet he could feel it, he could smell it coming. His fear never left him and compelled him to remain by Clément's side, even though he disliked the boy, envying him his privileged position close to Agnès. But Clément loved the good fairy, too, with a love that was true and pure, and the simpleton knew this. Clément had the brains which Gilbert lacked but in contrast possessed none of Gilbert's extraordinary physical strength. Together they could become their lady's knight in shining armour. Together they could fight off many dangers, perhaps even the beast itself.

The troubled mood that had overtaken him a few minutes before gave way to a burst of renewed confidence. He would pick a few more morels and then gather the medicinal herbs his fairy had requested. He knew so many plants and herbs with miraculous powers. Some healed burns while others could kill an ox. The trouble was he didn't know their names. He recognised them by their pleasant aroma or their nauseating stench, or by their flowers or the shape of their leaves. The previous winter, he had cured his lady's cough with a few simple decoctions. As soon as he had picked enough he would go back. He was already feeling hungry.

He knew exactly where to find a nice crop, just beyond that bit of undergrowth that looked so much bigger than last year. He lay on his belly beside the tangle of brambles and bindweed and slid his hand between the nasty thorns. What was that touching his fingers? It felt like cloth. What was it doing there in the middle of his good fairy's mushrooms? The snarl of weeds was so dense that he couldn't make out much, just a vague outline almost the size of a stag, except that stags didn't wear clothes. Gilbert pulled his sleeves down to protect his hands and tugged at the wild brambles until he had cleared a sort of tunnel through which he was able to crawl towards the shape.

Closed-eyed death. It wasn't staring at him for there were no eyes – only two puffy slits. Inches from the soft mass that had once been a face, the simpleton was breathless with terror. He crawled backwards, twisting like a snake and whimpering, his mouth closed. Fear clouded the few brains he possessed. He tried to stand up, the thorns from the blackberry bush spiking the flesh on his shoulders, arms and legs.

He ran like a madman towards the village, panting and clasping his bag of mushrooms to his belly. A single sentence kept racing through his head: the beast was here, the beast was upon them.

The corpse, or what remained of it, lay on a plank resting on two trestles in the hay barn at the Manoir de Souarcy. Agnès had sent three farm hands with a cart to bring it back. Clément had taken advantage of the general commotion to go in and take a look undisturbed. It was true that the state it was in was hardly an enticement to onlookers.

It was a man, in his thirties, fairly tall and well built. There was no sign of any tonsure to suggest he might be a friar. Clément did not trouble to go through the dead man's pockets, certain that the farm hands would have filched anything of value he might have been carrying, and then scattered the rest to make it look as if a thief had arrived there first.

The man had not been dead long, three or four days probably, judging by the state of the flesh that bore almost no signs of decomposition. In addition, the smell he gave off was still tolerable. On the other hand, it looked as though some animal had attacked him, unleashing itself on his face until it was unrecognisable, an exposed mass of mutilated flesh. Such a sustained attack by a carnivorous animal on one part of the body was inconceivable. The face is not the fleshiest part of the body – far from it. Predators and carrion feeders go for the buttocks, thighs, belly and arms, leaving the bony parts covered in skin or a thin layer of flesh for the insects or other small scroungers.

Were his deductions the result of his previous encounter with the corpse in Clairets Forest, or of the science he had been devouring over the past few weeks? Doubtless both. In any event the corpse made no impression on Clément and he walked over to it unflinchingly.

He lifted the tattered shirt hanging from the man's chest with the tip of his forefinger in order to examine the abdomen. The greenish hue had not yet spread over the entire stomach, although blisters filled with foul-smelling gases – a sign of putrefaction – were beginning to appear on the skin, bearing out Clément's first speculation as to the time of death. He walked around the table so that he was standing directly behind the man's head. It looked as though a set of talons had ripped into his face, slashing his brow, cheeks and neck so savagely that even a close friend would have difficulty recognising him. He found one detail puzzling. How would an animal have gone about maiming its prey in this way? The direction of the wound was obvious from the way the slashes on the right cheek were neater by the nose and clogged with skin and flesh towards the ear. Examining the wounds on the left cheek, he noticed that the inverse was true. So this hypothetical creature must have lashed at one ear with its claws and ripped the flesh towards the nose and then done the opposite on the other side of the face. It couldn't be the result of a single movement of the claws slashing from right to left because the nose was intact. Another detail caught his attention. He had read, in the introduction to a work by a renowned eleventh-century Iranian doctor called Avicenna, that wounds inflicted post mortem were easily identifiable. They neither bled nor showed signs of inflammation. Exactly like those the man presented. The bloodless edges of the elongated contusions ravaging the victim's face cried out their truth to those who knew how to listen. The man had been attacked after he was dead.

The sound of a man's heavy gait accompanied by a lighter step, which Clément immediately recognised as Agnès's, interrupted his reflections. He dived behind some bales of straw stacked at the far end of the barn.

That man's death was not the work of any animal. His wounds had been inflicted post mortem in order to conceal his identity or divert suspicion. As for his attacker, the boy would have sworn it was a beast of the two-legged variety that drank from a cup.

The footsteps drew closer and then came to a halt. The silence was broken by the sound of heavy and increasingly irregular breathing. Clément deduced from it that the man was examining the corpse. A rustic accent declared:

'Confound it! It takes an angry beast to rip a fellow to shreds like that. Well then . . . I'll go and inform my master. He has to see this for himself.'

So the man worked for Monge de Brineux, Chief Bailiff of Comte Artus d'Authon. The boy heard the Dame de Souarcy give a deep sigh. He could sense her anxiety as soon as she spoke. She was counting on the man's stupidity and his agitation to attempt one last ploy. If she succeeded in convincing him, there was a good chance the investigation would end there.

'Since it is the work of an animal, it seems unnecessary to trouble Monsieur de Brineux and make him come all the way here. However, you are right and I shall order my men to track it down. It must be killed without delay. Follow me to the kitchens. A goblet of our wine will refresh you.'

'Hmm . . . An animal. With all due respect, Madame, I'm not so sure. An animal would have eaten more of him than that.'

A heavy sense of foreboding warned Clément that their troubles had begun, and he blamed himself for his lack of foresight.

Manoir de Souarcy-en-Perche, June 1304

WHEN Clément returned to the manor that morning, following another night of feverish reading and discovery, he was alerted by an unusual commotion in the courtyard. Three geldings, nearly the size of ceremonial horses, were tied to the wall-rings of the barn, and a few yards away a bay palfrey pawed the ground, snorting nervously. Clément studied the magnificent steed. It was rare in these parts to see one so fine. The exertion of galloping had left white streaks down its neck and sides. It had come a long way, and at speed. Who might ride such an animal and be accompanied by three others?

Clément slipped through the kitchens and down the passageway leading past the garderobe until he reached the small postern door the servants used to enter the great hall. He pressed himself against it in the hope of discovering who was visiting Agnès so early in the morning. He heard his lady reply:

'What can I say, my Lord Bailiff? Up until your arrival I knew nothing of these mysterious deaths, as you have described them. One of my servants was out picking mushrooms and discovered this poor wretch in a thicket.'

Monge de Brineux, Comte Artus d'Authon's Chief Bailiff, Clément thought.

'And yet, rumours spread fast, Madame. Had they honestly not reached you?'

'Indeed not. We are very isolated here. Four victims in two months, and all of them friars, you say?'

'Three out of the four — we know precious little about the man in your barn except that he met an identical fate . . .'

'Were all their faces slashed in that way?'

'All but the second victim, an emissary of the Pope, like the first. As you can imagine, his death has caused great upset in Rome. However, it is the first two deaths that are proving to be a real puzzle. It would seem both men were burnt, or at least that is what their black shrivelled skin leads us to believe. And yet their clothes show no sign of having been exposed to flames. Were they undressed before being tortured and then dressed again? It seems improbable.'

So there was another corpse before the one he had found in the clearing, Clément deduced. And his clothes bore no trace of having been destroyed by fire, any more than his hair or body hair.

'We were unable to find the message he was carrying. The Abbess of Clairets admits she wrote it, while not wishing to disclose the contents to us. According to her, the two other friars never reached the abbey. And as for the man lying in your barn, the brief description we gave her stirred no memory. So far we know next to nothing about any of them.'

'And yet you maintain they are friars.'

'That is correct.'

'How can you be so sure?'

'A detail that concerns only those charged with the

investigation,' replied the Bailiff in a polite but firm voice.

The tonsure, Clément thought instantly.

Agnès understood the warning. She remained silent for a few moments. When she spoke again, her changed tone alarmed the child pressed up against the other side of the door. It was sharper, almost imperious.

'What are you implying, my Lord Bailiff?'

'Whatever do you mean, Madame?'

'I have a curious feeling that you are being evasive.'

The ensuing silence made Clément uneasy. Monge de Brineux was a powerful man. His office and his authority came directly from the very influential Comte Artus d'Authon. A childhood friend of King Philip, the Comte had had the good sense to refuse the royal favours he knew to be fickle, and devote himself to the running of his estate. The attention he paid to his affairs had enabled him to preserve his friendship with the monarch, who mistook Artus's political circumspection for dignified disinterest, while making of his little county one of the richest and most peaceable in France. Clément reassured himself; Agnès's perceptiveness was equalled only by her intelligence. She must have taken the measure of her interlocutor before adopting such a strategy.

'Whatever do you mean, Madame?' he repeated.

'Come now, Monsieur, have the good grace not to under-estimate me. You and I both know that no animal is responsible for what happened to that poor wretch. I have not seen the others but your presence here is proof enough. At least three of these men were slain, and their slayer, or slayers, attempted to mask the crime by savagely clawing their victims' faces.'

By clumsily clawing their faces, Clément corrected from his spy hole.

There was another, briefer silence before Monsieur de Brineux confessed:

'I had indeed reached the same conclusion.'

'So why this urgent visit? For surely you did not ride all this way with three of your men simply to examine a mutilated body decomposing in a barn. In what way are these murders connected with Souarcy and its mistress? Come now, the truth, Monsieur.'

'The truth is . . .' The Bailiff paused. 'The truth, Madame, is that we found a letter scratched in the ground under the bodies of two of the victims. My men are presently combing the thicket your man Gilbert showed us to make sure there is . . . no letter.'

My God! The *A* in the ground under the Pope's emissary, which he had instinctively brushed away with his hand.

'A letter? What sort of letter?' asked Agnès.

'A letter of the alphabet. An *A*.'

'An *A*? I see . . . *A* as in "Agnès"?'

'Indeed, or as in any number of words or Christian names, I grant you.'

He was cut short by an incongruous laugh. The Dame de Souarcy quickly pulled herself together before adding:

'Plenty indeed – why, I could give you thirty without even having to think about it! Well, Monsieur? Do you really see me running through the forest armed with a claw and attacking men twice as heavy as I, if the size of the one lying in my outbuilding is anything to judge by? Moreover, you must suppose that my victims know me well enough to know my Christian name and do not hesitate to use it to incriminate me. If the situation were not so serious, your suppositions would be purely grotesque. Lastly, and if I may be permitted to say so, I would be most foolish to have proceeded in this way.'

'I do not understand what you mean.'

'And yet it is very simple. Now, let us just suppose that for some unknown reason I am a bloodthirsty monster. I do not know why, but I kill men. And I try to make my crimes look like the work of a wild beast. A bear perhaps; they are to be found in our forests. Would I really be so foolish as to simulate an attack by setting about the face and nothing else, not even the clothes? Why, any serf or huntsman would see through it immediately. Even your half-witted sergeant was not fooled! A five-year-old child could see that this was no animal. And this leads to my question: is the killer a simpleton, or much cleverer than you imagine?'

'What are you insinuating, Madame?'

'I insinuate nothing; I suggest. I suggest that this evil criminal wanted, on the contrary, to draw attention to these murders. In fact, do you not find it strange that all four were discovered within such a short time? Two months, did you say? Many, I am sure, who are tossed into ravines, buried in caves, weighted down and thrown into rivers for the fish to colonise, or reduced to ashes will never be found. You must confess that the connecting threads in this case are glaringly obvious.'

Clément could not see the smile that played across the Bailiff's lips. The man was astonished, not by a woman displaying the kind of intelligence and quick wits he wished more of his men possessed – after all his own wife Julienne was his most valuable counsellor – but that she did not hesitate to contradict him openly.

He rose to take his leave, remarking in an amused voice:

'You would delight my master, the Comte d'Authon, Madame. He has reached the same conclusion as you. The fact remains that we have four bodies on our hands, three of whom are friars – who knows, perhaps even four – and a persistently recurring letter that may have been scratched by the victims or by their aggressor.'

His smile faded and his pursed lips betrayed his perplexity.

'There is one other detail I hesitated to mention . . .'

He pulled a tiny pale-blue square of cloth from his leather shoulder bag and unfolded it before her.

'Do you recognise this linen handkerchief, Madame? It bears your initial in the corner.'

Mabile, or even Eudes himself. Clément was convinced. Agnès's half-brother could have taken the handkerchief during his last visit. The timing was not impossible.

'Indeed I do, it belongs to me,' declared Agnès.

'We found it hanging from a low branch, two yards from the second victim.'

'So in addition to being bloodthirsty and extremely foolish I must also be very careless to run through the woods with a linen handkerchief in one hand and a set of claws in the other! What a flattering picture you paint of me, Monsieur.'

'No, Madame, to be sure, I would be a fool myself to suggest such a thing,' Monge de Brineux chaffed. 'I must set off again. The journey to Authon is a long one. Believe me, this meeting has been more of a pleasure than I anticipated. I take my leave of you, Madame. Pray do not trouble yourself . . . I can find my own way to my horse.'

Clément listened to the Bailiff's footsteps walking off towards the main door that opened onto the courtyard. The footsteps halted.

'Madame. I confess I am still unsure of the facts. But if what you say is true then I strongly recommend you to be on your guard.'

A few seconds later, Clément emerged from his hiding place and approached Agnès.

'You were listening?'

'Yes, Madame.'

'What do you think of all this?'

'It worries me. The Bailiff is right – we must be doubly vigilant.'

'Do you think Eudes might be behind this plot?'

'If so, I doubt he is the instigator. He is better suited to spying on you in your home. He has no head for strategy.'

'Someone who has might be guiding him. Moreover, how did my handkerchief find its way into the forest?'

'Mabile?'

'Why not? She is cunning, and I think she nurses some kind of hatred towards us – the hatred of the weak who prefer attacking other prey rather than risk being caught in the jaws of the predator.'

'I was intrigued, not to say alarmed, by the turn you gave to that . . . conversation, Madame.'

She looked at him and grinned.

'Do you mean to say, assertive . . . Confrontational?'

'That's right.'

'You see, Clément, by dint of being subjugated by them, women learn to recognise the tracks men leave behind them – similar to wild game. You will understand it better as you get older.'

'And what species might he be?'

'Hmm . . . a young boar in his prime perhaps.'

'They are lean and muscular and prefer scaring off to attacking.'

'But when they attack, nothing can survive their charge. Monge de Brineux was testing me. It became clear after only a few sentences. I do not know why. What I do know is that nothing I said to him came as a surprise. It remains to be seen what his true motive for coming here was. Furthermore, I could not allow him to sense my apprehension.'

'They say the Comte d'Authon is very powerful.'

'Indeed, he is.'

'Your half-brother is a feudal baron and his vassal.'

'As I am my brother's, which makes of me the Comte's under-vassal.'

'Have you ever met him?'

'I remember a tall young man, serious and reserved, who came to pay the late Baron Robert a visit once. That is all. I was still a girl.'

'Madame, could you not demand his direct protection?'

'You know as well as I that a liege lord will not intervene directly in the affairs of another liege lord's vassal, except in cases of injustice or wrong judgement and we have not reached that stage yet. Artus d'Authon will not involve himself in a family dispute at the risk of sparking a political row that could prove injurious to him. Eudes is admittedly only a member of the lower nobility, but he holds an important trump card: his iron mines.'

'You mean, his iron mine, his last, which they say is almost exhausted,' corrected Clément.

'He extracts enough ore from it to keep the King happy. Clément . . .'

'Yes, Madame?'

'I do not like to involve you in such schemes, but . . .'

He understood at once what was troubling her and informed her:

'Since her visit to the chapel, Mabile has not been out for quite some time and has encountered no one likely to take messages to your brother.'

She reached out her hand, and he closed his eyes as he laid his cheek in her palm.

Towards the middle of the afternoon a second visitor did little to lift Agnès's spirits. Jeanne d'Amblin from Clairets Abbey was making her monthly rounds. Usually, Agnès found the jolly Extern Sister delightful. Her ready supply of stories and harmless gossip about her encounters with the wealthy burghers, merchants and farmers or even with the local nobility amused the younger woman. The nun brought her news of the outside world, its births, marriages, deaths, pregnancies and its harvests. Today, however, the good sister's unease was palpable. They sat in the little anteroom outside Agnès's quarters, furnished with a small round table and two chairs. Agnès's veil fluttered in a gentle current of air and she looked up at the high window. Several of the diamond-shaped panes were broken. By birds? When? She only ever passed through this tiny room, never stopping to sit there unless a lady visitor came, which was rare. What a day it had been! Glass was so costly and difficult to come by. The few glazed windows at the manor were the only reminder of Hugues's extravagant tastes. When winter came the rest would be stopped up with hemp or hides. How would she find the money to pay for the missing panes? Presently . . . She made an effort to attend to her visitor.

'Would you accept a cup of hippocras?'

'I never refuse good hippocras, and the one you make here is among the best.'

'You flatter me.'

The nun's smile lacked conviction, and she went straight to the point:

'I hurried here as soon as I learnt of the Bailiff's visit.'

'News travels fast,' observed Agnès.

'Not really. Monge de Brineux stopped off at Clairets Abbey on his way. Just after lauds.'*

'And why did he go to the abbey before dawn?'

'He desired a meeting with our Abbess. That is how we knew he was setting off afterwards for Souarcy. I can tell you precious little else. The Abbess asked me to come here to make sure that you were safe and sound – which I would have done anyway had her thoughts not anticipated my own,' Jeanne d'Amblin added. 'What wicked murders, for they are murders, are they not?'

'Everything would suggest it.'

'Wicked,' repeated the nun, clasping the large wooden crucifix hanging round her neck. 'Friars . . . Sister Adélaïde was right. This matter of the tonsures is so mysterious . . . I mean, why did those three friars, if not four, let their hair grow?'

'So as to blend in, to go unnoticed, I suppose.'

'Hmm . . . A convincing theory. At least it seems fitting in the case of the second victim, the papal emissary who met with our Abbess. She was terribly upset after he left. Naturally, it was only much later that we connected her distress with his visit, since we knew nothing of his mission.'

'What became of the missive he was carrying?' Agnès asked, even though thanks to the Bailiff she already knew the answer.

'Vanished into thin air. Our Abbess is worried sick about it. She refuses to disclose the contents and, knowing her as I do, I am certain she has every good reason.'

'And did the other victims . . .'

'. . . No, they did not visit us, if that's what you were going to ask. Few men besides the chaplain and the young pupils are allowed within our walls, otherwise it would be difficult for us to be so sure. The state of their faces made any identification virtually impossible.'

She paused, and looked at Agnès with a grave expression on her face before continuing:

'Something terrible is being hatched, I can sense it. And I am not the only one. Thibaude de Gartempe, our guest mistress, is anxious too. And others. Even Yolande de Fleury, who never seems upset by anything. Our Abbess's desperate silence contributes to our concern. For it is desperate. She has retreated

147

into herself in order to protect us, her girls, from what I do not know. We are afraid, Madame . . .'

Agnès did not doubt it. An unshakeable gloom seemed to have clouded the Extern Sister's usually bright happy face. She continued:

'I am afraid of an unknown entity whose form I cannot make out . . . It feels as if a deadly fog were about to engulf us, as if an evil beast were approaching by stealth. You will think me raving like some mad superstitious old woman.'

'No, indeed. You have described my own instinct. I too dread . . . I know not what.'

This was only half true. She had in some measure identified her fear: Eudes. And yet, like the nun, Agnès sensed something far more terrifying was secretly preparing to strike them and with great force.

Jeanne d'Amblin appeared to pause before deciding to speak:

'I did not only come here today to see how you were, but also to . . . how should I say . . . ? Well, we were wondering whether my Seigneur de Brineux had confided in you . . . some detail, anything that might help us to see more clearly, to have some idea, to console our Abbess, perhaps even to help her, to save other wretched victims?'

'No, and to be very honest I had the impression that he, like us, is groping in the dark.'

Shortly after the Extern Sister had left, Agnès resolved to take her mind off things by going to see if Vigil had come back from his latest jaunt. He had the habit of disappearing for a day at a time but always returned to the pigeon-house in the evening to guard his females. She had not seen him the previous evening, and a vague concern for the cocky bird added to the dark mood that never left her. Some huntsmen were quick to take aim and had few scruples.

Vigil was neither in the pigeon-house nor perched on the rooftop of the manor. The angry and unexpected peck she received from one of his mates as she tried to stroke it seemed to her a bad omen.

Béthonvilliers Forest, near Authon-du-Perche, June 1304

IN response to the pressure of his rider's leg the magnificent stallion came to a halt, statuesque. His immaculate black coat gleamed with sweat. He breathed without a single tremor of his powerful neck muscles, aware that the archer on his back was flexing his Turkish bow, made of two ox-horns joined by a metal spring.

The three-foot-long fletched arrow whistled through the air. It would have continued its flight for a hundred yards or so had it not struck the target, whose wings spread out in shock and pain as it plummeted in a swirl of feathers towards the archer. The rider swiftly dismounted and stooped to pick up the bird. The arrow had run it through, piercing the breast and exiting behind the wing joint. The huntsman's gloved hand paused an inch from the handsome pinkish-purple neck, now bloodied bright red. One of its sturdy feet was ringed; the other had a message attached. The huntsman pursed his lips in an expression of displeasure. He had shot a carrier pigeon – a superb animal whose loss the rightful owner would regret. What a fine haul! He would be obliged to compensate the lord or convent that owned the pigeon, despite having shot it down on his own land. A second infuriating thought occurred to him: his eyesight was waning. He who had been capable of following a falcon during the hunt without ever losing sight of it would soon be unable to tell the difference between a pigeon and a common pheasant! The silent devastation wrought by age. He became more aware by the day of its undermining effect. He would soon be forty-three. True, he was still a long way from old age, having only just passed the forty-year threshold signalling the end of youth. And yet, his joints would grumble after a day spent in the saddle, and he no longer had the urge to sleep out in all weathers. If he were to believe *The Four Ages of Man*, the treatise written forty years before by a lord of Novara, he still had a few good years before he entered old age. Artus d'Authon slipped off his right glove and pinched the skin on the back of his hand. Weathered from decades spent outside and leathery from handling weapons, it had grown more slack and seemed to want to come away in places from the flesh underneath. As for his wrist, it had lost some of its musculature.

'A pox on the years,' he muttered between his teeth.

The years had passed so quickly and yet he had been so terribly bored throughout, one day running into the next so that in the end he was barely able to tell them apart.

Born under the reign of Louis IX, he had grown up during that of Philip III, the Bold, under whom his father served as supreme commander of the French armies for some years before dying prematurely. He was nine years old at the birth of Philip, who would later become the fourth monarch to bear that name. He had initiated the young future king into the art of hunting and handling a bow. The inflexibility, the severity of the man, who would later be given the sobriquet 'the Fair', were already apparent. Artus was convinced that he would make a good king if he received good counsel, but a king he would prefer to admire from afar. Thus he had declined the honour of taking up the onerous post filled by his father, which would have been conferred on him owing to his friendship with the monarch, but also because its bestowal had become almost hereditary. Artus had then ridden halfway around the world, fighting wherever fortune or his fervour took him until he reached the Holy Land. It had brought him some subtle surprises, a few furious rages and a fair share of wounds that flared up in stormy weather. He had defended causes with both his brains and his brawn, but none had convinced him sufficiently for him to embrace any one completely. He had returned to France without having experienced the hoped-for transformation and had sunk back into the repetitive tedium of every day seeming the same.

Thereafter, the running of his small county had taken up all his time. His father's fascination with royal politics had led to its neglect, and it fell to Artus to put his house in order, to bring to heel, with more or less recourse to force, the lower nobility who were at each other's throats over the systematic carving-up of land that was not theirs. Widowed at thirty-two, he had all but forgotten the features of his ghostly wife who had died bearing him a son. Little Gauzelin had inherited his mother's frailty and, too weak to live, had died aged four. A father's grief had turned into a destructive animal rage. He had stormed the castle for weeks on end, sending the servants scattering for cover like mice whenever they heard the madman approach. Two deaths. Two pointless deaths and no heir. Only a terrible loneliness and regret for what had not been.

He pulled himself together. If he let his thoughts go down

that bitter path again the day – yet another day – would be irrevocably ruined.

He picked up the pigeon and examined the ring, pausing before he removed the long arrow implanted in the still warm flesh. A capital *S* was followed by a small *y*. Souarcy. The animal was the property of the young widow, Eudes de Larnay's half-sister, born of an adulterous liaison. He could not remember ever having met her, though Brineux had described her briefly and with a roguish glint in his eye.

A few days earlier, when his Chief Bailiff, Monge de Brineux, returned from his inquiries, Artus had asked him:

'And what of the cornered doe you ran down?'

'If she's a cornered doe then I'm a newly hatched gosling. The lady was not ruffled in the slightest by my visit – either that or she's a brilliant actress. That woman is more like a lynx than a doe. She's cautious, bold, clever and patient. She lures her prey into her territory by feigning sleep. As for the hunters, she plays with them, pretending to show herself while in reality protecting her young, covering her rear and preparing her escape.'

'Do you believe she is involved in these murders?'

'No, my Lord.'

'You seem very sure.'

'I can read men's souls.'

'Those of women are harder to decipher, my friend, especially,' the Comte added with a half-smile, 'when they are lynxes.'

'Goodness me, yes! She was fearful but not because of any guilt. Her show of arrogance was intended to convince me of the contrary. In my opinion she has nothing to do with these murders. And so the question we must now ask is glaringly obvious: how did her handkerchief come to be in those bushes? Somebody placed it there, but who? With the aim of implicating her, but why? I have gathered some reliable information. She possesses no great fortune; on the contrary. Souarcy is nothing but a large farm and rather less splendid than most of those belonging to our wealthy farmers in and around Authon. Moreover, the manor and its land are part of her dower. She owns nothing in her own right. If as a widow she were to lose the usufruct of the property it would revert to her half-brother, until her only child, Mathilde, Hugues de Souarcy's heir, comes of age. Having said this, the property in question would hardly be enough to attract the wealthy Eudes de Larnay, even though he scatters his fortune and that of his wife to the four winds.'

Eudes de Larnay. The mere thought of his vassal's name put Artus in a bad mood again. Eudes the rat. Beneath his bulky physique and his virile, seductive exterior he was a coward and a vile scavenger. Any man who beat the women he bedded was not worthy of being called a man. This at least was the wretched reputation of the feudal Baron as it had reached Artus's ears.

He paused for a moment, stroking with his forefinger the tiny roll of paper wrapped round the dead bird's leg. No. This message had been sent by the Dame de Souarcy or was intended for her, and it would be unseemly of him to read it without her permission.

'Let us go and take a look for ourselves, Ogier, my beauty,' he declared to the destrier, who pricked up his ears on hearing his name.

Artus d'Authon pulled out the arrow and made himself look at the blood that dripped from it. He remounted and gently squeezed the flanks of his horse, who took off towards the north. After all, it was as good a way as any to end a new day and he had to confess that Monge had excited his curiosity.

The Comte did not entirely trust his Bailiff's enraptured description of the lady. Brineux felt a mixture of affection and admiration towards women, which his marriage to a very quick-witted mischievous member of the burgher class from Alençon had done nothing to allay. Julienne might not have been the most beautiful girl in Perche, despite her pretty face and attractive figure, but she was incontestably the most entertaining, and had made him and Monge laugh many times with her gift for mimicry that bordered on genius. The way she impersonated Comte Artus right under his nose, frowning solemnly and lowering her pensive brow, crossing her hands behind her back and stopping as she walked, as though embarrassed by her great height, had the man himself in stitches, but he would never have accepted this playful mockery from any other.

It was a three-hour ride to Souarcy – a little less if he kept up a good pace. Madame de Souarcy could not refuse her liege lord lodging for the night, should he require it. As soon as he had satisfied his curiosity he would return home.

Manoir de Souarcy-en-Perche, June 1304

A FARM hand, overcome by panic on hearing his name, had spluttered directions to the forest where he would find the lady of the manor.

Ogier walked at a slow pace, sensing his rider's hesitancy in the slackening of the reins and the bit.

'It's not too late to turn back,' Artus d'Authon muttered, as though seeking his horse's approval. 'What a ridiculous fool to have come here at all. No matter. We shall finish what we have begun, so be it!'

Ogier lengthened his step.

A good thirty yards away, a blanket of smoke caught his attention. Two men, one tall and heavily built, the other slender, were gesticulating in its midst. Two serfs, judging from their short tunics, tied at the waist with a wide leather strap, and their thick linen breeches. The two men both wore gloves and a peculiar bonnet on their heads with a fine veil bunched at the neck.

Artus was alerted by his horse's sudden jumpiness. Why was a swarm of wild bees coming towards them? Hives. The two serfs were smoking out hives. He pulled up short and made Ogier walk back a few paces before dismounting and continuing alone on foot.

He was only a few yards from the two servants, yet they were seemingly so absorbed in their task that they did not notice his arrival. No doubt the strange protective garb they wore made it difficult to hear.

'Hey there!' he cried, alerting them to his presence while driving away the surrounding bees with a gloved hand.

The slender figure turned a veiled head towards him and a youthful, boyish voice spoke in a brusque tone that surprised the Comte:

'Stand back, Monsieur, they are angry.'

'Are they defending their honey?'

'No, their king, and with a ferocity and self-sacrifice that would be the envy of many a soldier,' replied the sharp voice. 'Stand back, I tell you. Their sting is fierce.'

Artus obeyed. This was no boy but a woman, and a very comely one at that, in spite of her outlandish costume. So Agnès de Souarcy had of necessity become a beekeeper. Monge de Brineux was right, the lynx was brave, for those bees when they attacked could prove lethal.

A good ten minutes elapsed, during which he did not take his eyes off her, studying each of her precise, agile movements, admiring how calm she stayed in order not to alarm the bees, listening to the patient way she instructed her farm hand, who towered above her like a giant. Artus felt half amused, half embarrassed. It would doubtless grieve her to be caught wearing breeches, though these were certainly far better suited to collecting honey than a robe. Even so, the wearing of men's clothes by women, for any reason, was strongly censured, although the doughty Eleanor of Aquitaine had done so in her day.

At last it appeared the two beekeepers had finished with the hives. They made their way towards him, the farm hand carefully carrying two pails brimming with the amber crop while the Dame de Souarcy loosened her protective veil, revealing two strawberry-blonde braids, which unfurled on either side of her pretty head.

As she walked up she addressed him blandly: 'They will calm down now and rejoin their king.' Then her tone changed suddenly, became scathing. 'You surprised me wearing unsightly and improper clothing, Monsieur. It would surely have been more appropriate for you to have sent one of my servants to announce your arrival and to have waited until I returned to the manor.'

He had seldom seen a woman so completely beautiful right up to her high, pale brow with the hairline set slightly back, according to the fashion of the time. He opened his mouth to utter the apology he had prepared but she cut across him:

'Souarcy is only a farm, I'll grant you. However, I insist on a modicum of good manners and couth behaviour! Your name, Monsieur?'

Good gracious, the woman's temper was beginning to unsettle him, and he a warrior and huntsman and one of the most redoubtable swordsmen in the kingdom of France. In truth he was quite unaccustomed to being snapped at like this. He recovered his poise and declared in a calm voice:

'Artus, Comte d'Authon, Seigneur de Masle, Béthonvilliers, Luigny, Thiron and Bonnetable, at your service, Madame.'

A shiver ran down Agnès's spine. The one man she ought never to have snubbed, much less offended. Admittedly, she had always doubted he would intervene on her behalf, and yet this powerful figure in the shadows had become like a magic spell she could never invoke for fear it might not work. Her inaccessible lucky charm. Indeed, this was the main reason why she had always refused to call upon him or his justice. If, as she feared, he were to turn her away then she would be completely helpless, alone against Eudes and no longer able to delude herself into believing that some miracle might save her. And yet now more than ever she needed to believe it.

She closed her eyes and breathed a sigh, her face white as a sheet.

'Are you unwell, Madame?' he enquired, concerned, and offered her his hand.

'It is nothing, just the heat and my fatigue.' She collected herself and continued, 'And the Seigneur de Souarcy. You forgot Souarcy.'

'Souarcy is under the protection of Baron de Larnay, Madame.'

'And he is your vassal.'

'Indeed.'

Agnès gave a polite if belated curtsey encumbered by her peasant's outfit.

'You are right to mention it Madame; I have behaved like an oaf . . . Are you finished with the bees?'

'Gilbert will see that they return to the hives. They like him. He is a gentle good soul. Would you be so kind, Gilbert?'

'Oh yes, my good lady, I shall fetch the honey and the wax, too, don't you worry.'

'You look weary, Madame. Pray let Ogier take you back to the manor. Allow me.'

He stooped, clasping his fingers to make a foothold for her. She was dainty and lithe, and mounted with a natural ease, sitting astride the saddle. Despite the inappropriateness of this position for a lady he found her fascinating. She was undaunted by his destrier, which was an awkward animal with anyone but its master. She sat admirably well on the huge black stallion, and horse and rider made an astonishingly handsome pair. Artus was beginning to think Monge had been right. He was reluctant now to mention the pigeon he had killed earlier, afraid of spoiling this singular moment.

Too soon for his liking, for he had been savouring their silent walk, they reached the courtyard of the manor. Agnès did not wait for his helping hand but slid from the saddle down Ogier's motionless flank.

Mabile had come running and the pale look on her face convinced Agnès that she was right in believing this man a godsend.

The girl gave a deep curtsey. So she had already seen him at her master's residence.

'Pray excuse me, Monsieur, while I change. Mabile will fetch you some refreshments and a bowl of fresh fruit.'

'I have something to show you, Madame,' he began in a faltering voice, tapping the leather game bag that was attached to his saddle, 'something I regret with all my heart.'

'Some wild game?'

'A terrible blunder.'

He pulled out the pigeon, stiff now, its silky throat stained with a layer of dried blood.

'Vigil . . .'

'He is yours, then.'

'Indeed,' Agnès murmured, fighting back the tears that veiled her eyes.

'Madame, I am truly regretful. He was flying through one of my forests, I took aim and . . .'

Mabile made a mad rush for the animal, crying:

'I'll take him, Madame, don't . . .'

'Stop!'

The order resounded. Agnès had seen the message round the animal's leg.

'Leave it. I will deal with it.'

The girl retreated under Comte d'Authon's baffled gaze. Agnès understood from her darting eyes and trembling lip that she was the author of the message, but she managed to keep her composure.

Her lucky charm. This man had already made a small miracle happen, for she was certain the message was addressed to Eudes. Now she knew how the plotters communicated: thanks to the beautiful trained bird, a generous gift from her half-brother. Her sadness at Vigil's loss quickly faded and she turned, smiling, to face the person who had no notion of the enormity of the good turn he had just done her.

'I am . . . an oaf. Pray believe me, Madame. I mistook it for a small pheasant. It was flying quite high and . . .'

'Do not mention it, Monsieur. Your blunder saddens me for I was fond of the bird, but . . . not everyone would have shown your consideration by returning the animal to me. Pray excuse me a few moments. I shall rejoin you shortly.'

She clutched Vigil and went up to her chamber. Before entering she called out from the bottom of the rickety ladder.

'Clément! I need your help.'

'I'm coming, Madame.'

She heard a quiet patter of feet and a face peered through the trapdoor opening.

'Vigil!'

'Yes. Come down. He's carrying a message.'

'So he was their messenger!'

'The huntsman is no other than Comte d'Authon. He is waiting for me in the great hall. Hurry.'

The child hurled himself down the ladder and joined her in her chamber. She briefly explained the unexpected encounter, which she dared not as yet consider a timely one. He listened with a smile on his lips that was betrayed by the gravity in his blue-green eyes.

'Change out of your clothes, Madame. I will remove the message from the bird's leg.'

Agnès paused. She had only a few minutes left in which to dress. What should she wear? Not the ceremonial robe she had fashioned from the sumptuous piece of silk Eudes had given her. Finery was not sufficient to charm this man. And charm him she must, her life depended on it. It was something at which she excelled and yet today she felt hindered by an unusual apprehensiveness.

'It is written in code, Madame. Each number stands for a letter, except for these Roman numerals – they probably represent real numbers. It doesn't need a genius to work out what they stand for: XXVIII – XII – MCCXCIV: 1294, the date of my birth. Mabile was sending him the information she found in the chapel register. The message might contain other clues that throw light on their plan.'

She turned towards Clément, who, out of a sense of modesty, was looking in the other direction over at the narrow window in the stone wall of her closet.

'Will you be able to decipher its secrets? You must, Clément.'

'I shall do my utmost. It is common to use a reference book and the few there are at Souarcy would mostly be inaccessible to the servants. My first choice would be the translation into French of the psalter you gave them. My only worry is that the two plotters might have been cleverer than we supposed. You see, the accomplices agree on a page and then number all the letters on that page. The ingenuity consists in beginning a few letters or lines into the page instead of with the first letter of the first line. It makes the job of decoding far more laborious and time-consuming.'

'Where did you obtain all this knowledge?'

'From books, Madame – they contain many marvels.'

'Indeed, but they are difficult to come by, and I was unaware that our modest library possessed so many treasures.'

'May I leave you to finish dressing, Madame?'

'You may, but do not vanish as is your custom.'

'Not tonight, Madame. I shall be watching over you.'

She stifled a smile. And yet what would she do without him, without his vigilance and his intelligence, which she saw new facets of every day?

Before leaving the room he whirled round and said in a hushed voice:

'And what type of game do you think this one is, Madame? A stag?'

'He is certainly strong and noble enough, but no, he possesses far more cunning. The stag runs until he hears the sound of the mort and then bravely but foolishly turns before charging. This one weighs up, thinks ahead. He knows when to renounce strategy in favour of strength, never the other way round. No. Not a stag, a fox, perhaps.'

'Hmm . . . A worthy animal, though almost impossible to tame.'

He closed behind him the heavy, studded door.

The pale-grey robe she wore for mass would do perfectly. She covered her braids with a long fine veil fixed at her crown by a small darker-grey turban. The fluid contours of the robe enhanced her graceful figure and made her look taller, which was acceptable given the height of her guest. She had matched the elegant austerity of her clothes to her perception of him. She chewed a pinch of *épices de chambre* to scent her breath, and put a drop of the belladonna Eudes had brought from Italy the year before in the corner of her eye. She had used the contents of the little phial studded with grey pearls and miniature turquoises but once, to see the effect it had. The eyes seemed to dissolve, becoming strangely deeper, like two languid pools.

Agnès walked back via the kitchens where she knew she would find Mathilde. The little girl was greedily watching Adeline and Mabile prepare the food.

'My lady daughter, the Comte d'Authon, an important man, has honoured us with his presence. I would like you to make an excellent impression, and then to take your leave without needing to be asked.'

'The Comte d'Authon here, Madame?'

'Indeed, it is no small surprise.'

'But . . . my dress is old and ugly and . . .'

'It is perfect. Besides, neither of our dresses could compete with those of the ladies in our lord's entourage, and so we must content ourselves with being dignified, which is a woman's best finery. Go and comb your hair and come back down at once.'

When Agnès rejoined the Comte in the great hall he was sitting on one of the sideboards playing with the dogs.

'Fine beasts, Madame.'

'They are fearsome guard dogs . . . Or at least they were until your arrival.'

He smiled at the mild compliment and replied:

'Animals seem to warm to me. No doubt it is on account of my good manners.'

She offered no apology for her earlier rebuke. It would be a mistake, for he would instantly detect her servility. The simple fawning she used so abundantly with Eudes would never work on this man. On the contrary it would almost certainly repulse him.

A moment later, Mathilde made her entrance as agreed. She was struggling to catch her breath from running, but walked with a calm, measured step towards her liege lord.

'Monsieur,' she began, curtseying gracefully, 'your presence within our walls is a rare pleasure indeed. And the honour you confer upon us brightens our humble dwelling.'

He went over to her, suppressing a good-natured chuckle.

'You are utterly charming, Mademoiselle. As for pleasures and honours, believe me, they are all mine. Had I known that two of the most precious pearls in Perche lodged here at the manor, I should not have delayed so long in coming. It is an unforgivable oversight on my part.'

The little girl's face flushed with joy at the immense flattery, and she took her leave, curtseying again.

'Your daughter is delightful, Madame. How old is she?'

'She is twelve. I try to teach her refinement. I hope she may enjoy a more . . . a more sumptuous life than the running of Souarcy.'

'To which you have nonetheless devoted yourself.'

'Mathilde was not born between two beds in the servants' quarters, albeit the servant in question was a lady's maid.'

Artus knew of the Dame de Souarcy's illegitimate birth. It disconcerted him that she would flaunt it until he realised that by making light of it she was defending herself against gossip or, worse still, ridicule. She really was a fine lynx. And she pleased him greatly.

The dinner began on a note of delightful banter, notwith-standing the miserable expression Mabile wore as she served the *cretonnée* of new peas, freshly picked; the creamy soup thickened with egg yolk beaten in warm milk looked appetising.

Artus perceived that the lady was cultured, lively and intelligent and had a facility for repartee rare in a woman of her social standing.

When he complimented her on her composure earlier in the middle of a swarm of unfriendly bees, she told him of her first harvest with a playful look:

'. . . A column of bees was coming towards me. I shrieked and in a moment of foolish panic threw the pail of honey at them, half believing that if I gave it back they would leave me alone. Nay! I was obliged to hitch up my dress and run as fast as my legs would carry me back to the manor. You should have seen me in my crooked turban with my veil half torn off. I even lost a shoe. One of the fierce sentinels flew under my skirts and stung me – well, above my knee, and hence the breeches. In short, I made an utter fool of myself. Thankfully Gilbert was the only witness to my pitiable retreat. He bravely drove back the bees, thrashing his arms in the air like an angry goose to protect me. He came back covered in swellings and running a temperature.'

Artus burst out laughing as he pictured the scene. How long since he had laughed like that and above all in the company of a woman?

His mind grew troubled by a memory. The small frightened face of the frail young woman he had married when he was nearing his thirtieth birthday. Madeleine, the only child of the d'Omoy family, was eighteen, a perfectly decent age for becoming a wife and mother. And yet she still played with dolls. Her weeping mother and her father, who would have gladly continued treating her as a child for a few more years if he had not needed to secure a commercial transaction with the Comte, agreed to her marriage to Artus. Normandy and its ports, which supplied large areas of the hinterland via an extensive network of waterways, was vital to the flourishing of Artus d'Authon's commerce, all the more so since the region was equally rich in iron ore. As for Huchald d'Omoy, an impoverished yet distinguished nobleman, the Comte d'Authon's gold would allow him to regild the family crest, tarnished following a series of ruinous investments. The young Madeleine d'Omoy sealed their contract. Anyone might have thought she had been abducted by a barbarian. For her their marriage began as a betrayal then turned into an ordeal when she realised that the physical distance separating her from her parents meant she would rarely see them. Artus could picture her now languishing in the room she almost never left, sitting on a chair under one of the arrow slits staring up at the sky, watching out for he knew not what. If he enquired she would invariably turn her ashen face towards him, forcing a smile, and reply:

'The birds, Monsieur.'

'You would glimpse them more easily from the garden. It is warm outside, Madame.'

'No doubt it is, Monsieur, but I am cold.'

She stayed where she was.

His visits to his wife's bedroom became more infrequent. He felt unwelcome there, and had it not been for his need of an heir he would doubtless have ceased inconveniencing Madeleine with his presence. He had never felt any desire for her. That skinny angular body, which he hardly dared touch for fear it might break, inspired a sort of pity in him that had gradually become mingled with repulsion.

The birth had been a nightmare. For hours on end he had listened to her groans from the lobby of her chamber.

Immediately after the delivery she had nearly succumbed to a haemorrhage that all but drained her weak blood. Despite the attentions she received from the physic and the midwife, which appeared partially to revive her, she doubtless had little will to live and three weeks after Gauzelin's birth, without a last word or even a gesture, her frail existence was snuffed out like a candle.

He surprised himself casting furtive glances at Agnès. She was strikingly beautiful and graced her speech with elegant gestures. Underneath all this refinement he was sure she possessed a rare strength of mind. Hugues de Souarcy had been a fortunate man when he married her at Robert de Larnay's request – she much less so. Not that Hugues was a bad man – on the contrary – but he was a coarse man whose rough edges had hardly been refined by wars and the tireless frequenting of taverns. Moreover, he was already quite advanced in years when they married. How old had she been then, thirteen, fourteen perhaps?

They talked of this and that, making each other laugh and jumping from one subject to another in an atmosphere of humorous repartee. She paused, concluding:

'With their *Roman de la Rose** Messieurs de Lorris and de Meung left me, how should I say . . . disappointed. The beginning and the end were so different. I found parts of the first story conventional, not to say over-indulgent, while the second, the satire on "feminine etiquette" by Ami et la Vieille, grated on my nerves.'

'The second author was a Parisian scholar and not always successful in avoiding the pitfalls of his education – which he was fond of parading – or of his milieu, or indeed those of farce itself.'

'In contrast, I confess to being extremely partial to the ballads and fables of Madame Marie de France.* What wisdom, what finesse! The way she makes the animals speak as though they were humans.'

Artus could not resist seizing the opportunity.

'I, too, admire the lady's finesse and use of language. And what did you think of the poem entitled *Yonec*?'

Agnès immediately understood the reference. In that enchanting poem – the pretext for a discourse on true love – a woman who has married against her will prays to heaven to send her a sweet lover. Her wish is granted and the lover arrives in the form of a bird which turns into a prince.

She took her time responding, lowering her gaze towards the snail, herb and onion pâté which, enthralled as she was by their conversation, she had hardly tasted. He reproached himself for her silence:

'The term uncouth would seem perfectly suited to me this evening. Pray forgive my tasteless question, Madame.'

'Why, Monsieur? Indeed, my Seigneur Hugues was not the husband of a young girl's dreams, but he was courteous and respectful towards his wife. Besides, I did not dream. Dreams were a luxury I was scarcely permitted.'

'More's the pity, Madame.'

'Indeed.'

The acute sadness his idiotic question had caused the young woman wounded him.

'I feel I have behaved like an insensitive oaf.'

'No, for, with all due respect, I would not have allowed that. Hugues was my life raft – I believe that is the name sailors give it, and he was no less dependable. I was thirteen years of age. My mother had left this world when I was still a child and as for the Baroness, God rest her good soul, she was more interested in astronomy than matchmaking. In brief, I knew nothing of the role of wife . . . nothing of the duties involved.'

'Some of which can be pleasurable.'

'So I believe. In any event, Hugues never lost his patience with me. His only failing in my eyes was that he allowed Souarcy to go to rack and ruin. He was no farmer, even less an administrator, he was a soldier. Most of the land had turned into a wilderness and parts of it had become barren.'

'Why did you not seek your brother's protection after your husband's death? Life at Larnay would surely have been less arduous for a young widow and her child.'

Agnès's face froze, and her pursed lips spoke louder than any words. He quickly changed the subject. Now he knew the answer to the question he had been asking himself all evening.

'The snail pâté is divine.'

He sensed the effort she needed to make in order to return to polite conversation and he was overcome by a strange tenderness.

'Is it not? The little animals are very partial to the baby lettuce we grow here. It gives them a sweet flavour, which we bring out with sautéed onion. And what they don't eat we use in soups or salads.'

Next, Mabile served roast rack of wild boar in a glistening sauce made of verjuice, wine, ginger, cinnamon and clove, served with broad bean purée and stewed apple. As soon as the servant had returned to the kitchen Artus declared:

'That girl is peculiar.'

She is afraid I might find out the meaning of the message Vigil was carrying, that is why she is peculiar, thought Agnès. She fixed the Comte's dark eyes with her grey-blue gaze and said:

'A gift from my half-brother Eudes.'

It was clear to him from her voice that it was one she would have gladly refused and that she mistrusted the girl.

The dinner continued. Agnès put the conversation back on a pleasant light-hearted footing. Their amusing exchanges were once again punctuated by repartee, learned observations and poetic quotations. Not that the Comte's earlier seriousness had annoyed the lady, on the contrary it had allowed her to let him glimpse the aversion she felt for her half-brother. She had said nothing to compromise herself, and if the Comte were on friendly terms with Eudes she could always maintain that he had misinterpreted her mood. The cause would once again be attributed to the fickle nature of women's disposition.

Having achieved her aim of gratifying him with her company and her conversation, Agnès now studied him properly for the first time. He towered above her by a head and a half, though she was tall for a woman. He had dark hair and dark eyes – rare in a region where men tended to have light-chestnut or blond hair and blue eyes. He wore his hair shoulder-length, as was the fashion among the powerful. It was wavy and flecked with grey. He had a good, straight nose, and a chin that revealed authority, and intolerance, too. He moved with rare elegance for a man with such a muscular build. His brow was deeply furrowed, weathered from years of riding. A fine specimen indeed.

'You are examining me, Madame,' a deep voice said, not without a hint of satisfaction.

Agnès's cheeks flushed and she dissembled:

'You have a hearty appetite. It is a pleasure to receive you in my home.'

'Believe me, the pleasure is all mine.'

She detected an amused sparkle in his eye.

All at once, the Comte's smile faded, and he instinctively raised his hand to tell her to be quiet. He strained his ear in the direction of the postern door.

Agnès swallowed hard. Clément.

Artus d'Authon rose to his feet and crept cat-like over to the door. What should she do? Feign a sudden attack of coughing? Warn the child by crying out: 'What is it, Monsieur!' in a loud voice? No. The Comte would see through the ruse and the evening had been going too well to risk ruining everything now.

He pulled hard on the door, and Clément toppled into the room like a sack of potatoes. He hauled him up sharply by the ear.

'What are you doing here? Were you spying on us?'

'No, Monsieur. No, no . . .'

Clément shot Agnès an alarmed look. Artus would be within his rights to flog the hide off him if he saw fit. He was trapped. The Dame de Souarcy thought quickly.

'Come over here, Clément, my dear.'

'Is he one of your servants?'

'The very best. He is my protector. He was keeping a watch on you to make sure his lady was in no danger.'

'He is a little on the small side to offer much protection.'

'Indeed, but he is brave.'

'And what would you have done, my boy, had my wicked intention been to pounce on your lady?'

Clément pulled out the carving knife he carried on him at all times, and declared in a solemn voice:

'Why, I would have killed you, Monsieur.'

The Comte burst out laughing and, amidst gasps of merriment, declared:

'Do you know, young man, I believe you capable of it! Now off to bed with you; nothing untoward will happen to your mistress, upon my honour.'

Clément stared at Agnès, who nodded in agreement. He vanished as if by magic.

'You stir passionate loyalties, Madame.'

'He is still a child.'

'A child who would have stabbed me to death if necessary, I am sure of it.'

A bewildering thought flashed through his mind. This woman was worth risking life and limb to protect.

Just then Mabile entered the room, her eyes bright with curiosity.

'A thousand pardons. I thought you might be in need of assistance, Madame.'

'No. We are waiting for the third course,' Agnès replied curtly.

The girl bowed her head, slowly enough for the Dame de

Souarcy to be able to glimpse the spite in her eyes.

The dessert of fruit and nut rissoles soon appeared. Mabile's face wore a more friendly expression. Even so, Agnès would have to put a stop to this girl and the façade they had been keeping up for months, and the thought worried her. Up until then, she had been able to manipulate Eudes by pretending she admired and trusted him. The incident with the pigeon had undermined this strategy, which, however dishonest, had succeeded over the years. The secret battle between her and her half-brother was about to burst out into the open and she was unprepared. She would be defeated. She had acted rashly and foolishly by demanding the carrier pigeon be returned to her. Restraining herself would have enabled her to keep up the pretence of not knowing Eudes's true intentions a little longer. Comte Artus's miraculous arrival and the obvious pleasure he had derived from their evening together only increased her anger with herself. With a little more time she might have gained in him an important ally. Her reckless anger towards the girl had spoiled everything. Agnès silenced her anxieties.

The last course was a thick cherry cream with wine, served on crepes.

'You have treated me to a veritable banquet, Madame.'

'A modest one for a nobleman of your standing.'

He was surprised by this formal courtesy coming from her lips, but understood when he looked up and saw the servant now waiting on them. It was no longer the sullen, miserable-looking woman from before but a rather ungainly, stocky young girl.

'Adeline, you will prepare the master bedroom in the South Wing for Seigneur d'Authon.'

The young girl mumbled her consent and curtseyed clumsily before scurrying from the room.

'She is not very bright, but she is trustworthy,' Agnès explained.

'Unlike Mabile, do you mean?'

Agnès responded with a vague smile.

'I regret having put you to so much trouble. I fear I have outstayed my welcome. I shall leave at dawn. Pray, grant me the favour of not troubling yourself to attend my departure. One of your farm hands can saddle my horse.'

'And I am obliged to you for the rare and all too brief entertainment your visit has brought me. The evenings here at Souarcy are long, and your presence has lifted the customary dullness that descends upon them.'

He stared at her, hoping that her glib speech was more than just a mark of exquisite politeness.

Less than an hour later, he was settled in what had been Hugues de Souarcy's chamber, which Adeline had gone to great pains to prepare – even starting a fire in the grate although the evening was mild. He walked over to the metal sconces in order to blow out the candles. Their sheer number attested to their having been lit in his honour. No small luxury for such a modest household, for even if her hives produced wax Agnès probably sold it instead of using it. After removing his surcoat, he stretched out on the bed without taking the trouble to undress or even to take off his shoes, and lay with his eyes open, staring into the darkness.

Artus acknowledged his confusion. What had started as mere curiosity on his part had turned into something quite unexpected. He had even forgotten about the gruesome murders.

Clearly the lady pleased him greatly, and this type of attraction had become rare enough in his life for it to unsettle and surprise him. Was his life really so empty that the Dame de Souarcy could fill it this easily? His life, it was true, had become a wilderness. In reality, it had always been one – a wilderness full of obligations and interests, which helped him to forget the painfully slow passing of time. And now eight hours had just gone by in a flash. Over the course of a single evening, time had regained its urgency. This lady had cured Artus's boredom and, what was more, his expectation of boredom. Her victory had been a swift one and yet she suspected nothing.

He was mistaken. Agnès was fully aware of the gains she had made during the course of their dinner. And, although she felt triumphant, she was clear-sighted enough to realise that she had won only a simple battle and that the real war was yet to come.

After leaving instructions for the Comte to be woken, she went back up to her chamber, pretending not to notice Mabile's absence from the kitchens. Perhaps the evil creature had run to seek refuge with her former master? Nonsense! Not in the night and on foot.

The glow of an oil lamp made her pause at the top of the stone steps.

A voice whispered:

'Madame . . .'

'Are you not asleep yet, Clément?'

'I was waiting for you.'

He went ahead of her into her room, which was sparsely lit by a few tallow lamps. The resin torches, which blackened the walls, were reserved for the long bare stone passageways or for the cavernous halls.

'Has something bad happened?' Agnès asked, after pushing the heavy door closed.

'You could say that. Somebody removed the pigeon and the message from your chamber this evening.'

'But you took it up to your attic with you,' objected the lady.

'Only while I copied out the message. Afterwards I rolled the strip of paper carefully round the bird's leg and replaced him in your quarters, on the dressing table.'

'You knew she would take it, didn't you? So that is where she went between courses.'

'I could have sworn it,' the boy retorted. 'Madame, we are not ready to confront the Baron head on. Mabile cannot be certain you saw the message or, even worse, that you suspect it comes from her. It suits her purposes not to know, to turn a blind eye. Otherwise she would be obliged to tell her master that their plan has failed, and he would not thank her for it. We need to gain more time in order to prepare for this fight, especially now after the Comte's unexpected visit.'

Agnès closed her eyes in relief, and bent down to embrace the child.

'What would I do if it weren't for you?'

'Were it not for you I would be dead, Madame; were it not for you I would die.'

'Then let us both do our utmost to stay alive, dear Clément.'

She planted a kiss on the boy's forehead and watched him leave the room noiselessly, her eyes moist with tears.

She stood still for a few moments, struggling against the memory of years of sadness and privation, of loneliness and fear. She fought off, inch by inch, the stubborn desire to surrender, to abandon herself.

A sudden voice, a voice she knew as if it were her own, floated into her consciousness. A sweet, gentle, but firm voice whose words she had treasured, the voice of her good angel, the Baroness Clémence de Larnay. How could she have almost forgotten her own mother when Madame Clémence's every gesture, smile, frown or caress was imprinted on her body and soul? God only knew how much she had loved that woman, so much that there were times when she thought of her as her only mother because they had chosen each other. God only knew how bereft she had felt when the woman died.

Her eyes brimmed with burning tears and she heard herself murmur:

'Madame, I miss you so very much.'

Agnès let herself be engulfed by all the years of lessons, laughter, secrets and affection they had shared. Madame Clémence had insisted the little girl choose a constellation for them. Agnès had taken a long time deciding between Virgo, Orion, the Plough and countless others, plumping finally for Cygnus, which shone so bright in early September. It was Madame Clémence who had read and re-read the ballads of Madame Marie de France to her. How they had both relished the poem *Lanval*, about a brave knight to whom a fairy promised her love on condition that he kept it secret. The

Baroness had taught her how to play chess, roguishly warning her: 'I confess to cheating. However, for love of you I shall try to play fairly for the first few games.'

Had Madame Clémence been happy? Perhaps, during the first few years of her marriage, though Agnès could not know for sure. In fact, it was their mutual loneliness that had first brought them together. The loneliness of a beautiful lady declining in years, whose husband and son appeared to treat her like a piece of furniture, addressing her with frosty politeness, and of a little girl terrified by the thought of being abandoned after her mother's death, tormented by Eudes, who had dinned it into her that she would do well to obey him if she did not want to find herself out on the street. Deep down, Agnès realised that she had always been afraid, except when Madame Clémence's presence had given her the courage to keep going, to face her fears.

She recalled a long-forgotten scene. What had happened exactly? No doubt Baron Robert had returned to Larnay after one of his amorous encounters, the worse for drink and reeking of the female sex. He had charged into his wife's chamber without taking the trouble to knock, intent on gratifying one last urge. Agnès was sitting at Madame Clémence's feet being read a story. At her husband's rude drunken entrance the Baroness stood up. He muttered a few words that caused Madame Clémence's face to turn pale, but which the little girl did not understand.

Agnès could still hear the cold, sharp voice ringing in her ears:

'Leave here this instant, Monsieur!'

The Baron had staggered over to his wife, his hand raised as though to slap her. Instead of backing away or crying out she had moved towards him and, seizing him by his coat collar, had growled:

'You do not scare me, Monsieur! Do not forget who I am or where I come from! Who do you think you are, you pig? Go and mount your whores if it pleases you and leave us in peace. I do not wish to see your face until you are sober and penitent. I command you to leave here at once, you uncouth drunkard!'

Agnès remembered seeing the Baron visibly recoil, his shoulders hunched, his drunken red face turning a greyish-green. He had opened his mouth, but no sound had come. The Baroness stared at him, unflinching, standing her ground.

He had done as she asked, or more precisely, as she commanded, muttering feebly for a man of his pride: 'You've gone too far!'

As soon as the door to her quarters had closed, Madame Clémence had been seized by a fit of trembling. She had explained to the alarmed and confused Agnès in a voice that was once more gentle:

'The only way to bring a dog to heel is to growl more fiercely than he, to raise your ears and tail and bare your teeth.'

'And then he won't go for your throat?'

Madame Clémence had smiled and stroked Agnès's hair.

'In most cases he will back down, though sometimes he will attack, and when that happens you must fight.'

'Even if you are afraid he might bite you?'

'Fear will not save you from being bitten, my dear. On the contrary.'

To fight.

Up until then, Agnès had always tried to avoid conflict by outwitting her enemy, by using her guile. For years the strategy had seemed to work. Though not entirely, for she now found herself in an even more dangerous position than the one she had been in before her marriage or just after Hugues's death.

Guile? That was what she had always told herself. But why not admit it: she had no guile; she was simply afraid. She had comforted herself with the thought that as a woman it was more appropriate, more becoming, to take a defensive position. But vultures such as Eudes made no exceptions for women. On the contrary, women inflamed their thirst for blood because they counted on a woman's weakness and fear to provide them with a swift and painless victory.

To fight. There would be no more evasion, no more pretence. It was her turn to attack and she would show no more mercy than her enemy.

The iron mine, Eudes's mine, which rumour had it was almost exhausted. Her half-brother and his ancestors before him had built the Larnay fortune on it and, more importantly, had received the self-interested benevolence of the monarchs they served. What if King Philip were to learn that the deposit was nearly depleted? Unquestionably the small favours its owner enjoyed would soon dry up, too. Eudes would be alone and defenceless. Artus d'Authon would once more be his all-powerful liege lord, and Artus liked Agnès, she knew. It is easy to observe when emotion takes a sincere man by surprise. No more guile, she had said. But there was nothing wrong with her using her feminine wiles. They were a weapon, one of the few that a woman was still permitted to wield.

To growl more fiercely, to raise her ears and tail, and bare her teeth. And above all to be ready to leap at her enemy's throat. To prevail.

How would she reach the King? The answer was simple: anonymously. The only intermediary the Dame de Souarcy could think of was Monsieur de Nogaret, of whom it was said he watched over the interests of the kingdom as if his own life depended on it.

She felt a sudden release and let her body slowly slide to the floor. She let out a long and peaceful sigh:

'Thank you, my angel, thank you, Clémence.'

It was not yet daybreak when Artus climbed back into the saddle the following morning. There was no reason for him to leave so early other than an irrational fear of meeting again, so soon, the woman who had robbed him of his sleep. For he had lain awake the whole of that short night, smiling one minute as he recalled her almost girlish hilarity, troubled the next by his strange infatuation.

A regular popinjay! He chuckled at the image of himself, a man over forty years of age behaving like a foolish love-sick youth! What a miracle! What a delightful miracle!

He sat up straight, trying his best to put on a sombre face in keeping with his reputation.

A few moments later he was riding across country, intoxicated by the powerful supple speed of Ogier, who was refreshed after his night's rest. A sudden anxious thought sobered him: what if he were making a mistake? What if she were a mere illusion and not the ideal woman he had, until then, never allowed himself to believe in?

He slowed his horse to a walk, troubled by the notion.

A hundred yards on he was smiling again as he recalled her account of her first honey harvest that had ended in a farcical failure.

The riotous flurry of emotions startled him. Zounds! Could he be falling in love? So soon? The attraction was clear, at least as far as he was concerned. However, attraction of the senses was, in everyone's opinion, commonplace and arbitrary enough for it not to cause him any great concern. But love and love's pains . . . In all honesty he could not say he had ever experienced them.

A sudden fit of laughter threw him onto the pommel of his saddle and against Ogier's neck. The horse gave a friendly shake of its mane.

Rue de Bucy, Paris, July 1304

I N the implacable calm of that early evening, the echo of feet on a stone floor. Francesco de Leone strained his ears to hear where the sound was coming from, only to realise all of a sudden that the footsteps were his.

He was walking along the ambulatory of the church. His sleeveless black coat flapped around his calves, occasionally brushing the rood screen shielding the chancel. A large white crucifix with eight branches fused together in pairs was sewn onto the garment, above his heart.

How long had he been advancing in this way? For a while no doubt, as his eyes were accustomed to the semi-darkness. He tried by the weak light filtering through the dome to study the shadows that mocked him. They seemed to be flowing between the pillars, lapping at the base of the walls, slipping between the balustrades. What church was this? What did it matter? It was not very big and yet he had been turning in it for so many hours he knew every last one of the massive stones whose ochre hue appeared tinged with pink in the gloom.

He tried to catch up with the silently moving figure, betrayed only by the faint rustle of fabric, of heavy silk. It was the figure of a woman, a woman hiding. A proud figure, almost as tall as he. Suddenly he noticed the woman's long hair. So long it reached below her knees, merging in a wave with her silk dress. A stabbing pain made him breathe in sharply. And yet the cold that reigned within those walls was biting. His breath condensed in the air, moistening his lips.

He was chasing the woman. She was not fleeing, only keeping the distance between them. She circled as he circled, always a few steps ahead of him as though anticipating his movements, staying on the outside of the ambulatory while he moved along on the inside.

He paused. A single step and then she stopped. He heard the sound of calm slow breathing, but he might have imagined it. As he moved off again so did his shadow.

Francesco de Leone's hand reached slowly for the pommel of his sword, even as an overwhelming love made his eyes fill with tears. He looked in disbelief at his hand clutching the metal pommel. Had he aged? Great bulging veins protruded under the pale skin, which was covered in a mesh of fine wrinkles.

Why was he chasing this woman? Who was she? Was she real? Did he wish to kill her?

Francesco de Leone woke up with a start, his face bathed in sweat. His heart was beating so fast it almost hurt and he was breathless. He lifted his arm and turned his hand. It was long and broad without being heavy. A layer of silky, pale flesh covered the subtle bluish maze of veins.

He sat on the edge of the canopied bed in the chamber Capella had allocated to him, struggling against the debilitating dizziness.

The dream, the nightmare, was becoming clearer. Leone was nearing his goal. The dream was the future, he was certain of that now.

He had to get out of there, to take advantage of the dawn and wander through the city streets. That chamber, that house oppressed him. The lingering stagnant odour choked him.

Giotto Capella was worried sick. Over the years he had developed a genuine aversion to honesty. This was not in his case because of any particular liking for vice; it was more out of superstition. Honesty had come to be equated in his mind with weakness, and to be weak was to be humiliated.

What could this handsome Knight from an eminent family possibly know of humiliation? Capella resented him bitterly. Not because of his noble birth or because he chose to disregard the privileges of such a birth, not even because of his implacable judgement of the betrayal at Acre. What did he think? That Giotto was such a fool that he had not weighed up his crime when he made his transaction with the enemy? Three hundred gold pieces for so many men, women and children, for so many screams, for so much blood? He had accepted the deal and been cheated. No. Capella resented him for having brought right into his study the proof that no memory can ever be entirely laid to rest. For in the end the usurer had managed to accommodate his. It was true that from time to time they would seep into his brain, above all at night. And yet these infiltrations had gradually become less frequent. Giotto owed his easy conscience to a convenient theory he had invented for himself:

after all, who could say that reinforcements would have arrived in time to save the citadel at Acre? What is more, someone else might have revealed the plans of the sewers if he hadn't. They would have died anyway in the end. And so the usurer had cleared his conscience by convincing himself that the massacre had been inevitable, and that he was one guilty party among a host of other potential ones. Now, thanks to the Hospitaller who had never known fear, the white walls at Acre never left his thoughts. Now, honesty was beating a pathway to his door accompanied by its ruinous counterpart: clarity. Now, here he was telling himself that but for his crime thirty thousand souls would still be alive.

In reality, as much as he hated Leone, his petty predator's instinct told him that this was not a man upon whom he could wreak revenge. He must be killed outright, and Giotto was too much of a coward to do that.

Before the arrival of Monsieur de Nogaret's envoy that afternoon he had entertained the foolish hope that some miracle, some sleight of hand might remove this troublesome guest from his midst. Each time he heard the man leave, as he had that early morning, he prayed he would never return. Countless people met their deaths in that city every day so why not the Knight Hospitaller? Giotto Capella knew this was foolish wishful thinking. There was another, less remote possibility: if he were to do nothing, why, the Knight would never meet Guillaume de Nogaret and might end up leaving. He could once again apply his favourite dictum: 'Always put off until tomorrow what people ask you to do today.' It had brought him fortune and riches up until then, but he was mindful that it might let him down now.

Capella's world, which he had worked so hard to build, was being trampled under the Knight's feet. In the space of a few days he had lost his appetite for life; even the lure of easy profit no longer filled him with feverish excitement. Why not admit it, since Leone was forcing him to be honest: it was not remorse that was demoralising him so much as the fear of his faults being imminently made public. A fault confessed is half redressed. Poppycock! Only those you succeed in burying never come back to haunt you.

Dressed in his nightclothes and a flannel nightcap, Giotto Capella was worried sick, plunged into despair for the past few minutes by the thought that his fear of reprisal prevented him from striking back. This impossibility had taken away his appetite for his supper and he was livid. Monsieur de Nogaret's messenger had left discreetly a few hours earlier and Leone could not have seen him sneaking out of the service entrance to the building. Monsieur de Nogaret had requested Giotto's presence two days later. The matter could only relate to money. King Philip did not baulk at borrowing vast sums of money even if it meant later on having to expel the moneylenders in order to avoid repaying the debts of the realm. If that meant money could be made by practising a barely concealed usury on, among others, the King's barons, then all the better. Since the man had left, Capella had been dragging his feet. What if he went to the meeting alone and warned his Seigneur de Nogaret of the Knight's extraordinary request? After all, what did one more betrayal matter? And yet the memory of the Knight's silences dissuaded him. Silences reveal a great deal more than words. And those of this man declared that he belonged to that race of wolves whom God's love has convinced to watch over His flock. A wolf possessed of a terrifying purity.

A nervous servant girl entered, stammering unintelligibly:

'I . . . I . . . he wouldn't listen, master, it's not my fault . . .'

Francesco de Leone appeared behind the girl, and dismissed her with a gesture. He studied Giotto Capella's apparel. A man in a nightshirt and nightcap will give less resistance than the same man fully dressed. No. The Knight expected no opposition from the Lombard usurer. His threats had already turned Capella's face even more sallow. Would he carry them out if it proved necessary? He might. Only those capable of pity were deserving of it and this man had not hesitated to profit from the massacre of men, women and children.

'When do you plan to arrange my meeting with Nogaret, Lombard?' he asked, without troubling to greet his recalcitrant host.

The coincidence was too great and Capella understood that the Knight had seen the messenger sent by the King's Counsellor.

'I was waiting for the right moment.'

'And?'

'It has arrived.'

'When did you mean to inform me?'

'Tomorrow morning.'

'Why the delay?'

The Knight's calm voice alarmed Giotto, who protested in a rasping whine:

'What were you expecting?'

'From you? The worst.'

'Foul lies!'

'Take heed, usurer. I have killed many men who caused me no harm. You, I shall turn over. The King's executioners have an enthusiasm for torture that inspires . . . respect.'

The apparent irony of this last remark worried the usurer, who made a show of his sincerity, explaining:

'We shall undoubtedly be received by Guillaume de Plaisians. Do you know him?'

'Only by reputation and not very well. He was Nogaret's student at Montpellier, I believe, and then a judge at the royal court in that city before becoming seneschal at Beaucaire.'

'Make no mistake, he is Seigneur de Nogaret's *éminence grise*. He began working with him last year as a jurist under direct orders to the King. In this case the expression "right-hand man" would be inexact for no one knows whether Nogaret or Plaisians is the brains behind any reform. The two men are equally brilliant, but Nogaret is no speaker, while the other will harangue a crowd until it no longer knows whether it is coming or going, and then make it perform a volte-face. I still remember his extraordinary and fearsome diatribe against Boniface VIII. Their physical appearance is as dissimilar as their talent for oratory. Guillaume de Plaisians is a handsome fellow. In brief, he is no less of a man to be reckoned with than my Seigneur de Nogaret.'

A doubt flashed through Francesco de Leone's mind. Why had the prior Arnaud de Viancourt not mentioned Nogaret's *éminence grise* as Capella referred to him?

Environs of the Templar commandery at Arville,
Perche, July 1304

THE pitch-black stallion pawed the ground while its rider, a shadowy figure wrapped in a brown woollen cloak, scanned the gloomy forest in search of his prey. A shiny metal claw on the end of his right hand gripped the reins. The ghostly figure sat up in his saddle and gave a grunt of disgust. This time, the fools had chosen a slip of a girl as a messenger. Did they really think she stood more of a chance than the men they had sacrificed up until then? The fools. And yet, having tracked her for more than half an hour, the ghostly slayer's contempt was gradually giving way to impatience, even to a sense of unease. The young girl moved swiftly and noiselessly. How could she not be exhausted? Where was she hiding, in which piece of undergrowth? Why had she not given in to her panic like the others before her? For they had not all been poisoned to the point of delirium. Why did she not make a run for it in a pathetic attempt to flee?

The figure tensed his calf muscles against the horse's flanks. The animal shifted restlessly, sensing the doubt creeping into the mind of its master.

What had brought this girl to Arville? Was her mission related to the Templar commandery? Hitherto all papal messages had passed through Clairets Abbey. The ghostly figure began to grow angry. He hated straying from his habitual hunting ground. He tried to calm himself by imagining what effect killing his first female would have on him. Would her face register the same expression of terror when she saw the metal claw? Would a woman's flesh tear more easily than a man's? Let it be done. Night was falling and the journey back was a long one.

The robed phantom scoured the brambles, shrubs and thickets. All the scheming, lies and murders he had been forced to tolerate and then to accept. For he did not revel in them, that was not his vice. Killing brought him neither pleasure nor displeasure. At best it was a hazard of the job, and at worst an unavoidable part of his mission, and if there was no other way . . .

The years of bitter disappointment, humiliation and needless hardship had placed his life on its present course. The exhilarating feeling of no longer being an insignificant person among others had achieved the rest. For the first time his existence had meaning, was becoming pivotal, and little did it matter in the end what cause he served. For the first time, he was no longer the victim of power but the one wielding it.

Lying flat on the forest floor some twenty yards from the horse's hooves, concealed under a mass of ferns, Esquive watched her pursuer, who had begun tracking her before she was able to deliver the message she was carrying. She had known of the dangers involved when she accepted the mission. Why had they chosen novices as messengers before sending her? The idea of taking a life was so alien to them that they preferred to sacrifice their own. Not she, who was a redoubtable swordswoman thanks to her father. The archangel Hospitaller would also have known how to fight the phantom and his pitch-black stallion, but he was still so far away. What did he remember of their meeting years before? Very little no doubt – at least with regard to her.

Esquive concentrated all her attention on the horse once more as it nervously sidestepped a few paces then came to a standstill. The evil phantom was growing anxious and communicating his alarm to the horse.

In spite of her faith, the strength of mind she had inherited from her father, and her immeasurable love for the archangel of Cyprus, Esquive had been seized with dread when she first caught sight of the enormous black stallion rising out of the evening mist. The animal had hurled itself at her and the spectre had raised his hideous gloved hand.

She had fled, her suppleness and speed giving her a head start. She had dug herself down into the earth and remained there motionless, like a root, in order to catch her breath and recover her presence of mind.

She could not allow herself to die now. She was less important than the information she was carrying. What then? Then God would decide. Death mattered little to her for she would be taking her archangel of flesh and blood with her.

At first the phantom saw only two pale amber pools, two almost yellow pools. Two immense eyes. Then a mane of long dark wavy hair. Finally a tiny heart-shaped mouth and skin as pale as moonlight. The command rang out even as a slender hand drew a short sword from a belted scabbard.

'Dismount. Dismount and fight.'

This unexpected reversal of fortune gave the phantom cause to hesitate. The young girl continued in a startlingly deep voice:

'Do you want my life? Come and take it. It will cost you dearly.'

What was happening? Nothing had gone according to plan.

What came next was so unexpected it caught the phantom off guard. The girl hurled herself at the horse, brandishing her sword, and thrust the sharp blade into the powerful chest of the animal, which whinnied in pain and surprise and threw its rider, rigid with shock.

A fierce joy made Esquive's strange eyes shine even brighter. She smiled, stepped back a few paces, and stood with her legs apart, ready to fight.

The phantom heaved himself up. Fear. The fear he had believed he could make vanish forever pervaded him again. That dreadful fear of death, of suffering, of being nothing again. He removed his glove, which felt ridiculous now, and tentatively drew his dagger. He knew how to fight, of course, but the girl's posture informed him he was dealing with an expert swordswoman.

He cast a desperate glance around him, choked by the self-loathing which up until a few minutes before he had believed himself rid of. He was a miserable coward, a weakling who had become drunk on the power of others, mistaking it for his own.

He hated the girl. She was responsible for resuscitating his past. She would pay for it; she would pay for his self-loathing. One day, he would take pleasure in killing her, in hearing her scream, then whimper, then die. One day. Soon.

Esquive sensed her enemy was about to flee. She hesitated a fraction of a second too long between her anger, her desire to slay the one who had killed so many of their own, and the over-arching importance of her mission. Did the phantom notice?

He bolted towards the big black stallion that had come to a halt a few dozen yards away, not quickly enough though to avoid the broad blade thudding into his right shoulder. The pain made him cry out, but fear and loathing drove him on. He heaved himself into the saddle with his left hand, and horse and rider vanished into the dark night of the forest.

Vatican Palace, Rome, July 1304

THE first days of July had brought with them a sweltering heat even more terrible than the one people had endured in June. The air seemed so rarefied that breathing it in required an effort. No breeze stirred to offer even a moment's reprieve.

Cardinal Benedetti had been overcome by the merciless heat. He had dozed off at his desk, his forehead resting on his left hand, his nose on the beautiful mother-of-pearl fan.

The figure paused and strained his ears. He was carrying a small basket, the arch of which was decorated with a white ribbon. The anteroom was empty, it being lunchtime, and the Archbishop's breathing was calm and regular. The figure glanced at the half-empty goblet of macerated sage and thyme, which it was the Cardinal's custom to drink every afternoon as a remedy against bloating and wind. The taste was unpleasant enough to mask the bitterness of the dose of powdered opium administered in order to induce extreme drowsiness.

Without a sound, without even stirring the air, the figure walked behind the desk inlaid with ivory, mother-of-pearl and turquoise. A gloved hand lifted a tapestry, which depicted a shy diaphanous Virgin surrounded by hovering angels, and concealed a low passageway between two thick walls. At the far end was the Pope's council chamber.

The figure stooped and crossed the ten yards separating him from the conclusion of his mission.

The vast chamber was empty, as predicted. Benoît XI had not yet returned from his midday meal. He was not known for his vices, with the exception of his fondness for food, especially anything that reminded him of the pleasant years he had spent as Bishop of Ostia.

The figure moved forward, crossing the luxurious carpet with its purple and gold motif that covered almost the entire expanse of marble floor. The consular table evoked the Last Supper and was dominated by the heavily ornate papal chair perched on a white dais in the centre. As he set down the basket directly opposite it on the table he grimaced from the pain he still felt in his shoulder. Figs. Splendid, perfectly ripe figs. Nicolas Boccasini had been very partial to them before he became Benoît.

The afternoon meeting began late as a result of Benedetti needing to be roused. His face had a sickly pallor and his head was swimming. As for his garbled speech, it shocked the others coming from the lips of a man renowned for his oratory skills. Nevertheless, the Pope listened attentively to his Cardinal's counsel. Honorius was undoubtedly the only friend who had remained true since his election. He was all the more grateful because the prelate had made no secret of his admiration for Boniface VIII. Benoît was ready to admit that he possessed neither the authority nor the Olympian nature of his pre-decessor, nor did this man whose eyes filled with tears at the evocation of Christ's torment or Mary's flight share the same imperial vision for the Church. And so the Cardinal's unfailing support, at first invaluable to him, he now cherished.

The Pope was uneasy. Guillaume de Nogaret's excommunication would greatly displease the King of France. And yet he had to show his authority. A failure to administer punishment would betray his fear of the ruthless monarch, and might further undermine their political influence. Honorius Benedetti had persuaded him that a direct attack on Philip the Fair could prove suicidal. Nogaret, on the other hand, made a good scapegoat. Benoît listened to each of his counsellors in turn as he ate his figs. His discomfort was such that they seemed unusually bitter and he did not derive his customary pleasure from them.

Louvre Palace, Paris, Guillaume de Nogaret's chambers,
July 1304

THEY left Rue de Bucy shortly after none.

The Knight Hospitaller Francesco de Leone, his head bowed, followed two steps behind Giotto Capella as a mark of subordination.

The construction work on the Île de la Cité palace requested by Saint Louis having not yet commenced, all the state powers were housed under the roof of the forbidding Louvre citadel, located just outside the city walls near the Saint-Honoré gate. They crowded as best they could into what remained the simple keep built by Philip II Augustus to centralise the Ministry of Justice, the Courts and the Exchequer.

They proceeded down Rue Saint-Jacques, which took them as far as the Petit Pont, and from there crossed Île de la Cité until they reached the Grand Pont, still known as the Pont au Change, which opened onto Rue Saint-Denis. Then they turned left, crossing to the Right Bank and backtracking in order to arrive at the Great Louvre Tower. A motley crowd of merchants, fishermen from the Seine, passers-by, beggars, women of easy virtue and street urchins jostled, called out and hurled abuse at one another in the maze of narrow streets filled with the stench of refuse. Metal-beaters[25] and millers blocked the alleyways with their handcarts, arguing over who had arrived first and therefore had right of way.

Giotto complained — more out of habit than because he hoped to engage his silent companion in conversation:

'Look at these encumbrances! It is growing steadily worse! Will they ever get around to widening these bridges? The Louvre is but a few hundred yards from Rue de Bucy as the crow flies, and yet we have walked thrice that distance.'

The Knight was content to retort in a good-natured voice:

'Are there not boatmen who ferry passengers and goods between the Louvre and the Tour de Nesle?'

Capella glanced at him with a hangdog expression before admitting:

'Yes . . . but they take your money.'

'Is avarice to be counted among your vices, then? And there was I thinking that the frugal meals you have been sending up to me were a sign of your consideration for my health.'

Capella was not about to pay for two crossings on top of everything else! The pain of his gout was throbbing in his foot and in his calf up to the knee, but it couldn't be helped, they would have to walk slowly.

The usher's pompous expression betrayed the satisfaction he derived from his lowly position. They waited in Monsieur de Nogaret's anteroom for a good half-hour in stony silence.

Finally they were shown in. Leone found himself face to face with their gravest enemy, for this could not be the same Guillaume de Plaisians whom Giotto had described as a handsome fellow. The man of at least thirty years of age who was seated behind the long cluttered table that served as a desk was small, almost puny-looking. He wore a fine indigo felt bonnet that covered his head and ears, sharpening an already emaciated face, out of which stared two intense eyes rendered almost repulsive by their lack of eyelashes. Despite the vogue of the period for extravagant and ostentatious dress, and the fashion for shorter men's clothes, Nogaret had adhered to the long austere jurist's robe. Over it he wore a sleeveless coat open down the front, whose only embellishment was a fur trim.[26] A fire blazed in the hearth and Leone wondered whether Nogaret might not be doing them the kindness of suffering from some serious ailment.

'Pray, have a seat, Giotto, my good friend,' Guillaume de Nogaret bade him.

Francesco remained standing, as befitted a moneylender's clerk. Finally, the jurist appeared to notice him and, without so much as a glance in his direction, enquired:

'Who is your companion?'

'My nephew, the son of my dearly departed brother.'

'I did not know you had a brother.'

'Who does not, my Lord? Francesco. Francesco Capella. We have every reason to be proud of our nephew . . .'

Nogaret, who found polite conversation tedious and who was not renowned for his drawing-room manners, listened with a forced smile. The thirty thousand pounds he was hoping to borrow from the usurer were worth a small amount of indulgence.

'. . . for three years he was chamberlain to our dearly departed Holy Father, Boniface . . .'

A spark of interest lit up the strange staring eyes.

'. . . and then a scandal involving a woman – a brawl. In brief, a fall from grace.'

'When was this?'

'Not long before the death of our beloved Pope – God rest his soul.'

Nogaret nodded, adding in a bitter voice:

'If indeed His judgement will wash away so many sins.'

Nogaret was a man of faith, a rigorous faith that had made him loathe Boniface, whom he considered unworthy of the greatness of the Church. Unlike his predecessor Pierre Flote, who was intent on ridding the monarchy once and for all of the continual interference of the Pope's authority, Nogaret's aim was to allow the King to provide the Church with a faultless representative of God on earth. Leone knew of his role in the great religious disputes that had shaken France. Nogaret had subsequently abandoned the corridors of power and come out into the light of day. Most notably, the year before he had made a virulent speech denouncing Boniface VIII's 'crimes'. In other words, he was paving the way for the King's future pope, no doubt with Plaisians's assistance.

The names of one or two cardinals who had already been approached, that was what the prior and the Grand-Master needed in order to be able to intervene.

Nogaret's animosity towards Boniface had not diminished with the latter's death. The insult the supreme head of the Church had publicly hurled at him, referring to him explicitly as the 'son of a Cathar', still rankled. On learning of the Pope's death the Counsellor had simply murmured:

'Let him meet his Judge.'

Nogaret had not finished with the man whom he considered at best an appalling disgrace and at worst an emissary of the devil, hellbent on destroying the Church.

For the first time he studied the silent young man whose unassuming manner pleased him.

'Be seated . . . Francesco, is it?'

'It is, my Lord.'

'It was a great honour and a privilege to serve the Pope. And yet you threw it away – and for the sake of a girl, moreover.'

'A young lady – that is, almost.'

'How gallant! Very well, a young lady, then. And what do you recall most about the time you spent in that prestigious service?'

He had hooked the big fish. The prior had been right. Despite his intelligence, Nogaret was a zealot. He was zealous about the State, his king and the law. Zeal drives men but it also blinds them.

'Many things, my Lord,' Leone sighed.

'And yet this abundance hardly gives you reason to rejoice.'

'It is only that His Extreme Holiness was . . . Well. The love of our Lord should impose itself without . . .'

A smile played across Nogaret's thin lips. He had taken the bait. How much did this usurer's nephew really know? Even if it were only sordid malicious gossip he would feel gratified and confirmed in his loathing of Boniface. All the more so as chamberlains poked their noses everywhere, trading secrets of the chamber pot and the garderobe where some left evidence of the affairs of state: the evil-smelling colic of a great man could herald an impending succession. Turning once again to Giotto, he asked:

'And so your nephew will take up the torch of your profession?'

'Oh no, my Lord, regrettably he has no interest in business, and I doubt he has any head for it. Indeed, I am on the lookout among my prestigious connections for someone who would be willing to take him on. He is extremely intelligent, fluent in five languages, not counting Latin, and the unfortunate matter of the lady has chastened him enormously – why, anyone would think him a friar. He is highly trustworthy and knows that in our profession silence is golden.'

'Interesting . . . As a kindly gesture towards you, my friend Giotto, I might be prepared to try him out.'

'What an honour. What a great honour. How thoughtful, how generous . . . I would never have expected . . .'

'It is because I value our agreeable and rewarding association, Giotto.'

Leone feigned boundless gratitude, going down on one knee, his head bowed, his hand on his heart.

'Very well . . . I shall expect you tomorrow at prime* and we shall pray together. I know no better way of meeting than through prayer.'

At last Nogaret could broach the subject that most concerned him. A new loan, of thirty thousand pounds no less! Plaisians had calculated as precisely as he could. This was the amount they needed to fund the countless meetings with the French cardinals, and to pay the various intermediaries – not to mention the 'gifts' the majority of prelates would expect in return for renouncing their own greed for supreme power in favour of a single candidate: that of Philip. As for the King, he had no fixed preference. It mattered little to him who was elected as long as the man did not meddle in France's affairs. The monarch was willing to support and finance anyone who could guarantee this.

Neither Giotto nor Leone was taken in by the Counsellor's justification for the loan: to prepare a fresh crusade in order to reconquer the Holy Land. Philip had far too much on his hands with Flanders and the Languedoc to be able to deploy his troops elsewhere. However, it was only polite to applaud any new project of this sort and Giotto did not breach the rule.

'And what terms will you grant us, my Lord? For, while the sum is not vast, it is by no means insignificant.'

'The interest rate set by Saint Louis.'

Giotto had expected as much.

'And repayment?'

'Two years.'

'Really? Only, it is a long time and I am not sure my lenders will . . .'

'Eighteen months, that is my final offer.'

'Very good, my Lord, very good.'

Moments later they were walking out of the Great Louvre Tower. Giotto rubbed his hands together.

'So are you satisfied, Knight? You have your position.'

'Don't expect any gratitude from me, moneylender. As for my mood, it is no concern of yours. Incidentally, I shall be staying on at your house.'

Capella pursed his lips. He had imagined that he was finally rid of this presence, which he rarely encountered but which he could feel even in the cold air that crept over his skin. He pretended to be unworried and asked:

'And what did you think of this loan? The pretext of the crusade is very clever. It can be adapted to suit any circumstance. Thirty thousand pounds is a substantial sum but hardly enough to send an army of crusaders halfway across the world. Our friend Nogaret has other things in mind.'

'What could it possibly matter to you? You have been paid, have you not?'

'On the contrary, it matters a great deal to me. To read the minds of the powerful is to anticipate their needs and ward off their blows. We poor defenceless moneylenders are always expecting to receive the boot by way of thanks. Such is life.'

'I am choked with tears.'

The snub did not fluster the spiteful rat, who persisted:

'So what did you think?'

'I found it extremely interesting for reasons you perhaps have not yet fully grasped.'

'And what might they be?' demanded Capella.

'You have just betrayed Monsieur de Nogaret. You have set a trap for him, and if he comes to learn of it . . . you would do well to die fast.'

It was so glaringly obvious that it had not even occurred to Giotto. His usual cunning and shrewdness had failed to alert him to the fact that by escaping one danger he was exposing himself to another, even greater one.

*

Ten minutes after they had left, the usher showed a slim figure wrapped in a heavy cloak into Guillaume de Nogaret's office.

'Well?'

'We are nearing our objective, my Lord. Everything is in readiness in keeping with your wishes.'

'Good. Carry on with your work. You will be rewarded for your pains, as agreed. The strictest secrecy is essential.'

'Discretion is my profession and my passion.'

A sudden misgiving made Nogaret ask:

'What do you think of our affairs?'

'What I think depends on how much you pay me, my Lord. Consequently your affairs are of a most noble nature.'

Château de Larnay, Perche, July 1304

SEXT* had just finished when Comte Artus d'Authon dismounted in the interior courtyard of the Château de Larnay. He had instantly thought of Agnès, of her illegitimate childhood spent within those walls.

The ferment caused by his arrival might have amused him under different circumstances. However, he had spent the last few days since his encounter with the Dame de Souarcy in a state of tension, and his resulting moodiness was only made worse by the half-hour wait he had just been subjected to.

A matronly woman hurried towards him in a panic, fanning herself with her apron.

'My Lord, my Lord . . .' she stammered, almost kneeling before him. 'My master is away, you see. Oh dear God!' she howled as if the end of the world had come.

Artus was aware that Eudes de Larnay's business took him to Paris at the end of every month. Indeed, it was what had compelled the Comte to travel the fifteen leagues between Authon and his vassal's chateau.

'Might his good lady wife be ailing?'

The woman understood the reproach and clumsily explained.

'Nay, nay, she enjoys good health, given she has nearly

reached full term, that is, praise be to God. Since she learnt of your arrival she has been preparing to receive you properly. She was asleep and . . . Oh, but I am a chattering old fool . . . Pray follow me, my Lord. My lady will join you at once.'

Artus could picture the charming, featherbrained woman, whose customary silence concealed a lack of intelligence, fretting in her room, cursing her husband's absence and wondering what she should say, not say, avoid or offer in order not to earn Eudes's wrath upon his return.

At last Apolline de Larnay stepped into the room, preceded by a pungent smell of garlic. Her pregnancy had not been in evidence the last time Artus saw her and her appearance disconcerted him. She was not one of those women who radiate health when they are with child. Her usually delightful face was spoiled by a grey pallor and the rings under her eyes had a purplish hue. He offered her his hand so that she would not be obliged to curtsey, and greeted her with an untruth:

'Madame, you look radiant.'

'And you are too kind, Monsieur,' she rejoined, demonstrating that she was not taken in by his flattery. 'My husband is . . .'

'. . . away, so I have been told. It is unfortunate.'

'Do you have some urgent business to discuss?'

'Urgent would be putting it too strongly. Let us say I wished to speak to him about a project I have devised.'

Something about her had changed. The pretty little vacuous creature he had once known seemed filled with sorrow.

'Eudes's . . . My husband's affairs take up so much of his time that I have seen him only once in a month.'

'Mining is a complicated business.'

She lifted her gaze towards him and he sensed she was fighting back her tears. Yet she replied:

'Indeed, it is the reason he gives.' Then pulling herself together, she added, 'I am failing in all my duties. You must have found the heat oppressive on your journey. A bowl of cider will quench your thirst.'

'With pleasure.'

She gave the command while he took a seat on one of the benches at the main table. She sat facing him, her body turned sideways to accommodate her rounded belly. An awkward silence followed, which he was the first to break:

'Did you know that I met your sister-in-law, the Dame de Souarcy, recently?'

At the mention of her name the little grey woman's face lit up.

'Agnès . . . and how is she?'

'She seemed in fine health.'

'And Mathilde? It must be five years since I saw her last.'

'She has turned into a charming and very pretty young lady.'

'Just like her mother. Madame Agnès was always a great beauty and I regret that all those years ago she refused my husband's offer to come and live here at the chateau with her daughter. Life at Souarcy is so precarious and difficult for a widow with no experience of farming. We would have been sisters and I would have had company – and of the best kind, for she is so full of life, so lovely.'

'It would have been a perfect solution for all. So why did she refuse?'

Apolline de Larnay's eyes misted over. She was such a bad liar that he sensed all the sadness she was trying to conceal.

'I do not know why . . . Perhaps out of an attachment to her estate.'

His suspicion was confirmed: Eudes de Larnay's reasons for offering protection to his half-sister bordered on the profane. Up until then, the feudal Baron's self-conceit and cowardice, his boorishness towards women had simply angered Artus, but now his exasperation was replaced with the revulsion that such perversions inspired in him.[27]

Sweet Apolline's gentle frivolity had been reduced to ashes – grey like herself. This, too, was Eudes's doing. The realisation filled the Comte with an indefinable sorrow, and he felt angry at himself for having manoeuvred this young woman he had once considered rather foolish into revealing her half-secrets.

As he took his leave of her he experienced for the first time a feeling of tenderness towards her and counselled:

'Take good care of yourself, Madame. The child you bear is precious.'

She murmured a response:

'Do you think so, Monsieur?'

The journey back to Authon did nothing to dispel his unease. It was growing dark when he joined his Chief Bailiff, Monge de Brineux, who was waiting for him in the library.

The modest-sized room with the rotunda was one of Artus's favourite places. It contained a fine collection of books he had brought back from his restless wanderings across the world. He felt on his own ground there, surrounded by memories the details of which had paled over time. All the people he had encountered, all the names he had uttered, all the places he had passed through, and in the end so few attachments.

Monge was drinking fruit wine and gorging himself on quince and honey conserve. When Artus entered he rose to his feet, declaring:

'Oh, Monsieur, you have saved me from my own gluttony.'

'Must you eat those confections by the handful?'

'Their sweetness calms me.'

'Tell me the bad news, then.'

The Comte's perceptiveness hardly surprised Monge de Brineux, but the grave expression he wore troubled him.

'Is something worrying you, my Lord?'

'The question would be more apt in the plural. I am completely in the dark. Come along, Brineux, out with it.'

'One of my sergeants rode over here in a great hurry at midday. Another disfigured corpse has been found close to the edge of Clairets Forest. This one appears to have been killed recently.'

'Another friar?'

'It would seem.'

'Near the forest's edge, you say?'

'Yes, my Lord. The killer has been very careless.'

'Or very cunning,' suggested Artus. 'In this way he could be sure his victim would be found relatively quickly. Was there a letter *A* near the body?'

'Yes, right beside the corpse's leg, scratched in the ground.'

'What else?'

'For the moment that is all I know. I have given the order to make a thorough search of the surrounding area,' the Bailiff explained.

Monge de Brineux hesitated to pick up their earlier conversation. His admiration and liking for the Comte did not make of him a close friend, or even a companion. In fact there were few who could boast such a degree of intimacy with Artus. His lord was remote in a way that, while not hostile, discouraged familiarity. However, Monge knew the man to be just and good. He continued:

'Did your meeting with the Dame de Souarcy bear out my description of her?'

'Indeed. I do not see her as a bloodthirsty criminal. She is learned, excellent company and undoubtedly a pious woman.'

'And do you not find the young widow very beautiful?'

No sooner had Monge uttered these words than he cursed his indiscretion. The Comte would immediately see what he was hinting at. What followed proved him right. Artus glanced up at him and Monge detected a flicker of irony in those dark eyes.

'I do indeed. You wouldn't be playing at matchmaking, would you, Brineux?'

The Bailiff remained silent but beneath his stubble his face turned bright red.

'Come, Brineux, don't pull such a face! I am touched by your concern for me. Marriage agrees with you so well, my friend, that you hear the sound of wedding bells everywhere. Have no fear. Sooner or later I shall produce an heir, like my father before me.'

It was largely Julienne who was to blame for Monge's recent propensity to wish marriage on anyone whose happiness was dear to his heart. The Comte had been a widower for many years and had no direct heir, his wife had argued one evening. How sad it was to see a man of his distinction grow old alone, without the love of a woman, she had insisted. Monge had tempered his wife's redoubtable zeal for matchmaking with the observation: 'It all depends on the lady.'

'I did not mean . . .' Brineux stuttered rather ashamedly.

'Do you really think that Madame Agnès is one of those fine ladies one mounts in the antechamber? It is true that we have both enjoyed the favours of a few of those ourselves.'

'I think I had better take my leave of you now, my Lord, before I dig myself deeper and make even more of a fool of myself.'

'I am teasing you, my friend. On the contrary, I bid you stay. I need you to help me gain a clearer understanding. Nothing seems to make any sense in this affair.'

Monge sat down opposite Artus. The Bailiff could tell his lord was lost in thought from the way his eyes stared into space and from his tensed jaw and rigid posture. He waited. He was accustomed to these moments when Artus became immersed in deep reflection.

A few minutes elapsed in complete silence before the Comte emerged from the furthest reaches of his mind and said:

'It makes no sense whichever way you look at it.'

'What do you mean?'

'We agree on one point, Brineux, which is that Agnès de Souarcy played no part in these killings.'

'As she so ably made me see, I cannot imagine her running through the undergrowth armed with a claw, intent on slashing the faces of a few unfortunate friars – except perhaps in a fit of homicidal madness or temporary possession. Besides, these men – especially the last one – are twice the lady's weight.'

'If we include this last killing, four of the victims, it would seem, traced the letter *A* before they died, and a linen handkerchief belonging to the lady was found near one of them. Somebody is trying to implicate her, then.'

'I had reached the same conclusion.'

'Before posing the fundamental questions, namely who and why, let us consider the killer's intelligence.'

'Whoever it is must be a fool,' Brineux retorted.

'It seems likely, for there are far more convincing ways of incriminating Agnès de Souarcy – unless, and this is what I am beginning to fear, we have understood nothing of these murders and have been mistaken right from the very start of your investigation.'

'I do not follow.'

'I am a little lost myself, Brineux. What if it has never been the villain's intention to point us in the direction of the Manoir de Souarcy? What if the letter *A* means something entirely different?'

'And the linen handkerchief, have you forgotten about that?'

'Yes, you are right. There is still the question of the linen handkerchief,' admitted the Comte.

After a brief silence, Artus d'Authon continued:

'I wish to ask you a rather delicate question – or rather an extremely indelicate one.'

'I am at your service, Monsieur.'

'I would prefer you to answer me as a friend.'

'I should be honoured.'

'Are you aware of any stories, any malicious gossip concerning Eudes de Larnay's relationship with his half-sister?'

Artus understood from the way his Bailiff pursed his lips that some rumour had indeed reached his ears.

'Larnay is not a very pleasant man.'

'It comes as no surprise,' admitted the Comte.

'I mean to a degree that offends the ear. His ill treatment of his wife is infamous. The poor woman is more cuckolded than an Eastern queen. They tell me he thinks nothing of entertaining strumpets in the very chambers of the chateau. And that some of these women of easy virtue have been discovered brutally beaten after their encounters with him. None has been willing to recount their story to my men for fear of reprisals.'

'And what about his sister?'

'It would appear that Eudes de Larnay has a very loose notion of kinship and blood relationship. He showers the lady with lavish gifts . . .'

'Which she accepts?'

'She would be foolish to refuse. I heard he even gave her sweet salt.'

'Goodness me! The man treats her like a princess!' remarked the Comte.

'Or an expensive prostitute.'

'Do you think that they . . . I mean that she . . .'

'I admit having entertained the idea up until I met her – after all Larnay may be rotten inside, but he is still an attractive man.

No. I do not believe that she would rub herself against that miserable brute. Other facts concur.'

'And what are they?'

Artus d'Authon realised at that very moment that it was not only necessary but vital for him to be certain of Agnès's indifference towards her brother, and if possible her detestation of him.

'Agnès de Souarcy has always refused her half-brother's "hospitality", despite the true affection and compassion she feels for her sister-in-law, Madame Apolline. She goes out of her way to avoid meeting him. In addition, one of Eudes's mother's – the late Baroness de Larnay's – ladies-in-waiting confided that Agnès instantly accepted the first offer of marriage as a way of escaping from her brother's predatory instincts. Fate would have it that Hugues died prematurely, killed by an injured stag, delivering her once more into Eudes's clutches.'

'A fine catch, that Hugues de Souarcy, to be sure!'

'It was no doubt preferable in the lady's eyes to wed him than be bedded by her wicked brother.'

'How do you know all this?'

'I am your Bailiff, my Lord. It is my task, my duty and my privilege to keep my "big ears" – as Julienne calls them – open in order to serve you.'

'And I am grateful to you for it.'

Manoir de Souarcy-en-Perche, July 1304

CLÉMENT had spent the last few days trying to decipher the coded message he had copied out. He had gone through every possible combination, varying the pattern, beginning with the first word of each psalm, then realigning his transcription by moving along a few words or lines. But to no avail. He had a nagging suspicion: what if he was wrong and Mabile had used a different book? But if so, which one? The few there were at Souarcy were mostly in Latin, and Clément was sure Mabile had no notion of that language reserved for erudite people. Given that piety was hardly the servant's main virtue, she could have chosen something more suited to her, a work in French that would be more easily accessible. Where was she hiding it? Agnès was keeping the scoundrel occupied as they had planned earlier that morning.

When Clément walked into the kitchen, Adeline was sweeping the ashes out of the big hearth.

'I'm looking for Mabile,' he lied.

'She's with our lady.'

'Well, in that case I'll keep you company while I wait for her. Chatting lightens chores.'

'That's very true.'

'You work hard and our lady is pleased with you.'

Adeline looked up, blushing.

'She's a good person.'

'Yes, she is. Unlike . . . Well, sometimes I have the feeling Mabile isn't very nice to you.'

The girl's usually flaccid lips puckered.

'She's a nasty piece of work.'

'To be sure.'

Adeline became emboldened, adding:

'She's like a boil on the backside, she is! Only I tell you one thing and that is you can prick a boil and it'll stop hurting. She thinks she's so high and mighty, with all her simpering . . . Just because she's being . . .'

Adeline froze suddenly and her eyes darted anxiously towards Clément. She had spoken out of turn and felt afraid suddenly of Mabile's possible retribution.

'Just because she's being tupped by her former master it doesn't give her the right to lord it over the rest of us,' Clément concluded to make the girl feel at ease. 'This will be our secret.'

Adeline's broad face lit up with a smile of relief and she nodded.

'What's more, she puts on airs and graces just because she can read a little,' Clément continued.

'Yes. Well, I don't need to read to know how to prepare a dish. Whereas she . . . She's always got her nose stuck in that meat recipe book of hers just to show off. She is a good cook, mind you, it's just that . . .'

'So she uses a meat recipe book, does she!' exclaimed

Clément. 'And there I was thinking she knew it all herself . . .'

'No, she cheats!' affirmed Adeline. 'But not me. It's all in here, in my head, not in some book!'

'Well! I'd be interested to know if that's where she got the recipe for the sauce she made to go with the rack of wild boar, which so impressed the Comte d'Authon. For if she copied it from someone then the compliments shouldn't go to her.'

'That's the honest truth,' agreed Adeline, pleased with herself. 'Only she never lets that recipe book out of her sight in case anyone discovers her deception. She hides it in her room!'

'By Jove she doesn't!'

'She does,' Adeline assured him, puffed up by a sudden sense of her own importance, and with a glint in her eye she added: 'But I know where she keeps it.'

'I *thought* you were a crafty one!'

'I am, too. It's under her mattress.'

Clément stayed chatting with the girl for a while longer and then stood up to leave.

The door had scarcely closed behind him before he raced upstairs to the servants' quarters. He only had a few minutes left before Agnès would be forced to release Mabile, who was surely astonished by the sudden interest her mistress was showing in her.

He immediately found the recipe book hidden where Adeline had told him. There was some writing on the first page: 'Copied from Monsieur Debray, chef to his most gracious and powerful majesty Sire Louis VIII, the Lion King.'

The boy paused. Should he replace the book and wait until Mabile was absent again in order to compare it with the text of the message, or should he take it? Time was running out and he chose the second solution. If Mabile noticed it was gone before he had a chance to return it, she would no doubt accuse Adeline. Agnès would then need to protect the poor girl from the servant's wrath.

He climbed silently back up to his eaves and set to work at once. He must be quick. The conflict was steadily becoming clearer. He must return to the secret library at Clairets Abbey to try to throw light on another mystery: the notebook of the Knight Eustache de Rioux.

Vatican Palace, Rome, July 1304

CARDINAL Honorius Benedetti was deathly pale. Although he found the heat so insufferable, he was chilled to the bone.

Nicolas Boccasini, Benoît XI, lay gasping as he clutched the prelate's fingers with his clammy hand.

The front of his white robe was disappearing under the blood-streaked vomit. All night long he had been racked by griping pains, leaving him exhausted by the early morning. Arnaud de Villeneuve* – one of the century's most eminent doctors, whose ideas were a little too reformist for the Inquisition's liking – had not left his bedside. His diagnosis had been immediate: the Pope was dying from poisoning and no antidote other than prayer could save him. Thus, without holding out much hope they had tried fumigating with incense, praying, and Monsieur de Villeneuve had been against bleeding, whose ineffectiveness in cases of poisoning was well known since the time of Monsieur Galen.

Benoît made a feeble but impatient gesture signalling that he wished to be left alone with his Cardinal. Before he left the dying Pope's chambers, Villeneuve turned to the prelate and murmured in a voice trembling with emotion:

'Your Eminence will have understood the nature of yesterday's mysterious drowsiness.'

Honorius looked at him, puzzled. The practitioner continued:

'You were drugged and, judging from your disorientation and encumbered speech in the afternoon, I would wager it was with opium powder. Somebody needed you out of the way in order to reach His Holiness.'

Honorius closed his eyes and crossed himself.

'There was nothing you could have done, Your Eminence. These accursed poisoners always achieve their ends. I regret it from the very depths of my soul.'

Arnaud de Villeneuve then left the two men to their final exchange.

Benoît had heard nothing of this monologue. Death was in his chamber and deserved his full attention in the company of the only friend he had found in this palace that was too vast, too onerous.

The room was filled with a strange sickly-sweet odour – the odour of the dying man's breath. His end was approaching and with it a miraculous release.

'My brother . . .'

The voice was so frail that Honorius was obliged to bend over the Holy Father, fighting off the tears he had been holding back for hours.

'Your Holiness . . .'

Benoît shook his head in frustration.

'No . . . brother . . .'

'My brother?'

A smile played across the dying man's cracked lips:

'Yes, your brother. That is all I wished to be . . . Do not suffer. It was inevitable and I have no fear. Bless me, my brother, my friend. The figs . . . What day is it today?'

'The seventh of July.'

Soon after the extreme unction performed by his friend and confidant, the Pope sank into a coma punctuated by delirium.

'. . . the almond trees at Ostia, how wonderful they were . . . Every year a little girl would offer me a basketful . . . I was so fond of them . . . She must be a mother now . . . I join You, my Lord . . . It was a mistake . . . I tried to do my best, to foresee as best I could . . . The Light, behold the Light, It bathes me . . . Unto God, gentle brother.'

Nicolas Boccasini's hand gripped Honorius's fingers then suddenly relaxed, leaving the Cardinal cold and alone in the world.

There was a last sigh.

Eternal sorrow, infinite tears. Choking with sobs, Honorius Benedetti fell forward until his brow was resting on the large red stain soiling the deceased Pope's chest.

He trembled for a long moment against the torso of his dead brother before managing to stand up to go and notify the people crammed into the anteroom where a deathly hush reigned.

Manoir de Souarcy-en-Perche, July 1304

Dawn was breaking, pushing back the night. Clément had not slept for two days. His head was spinning with exhaustion, or was it the euphoria of success?

A thought suddenly occurred to him that tempered his complacency. The poisonous snake! In those few lines he had transcribed from the message Vigil was carrying when he was pierced by an arrow was all the hatred and jealousy in the world. The venom was concealed in one of Mabile's famously delicious recipes for broad bean purée.

Place the beans on the heat and bring them to the boil, then drain the water from the pot and add fresh water to cover the beans, salt according to taste . . .

Eudes and Mabile had made no effort of imagination, beginning their code with the first letter of the first line.

The deciphered text made Clément shudder with horror. Following the details of his birth, his lack of a surname, godmother and godfather, were the wicked words:

Chaplain Bernard bewitched by Agnès. Sharing a bed?

The evil scoundrel. She was lying shamelessly in order to please her master. Another more likely reason suddenly occurred to Clément. She was lying in order to hurt him, and also to take revenge. Eudes's deep-rooted hatred of his half-sister was so confused, so mixed up with his unrequited love and unsatisfied desire. He wanted Agnès to grovel even as he continued to believe that, were it not for their blood ties, she would have loved him more than anyone. Mabile was aware of this. Her hatred was keen and merciless, like the blade of a knife.

Clément waited another hour before stealing down to his mistress's chamber to inform her of his discovery.

Seated on her bed, the lady studied him. A flush of anger had gradually replaced the pallor on her face when she learnt the contents of the message.

'I'll unmask her and throw her out on her ear. I'll give her a good thrashing!'

'I understand your anger, Madame, but it would be a mistake.'

'She accuses me of . . .'

'Of sharing your chaplain's bed, indeed.'

'It is a crime, not a mere error of judgement.'

'I am well aware of that.'

'Do you realise what would become of me if anyone were to give credence to this monstrous calumny?'

'You would lose your dower.'

'And more than that! Brother Bernard is not a man, he is a priest. I would be dragged before the courts, accused of demonically driving a man of God to commit the sin of sensual pleasure. In short, of being a succubus. And you know what fate is reserved for them.'

'The stake.'

'After everything else.'

She fell silent for a few moments before continuing:

'Eudes is expecting this message. How many more has he received from the loyal Vigil since he offered him to me? No matter. The pigeon is dead and we have no way of replacing Mabile's original note. Worse still, I cannot even rid myself of her without rousing my half-brother's suspicions. What am I to do, Clément?'

'Kill her,' he proposed, with great solemnity.

Agnès looked at him aghast:

'What are you saying?'

'I can kill her. It is simple; there are so many plants I could use. I would not be guilty of committing a capital sin since she is not a human being but a snake.'

'Have you lost your senses? I forbid it. Killing is only justified when one's life is threatened.'

'She is a threat to us. She threatens your life, and therefore mine.'

'No. You will not taint your soul. Do you hear me? It is an order. If anyone is to send that witch to her damnation it should be me.'

Clément lowered his head and murmured:

'I refuse. I refuse to let you be damned. I will obey you, Madame, as I always obey, just to please you.'

Damnation? She had lived with the possibility for so long that she had ended up no longer fearing it.

'Clément. There must be some other defence against his evil. I need precise information about the state of Monsieur de

Larnay's mines. I will give the order to saddle a horse for you. Our draught animals do not go very fast, but the journey will be less tiring for you and its imposing physique will deter brigands.'

They were running short of time.

Returning to her room that evening, Mabile discovered sooner than expected that her recipe book was missing. She charged to the end of the passageway leading to the servants' quarters, and burst into Adeline's chamber like a fury. The evil woman set upon Adeline's sleeping form, tearing at her hair and punching her.

The portly girl tried to scream, but a brutal hand clamped itself over her mouth and she felt the tip of a knife pricking her neck and a voice growled in her ear:

'Where is it, pig? Where's my recipe book? Give it to me now! If you cry out I'll skin you alive. Do you hear me?'

'I haven't got it, I haven't got it, I swear on the Gospel! I didn't take it,' squealed Adeline.

'Who did then? Quick, out with it, you ugly cow, my patience is wearing thin.'

'It must've been Clément. He was asking me where you kept it – the recipe book, I mean! So I told him, I did.'

'A pox on that sneak of a boy!'

Mabile's thoughts were racing. She had been careless. They had certainly found the message meant for Eudes de Larnay – contrary to what she had believed so as to put her mind at rest. No doubt knowing that she would try to recover the dead pigeon, that loathsome dwarf had placed it in the Dame de Souarcy's chamber for her to find. The missing recipe book showed he had discovered the nature of the code and probably already deciphered it.

She must leave the manor. Agnès had sufficient reason to demand her punishment.

Why did that miserable bastard always triumph? And why did Clément love her so much that he was prepared to risk Mabile's vengeance? And Gilbert? And the others? Why?

A sudden calm came over Mabile. Up until then she thought she had hated the Dame de Souarcy, but she hadn't. She had been content merely to hurt her. True hatred, the hatred that destroys everything, was only just beginning. It drove her and nothing could withstand it. It eclipsed all fear, all remorse.

Adeline was still sobbing as the tip of the knife pulled away from her neck.

'Listen to me carefully, you little fool! I'm going back to my room. If I so much as hear you move before dawn or raise the alarm, you're dead. Do you understand? Wet the bed if you have to, but I don't want to hear a sound!'

The girl nodded her head frantically.

Mabile left the tiny chamber. She only had a few hours' head start to put a distance between her and Agnès de Souarcy's men.

Agnès was not surprised to learn the news of Mabile's disappearance. Even less so was Clément, to whom Adeline had confessed, her face puffy from crying.

'May she be torn apart by bears,' Clément began, as they

stood in the hay barn where the corpse that the Bailiff's men had brought back had lain.

'They, too, are wary of snakes.'

'Are you thinking of sending some men after her, Madame?'

'She has several hours' head start and they won't catch up with her on our draught horses. And even if they did find her what would I do with her? Remember, she is my half-brother's property. I would be obliged to hand her over in order for him to mete out justice.'

'Indeed, we would do better to let her roam in the forest. Adeline said she must have left in a great hurry. She took very little food with her and even less water and clothing. Who knows . . . ?'

'Do not hope for miracles, Clément.'

'Then the war is at our gates.'

Agnès ran her fingers through the child's hair, and murmured in a voice so weary it startled him:

'You have summed up our situation admirably. Leave me now, I need to think.'

He appeared to hesitate, but did as she had asked.

Agnès climbed the stairs to her quarters, her limbs weighed down by an immeasurable fatigue. No sooner had she closed the door than the façade of self-control she had kept up for Clément's sake fell away. If Mabile managed to spread her poisonous lies, Eudes would believe them or pretend to give them credence. If her half-brother then concluded that the irregularities in the chapel register regarding Clément's birth and Sybille's death were designed to conceal Sybille's heresy, Agnès was lost. Her supposed crimes would be brought before the Inquisition. Choked with sobs, she slumped to her knees on the stone floor.

What would she do – what could she do? Her mind was flooded with questions, each more insoluble than the last.

What would become of Clément? He would be handed over to the Baron de Larnay – unless she managed to convince him to flee. He would never leave without her – she would force him. Above all, he must not suspect the danger Agnès faced, or he would cling to her in the hope of saving her, forgetting about his youth, the circumstances of his birth and what he knew he must conceal.

And what of Mathilde? Mathilde must be protected – but where could she send her? The Abbess of Clairets might take her in for a while. But if Agnès were accused of having incited a priest to commit concubinage, she would be stripped of her dower and her parental rights . . .

A garbled prayer came from her lips:

'I beg you, Lord! Do not punish them for my sins. Do what You will with me, only spare them for they are innocent.'

How long did she cry like that? She had no idea. She fought against the exhaustion that made her eyelids heavy.

Fear will not save you from being bitten, my dear, on the contrary.

Agnès's fury roused her and she castigated herself.

Stop this at once!

Stand up! Who do you think you are, grovelling like this!

If you falter they will pounce on you and rip you to shreds like the hounds their quarry.

If you falter they will take Clément and Mathilde, your name and your estate. Think of what they will do to Clément.

If you falter, you will have deserved your fate and you will be responsible for what befalls the child.

Growl more fiercely, raise your ears and tail, and bare your teeth to ward off the dangers that threaten you.

Fight.

Taverne de la Jument-Rouge, Alençon, Perche, July 1304

NICOLAS Florin, the Inquisitor, had swapped his robe for breeches, a chemise, a fustian doublet[28] and a rather old-fashioned long dark-grey tunic that would help him to go unnoticed. A taupe-coloured cowl, the pointed end of which was wrapped round his neck, concealed the tonsure that would have drawn attention to him the moment he entered the tavern on Rue du Croc. There were few customers seated at the tables that early afternoon.

He identified the man who had requested the meeting by his affluent appearance, and walked over to his table. The man greeted him without a smile and invited him to sit down, beginning as soon as the innkeeper had served them another jug of wine.

'As my messenger told you yesterday, this is a delicate matter and requires the utmost discretion.'

'I understand,' Nicolas nodded, sipping his wine.

Something struck his knee under the table. He grasped hold of it. A nice full purse, as agreed.

'There is a hundred pounds, and a hundred more will follow when the trial is over,' affirmed Eudes de Larnay in a murmur.

'I am interested to know how you came to me.'

'There are only three appointed Inquisitors in the Alençon region.'

'This does not explain how you ruled out the other two candidates.'

'It hardly matters,' retorted Eudes, uneasily. 'What matters is that the information I was given turns out to be correct. However, if you are not interested in the . . . affair we shall let it rest,' he concluded weakly.

Nicolas was not fooled. The other man needed him or he would never have risked arranging such a meeting. And he was not about to let go of two hundred pounds – a small fortune. He agreed wholeheartedly:

'Indeed, you are right. Let us return to business.'

Eudes took what he hoped was a discreet gulp of air, before commencing the little speech he had rehearsed a dozen times.

'My half-sister Madame Agnès de Souarcy is a wanton woman of loose morals. As for her devotion to the Holy Mother Church . . . the least I can say is that it lacks conviction . . .'

Nicolas did not believe a word of Larnay's preamble. He had become very gifted at detecting liars and, aided by his own extraordinary talent for deception, was clever at discovering other people's motives. What a fool the Baron was! Did he really believe Nicolas needed a good reason for dragging some-body before an inquisitorial court? Money more than sufficed. As for evidence and witnesses, he was perfectly capable of pro-viding or procuring these himself. Yes, the wine was good and Baron de Larnay was the first real client on a list he trusted would be long and lucrative. There was no shortage of impatient heirs, vengeful or jealous vassals, or even ambitious or bankrupt merchants. It was worth spending a little of his time listening to this man spout his nonsense.

'She indulges in carnal relations with a man of God, whom she has no doubt led astray through witchcraft. The man in question is her young chaplain – a certain Brother Bernard. The poor fool is so in her thrall that he has betrayed his faith. Moreover, for some years she has carried on unspeakable dealings with a simpleton who is as faithful to her as a dog.'

Well, well. Here was somebody who might help him. His patience had been rewarded.

'Really? And what is the nature of these dealings?'

'Potions, poisons and philtres in exchange for her favours.'

'Do you have any evidence or witnesses to support this charge?'

'The testimony of a very devout person who lived in Agnès de Souarcy's household, and I'll wager we can find others.'

'I do not doubt it. Demonology is becoming more and more bound up with the pursuit of heretics. It is understandable – for what is the worship of demons if not the supreme form of heresy, an unforgivable offence against God?'

Eudes, who was uninterested in these finer points, continued:

'A number of friars have met their deaths under strange and terrible circumstances near to her estate.'

'Indeed! But is murder not a matter for the high justice of Seigneur d'Authon and his Bailiff?'

'They have made precious little progress since the bodies were discovered.'

'Are you suggesting that this lady might have cast a spell on Comte Artus and Monsieur de Brineux?'

'The possibility cannot be ruled out – though it would be difficult to bring the matter to light given the rank and reputation of the two men.'

'Indeed.'

Since his arrival at Alençon, Nicolas, who was a judicious manipulator, had spent part of his time familiarising himself with the powerful people of the region. It was out of the question for him to make an enemy of the Comte d'Authon, a friend to the King, and this reticence applied equally to Monge de Brineux. He continued his enquiry:

'Madame de Souarcy, then, enjoys the backing of influential men even if she obtains it by demonic means?' asked Nicolas Florin in a hushed voice.

Eudes realised he had made a tactical error. But his desire to drag Agnès through the mud blinded him. He tried to reassure the Inquisitor, correcting himself over-emphatically:

'She is only another of my father's bastard offspring. Why did he have to recognise her so late in life?'

His violent outburst caused some heads in the tavern to turn. He lowered his voice:

'She has almost no property of her own, and I doubt whether Comte Artus and Monsieur de Brineux would defend her if she were found guilty of witchcraft. They are pious men of honour.'

Eudes paused suddenly. He had for some moments had a niggling suspicion, but his thinking was clouded by resentment and emotion.

'Pray continue,' urged Nicolas.

The Inquisitor's soft voice made Eudes uneasy. However, he kept going:

'The final and, no doubt, most serious charge, my Lord Inquisitor, is that Agnès de Souarcy once offered her protection to a heretic and with such zeal that one wonders whether she herself did not espouse the same theories. Moreover, she brought up the woman's posthumous son whose devotion to her is such that he would lay down his life.'

A greedy smile formed on the Inquisitor's exquisite lips.

'The facts, for pity's sake . . . you are keeping me in suspense.' The sentence terminated in a sigh.

'In the chapel register there is no surname entered for the child, Clément, or his mother, Sybille, for whom no funeral mass was held. Nor is there any mention of the name and status of the child's godparents. Notwithstanding the cross planted on her tomb, Sybille was buried just outside the consecrated ground reserved for the servants of the manor.'

'That is extremely interesting,' Nicolas observed. Heresy remained the ideal grounds for accusation. The charges of witchcraft or demonic possession, which were more difficult to substantiate, suddenly seemed incidental.

Nicolas continued:

'In accordance with your wishes the lady will be tried for heresy and complicity in heresy. Do you wish her confession to be . . . drawn out?'

At first, Eudes did not understand the precise meaning of the words. And then it struck him with full force and the blood fled from his face:

'Let us be clear . . . it is out of the question for . . . for her . . .'

His voice had become so choked that Nicolas was obliged to lean over. '. . . Flogging will be sufficient. I want her to be afraid, to believe she is lost. I want her whipped until her pretty back and belly turn black and blue. I want her estate and her dower to be confiscated according to the law and to revert to her daughter, who will become my ward. I do not want her to die. I do not want her maimed or disfigured. The two hundred pounds are contingent upon this.'

The pronouncement dampened Nicolas's enthusiasm. The affair was already losing its appeal for him. He comforted himself with the thought that he would soon have plenty of other toys to play with. It was better to take the money – the cornerstone of his fortune.

'Everything will be done according to your wishes, Monsieur.'

'Let us part company now. It is better for us not to be seen together.'

He wanted to be alone, away from the seductive presence he found so disquieting.

Nicolas stood up and took his leave with a radiant smile.

The nagging doubt the Baron had begun to feel earlier was growing stronger. Something was not right – something was very wrong. He placed his hands on his temples then swigged down the rest of his wine.

How had it come to this? True, he wanted Agnès to grovel and beg. He wanted to terrify her and make her swallow the contempt she felt for him. He wanted her dower. But at such a cost?

Was it he or Mabile who had first thought of delivering her

into the hands of the Inquisition? He could no longer be sure.

Mabile had told him of her encounter with a friar who had refused to let her see his face and whose few words had been disguised by his thick woollen cowl. Was it this monk she had barely glimpsed who had suggested the name Nicolas Florin and the plot that was beginning to make Eudes increasingly uneasy?

Manoir de Souarcy-en-Perche, July 1304

M ATHILDE hurled her dress to the floor at the foot of the
bed.

'What's all this now, young miss?' bleated Adeline, rushing
to pick up the discarded garment.

'Out, you fool! Out of my room at once! That oafish girl will
be the death of me!'

Adeline did not wait to be asked twice, fleeing the chamber
of her young mistress whose tantrums she knew from
experience to be fearful. Mathilde had already slapped her on
several occasions, and without the slightest compunction had
one day thrown a hairbrush in her face.

Mathilde was seething. She felt she could burst into tears at
any moment. Rags were what she was forced to wear. What
good was it everybody thinking her pretty if she was made ugly
by shapeless tatters? She couldn't even bring herself to wear the
beautiful hair comb her dear Uncle Eudes had given her, it
would have clashed so horribly with the few unfashionable
shoddy garments she possessed. Her sweet uncle . . . at least he
treated her like a young lady.

All that filth, the insufferable smells, the dirty uncouth farm
hands she was forced to mix with . . . Life at the manor was an
ordeal. Only that beggar, the conceited Clément, could endure

it. What a half-breed he was. And he had the impudence to stick his nose in the air when she gave him orders, as if he only received them from the Dame de Souarcy, her mother.

Madame – her mother. How did Agnès de Souarcy put up with this life? What a disgrace to have to watch her go and collect honey dressed as a man, worse still, as a serf. How degrading to be reduced to counting new-born piglets like a common peasant. True ladies did not deign to perform such tasks. Her mother's hands would soon be as rough as those of a farm hand!

Why had her mother not accepted Baron de Larnay's generous offer of going to live at his chateau? The two of them would have enjoyed a life befitting their position. Her Uncle Eudes gave myriad parties where beautiful ladies and gallant knights mingled. He even hired troubadours to delight his guests during meals made up of delicacies and exotic dishes. There was dancing and merriment to the music of *chifonies*,[29] *chevrettes*[30] and *citoles*,[31] and the subject of love was discussed openly, though chivalrously.

No, Agnès de Souarcy had flatly refused, thus depriving her daughter of the happiness that was her birthright.

The young girl was filled with bitterness. Thanks to her mother, she would never wear magnificent furs and sumptuous robes. Thanks to her obstinacy, that life of sophistication would forever remain a mystery. Thanks again to her stupid resolve, her daughter Mathilde would no doubt also be deprived of the kind of marriage to which she aspired.

Her eyes became moist with tears and she trembled at the thought of the future that awaited her in that miserable pigsty,

Souarcy. A peasant's life spent rummaging in the soil with her bare hands for food, and dressing like a beggar to go and collect honey! What misery! She did not deserve such a fate. She hurled herself onto the bed in despair. The life she had been forced to put up with for years was a dishonour. Just because the mother was prepared to wither and die because of some inexplicable pride, it did not mean the daughter had to share the same fate.

Her sorrow gave way to rage.

Mathilde was born within the sanctity of marriage, and of noble blood – the Larnays' on her grandfather Robert's side and the Souarcys' on her father's.

She did not intend to fade away within Souarcy's damp, grey walls. She refused to count pigeons' eggs as if her life depended upon it. She would not stoop to bartering cords of wood for a few yards of linen. Never. Not like her mother.

As for Clément, Mathilde couldn't care less what became of him. He could die with his good lady if he wished. She had had enough of his superiority all these years!

CLÉMENT was overwhelmed by an almost painful anguish. Each passing hour weighed on him like a curse.

Agnès's silence had not fooled him. He knew that if Eudes chose to believe in an unpardonable liaison between the Dame de Souarcy and her chaplain and if he guessed the truth about Sybille, he could request the intervention of one of the Inquisitors at Alençon. The boy shuddered.

Clément recalled the scene as if it were yesterday. He was five years old. Gisèle, the nursemaid who looked after him, had taken him one evening to his lady's chamber before putting him to bed. For a long moment, the two women, whom he knew were very close, looked questioningly at one another. Agnès had murmured:

'Do you not think it is premature?'

And Gisèle had retorted:

'We cannot delay any longer. It is too dangerous. All the more so since she suspects the truth, even though she doesn't understand. I watch her closely and I know.'

At the time Clément had wondered who the two women were talking about.

'But she is still so young . . . I'm afraid that . . .'

The nursemaid cut across her in a firm voice:

'There is no place for such fears now. Think what would happen if anyone discovered our secret.'

Agnès de Souarcy had begun with a sigh. She had told him what it was he needed to know about his birth in order to understand that only complete secrecy could save them. At the tender age of fifteen, his mother, Sybille Chalis, had been seduced by the evangelical purity of the Waldensian Church. She had run away from her family, wealthy burghers from the Dauphiné region, in order to join her brothers and sisters in hiding and to be ordained a priest. Their tiny congregation had been denounced, but the young girl had just managed to escape. She hid, travelling by night, hardly knowing where she was headed, begging for bread in exchange for a few hours' labour. It was only a matter of time before disaster struck in the form of two drunken brutes who raped and beat her and left her for dead. Sybille already knew she was pregnant by the time she arrived at the manor one evening. Agnès took her in, oblivious to the fact that in doing so she was harbouring a heretic. But even had the young woman revealed the truth about her faith, the Dame de Souarcy would not have ordered her men to throw her out. Agnès had paused briefly before relating what for Clément had been the worst: his mother could not tolerate the idea of her soul being trapped in a defiled body and had let herself die of starvation and cold during the deadly winter of 1294.

Sensing that her mistress was unable to go on, Gisèle had concluded:

'She pushed you from her womb as she lay dying – that was on 28 December.'

Clément was overcome, great tears rolled down his cheeks. He could see from Agnès's staring eyes that she was reliving those nightmarish scenes. She had stroked his brow with a trembling hand before continuing in a choked voice:

'Clément, you are not a boy. That is why we insisted you never bathe with the servants' children and that you stayed away from them and did not join in their games.'

He – she – already suspected, having noticed that his body had more in common with those of little girls.

'But . . . why?' he had stammered.

'Because I could not have kept a motherless girl in my service, and you would have become one of the many offerings to God who end up in convents. Eudes de Larnay would have demanded it and I would have been in no position to refuse.' At this point Agnès had closed her eyes for a brief moment and when she spoke again her voice was firmer: 'Orphans of low birth have no other choice but to enter servitude – or worse, but you are still too young for that. They have no access to knowledge and their lives are harsh. I wanted to spare you. If my brother and his breed were to learn your true sex . . . That can wait. What you need to realise now, dear Clément, is that nobody must ever discover the truth about you. Never . . . Well . . . the day might dawn when . . . Your fate would be cruel. Do you see?'

Afterwards he – she – had cried all night long, wondering whether the mother he had so often imagined, so often pictured as a beautiful star or a gentle ray of sunshine had also wished him dead before he was born. What use was a life so worthless that even his mother had rejected it? The question had haunted him for weeks before he had had the courage to put it to his lady. She had gazed into his eyes, tilting her head to one side so that her veil brushed her waist, and smiled such a beautiful, desperate smile:

'Your life is terribly precious to me, Clément . . . Clémence. I swear on my soul.'

He had Agnès. His whole life depended on his lady. After all, she fed him and protected him like a mother. He knew she loved him. And he adored her.

As for the rest – this inversion of his sex – it hardly mattered to him in the end. His lady was right. A low-born girl, the orphan of a heretic mother, was nothing or worse than nothing. He would continue thinking of himself as a boy for his own and Agnès's protection. And besides, a boy's life was so much more exciting than that of a girl.

Clément wiped away the tears that had wet his lips and chin with his sleeve. Enough! Enough memories! The past was over. He must devote himself to the future. He must concentrate on living even as so many dangers were stacking up against them.

Why, whence the need he felt to penetrate the mystery of the diary belonging to the Knight Eustache de Rioux and his co-author? How might the crossings-out, question marks, blind searchings of these men, who were perhaps dead, help them – Agnès and him? And yet he was driven on by an instinct he found difficult to analyse. This astrology and astronomy, these mathematical calculations, furious or fervent jottings and hinted-at secrets were a nonsense to him:

The Moon will eclipse the Sun on the day of his birth. The place of his birth is still unknown. Revisit the words of the Viking, a bondi trader in walrus tusks, amber and furs chanced upon in Constantinople.

What were these words? Where did they come from?

Five women and at the centre a sixth.

A geometrical shape? A metaphor? What?

Capricorn in the first decan and Virgo in the third being variable and the consanguinity of Aries in any decan too great.

Was this a reference to a past or future birth, and if so whose? And what did 'consanguinity' mean in relation to a zodiac sign?

The initial calculations were incorrect, failing to take into account the error relating to the year of birth of the Saviour. It is a fortunate blunder for it gives us a little more time.

Could some error have been made concerning the date of Christ's birth? And more time for what? Clément leafed through the long notebook, fighting back his feelings of frustration and despair.

He must read it through from the beginning, pushing aside his impatience and his looming sense of panic.

What was the drawing with a line through it which he had been struggling for hours to comprehend? It was shaped like some sort of disc. In the margins on either side of it were columns of Roman numerals, preceded by some initials and symbols. The same sequence of letters – *E, Su, Me, Ma, V, J, Sa, GE1, GE2, As* – reappeared in various places next to the signs of the zodiac. It did not take a genius to work out that some of these initials referred to the planets – except for *GE1, GE2* and *As*, which meant nothing to him.[32] As for the Roman numerals, they represented the different astrological houses. Clément compared the two columns depicting astral or birth charts. They were almost identical except for the two planets Jupiter and Saturn. In one column they were in Pisces and Capricorn respectively and in the other in Sagittarius and Pisces. Capricorn. That was between 22 December and 20 January. Had it not been for the gravity of the situation the coincidence might have amused him. He was born on the night of 28 December.

The first time he had examined the scored-through drawing he had been devastated by the writing below it:

Equatoire[33] carried out in accordance with the measurements of the Arab mathematician Ibn as-Samh originated from the illogicality defended by Ptolemy. The figures obtained thus are unusable since the Earth is not stationary! Therefore they were all mistaken.

God in heaven! Was such an aberration possible? How could the Earth be anything but stationary? And if so where was it going?

The Greek astronomer and mathematician Ptolemy had affirmed that the universe was finite and flat and that the Earth was at its centre, fixed. The nearest planet to Earth was the Moon, followed in an almost straight line by Mars, Venus and the Sun. Everyone recognised the truth of this system – in particular the Church, and thus the schoolmistresses at the convent praised its importance. How, then, could Eustache de Rioux and his fellow author describe it as illogical? And yet the Knight – or whichever of the two wrote in a bolder, less flowing script – had reiterated at the bottom of the page:

It was necessary to do all the calculations again using Vallombroso's theory, which we did.

Clément could find no other mention of this Vallombroso, despite having trawled through the notebook several times.

On the back of the sketch that had given rise to Monsieur de Rioux's (or his co-author's) rage was a sentence they had been so keen to obliterate they had scraped away the letters with a knife. The paper still bore the marks, and Clément had carefully examined it, holding the page up to the oil lamp to see whether the light might expose its secrets. He had been able to make out some speech marks framing the scratched-out letters. So it was a quotation. The ink that had seeped into the layers of pulp revealed a few letters, but not enough to give any real clue as to the meaning of the words: 'b . . . me . . . re . . . au . . . per . . . t.'

Below the sentence was another drawing, of a rose in full bloom.

Were these the words of the Viking merchant which the Knight had earlier quoted?

Clément discovered something he had missed on his first reading of the journal: the bold script disappeared completely a few pages on, where some strange drawings the size and shape of almonds in the form of a cross had been traced by a fine hand. The words 'Freya's cross' at the top of the page provided no clue, since Clément did not know who or what Freya was. At the centre of each almond was one of the indecipherable cuneiform letters he had already come across in other works. These strange signs were transcriptions of ancient languages. Each had an arrow pointing from it to a strange word.

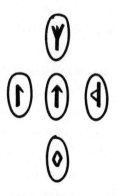

The almond on the left branch was called – or signified – 'Upright-Lagu' and the one on the far right 'Reversed-Thorn'. The almond at the centre of the cross was described as 'Upright-Tyr' and the one on the top branch 'Upright-Eolh'. The bottom branch was given as 'Reversed-Ing'. Although the actual names meant nothing to Clément the alternation of 'upright' and 'reversed' was implicit: it was some sort of prophesy, since fortune-tellers used similar terms for their cards.

Clément paused. He could memorise the letters and their corresponding names, as well as the two charts. However, he sensed that their precision was of paramount importance and was afraid of making a mistake when trying to reproduce them back in his eaves. He felt a strong temptation to go over to the lectern and make use of the hollow quill pen and ink pot standing there. He did not resist for long, promising himself he would take great care not to move anything, and above all to leave nothing behind that might draw attention to his intrusion. All he needed now was a piece of paper. He searched the library in vain. Paper was a luxury that was kept carefully locked away in cabinets. He struggled for a few seconds with a thought that kept going through his head. Why not tear out one of the last two pages of the diary – blank because the co-author's notes stopped before the end of the notebook? The gesture seemed to him so sacrilegious that it took him three attempts to pluck up the courage.

Satisfied with his copy, he removed all trace of his labours, cleaning the tube of the quill pen and his fingers with a corner of his tunic moistened with saliva.

In order to turn the calculation on its head and discover a date that would show him whether these combinations referred to a birth or a forthcoming event, he needed to find out which system the Knight and his companion had used – in other words: Vallombroso's theory. As for the cuneiform letters, their meaning must be recorded somewhere.

The child spent the last remaining hours of darkness consulting every manual on physics, astronomy and astrology and every glossary in the library, without finding anything resembling that name or that shed light on the symbols in the almonds.

Vallombroso, Vallombroso . . . He resumed the search. It was the small hours of the morning before he came across what he considered to be a sign from God. He had stumbled upon a copy of Gui Faucoi's[34] *Consultationes ad inquisitores haereticae pravitatis*, accompanied by a slim manual detailing a series of blood-curdling procedures.

Reading them left him beyond all rage, filled with dread.

Louvre Palace, Paris, July 1304

GUILLAUME de Nogaret had been awake all night since learning of Benoît XI's demise. He had spent hours weighing up the pros and cons, tossing and turning in his bed as he imagined the worst possible consequences for the kingdom of France. He was choked with rage at the idea that somebody could have stooped so low as to poison the Pope. Not that he had held the Holy Father in particularly high esteem. However, as a lover of the law, Nogaret required that all matters be settled by it. And the law served equally to depose a pope, making it unnecessary to kill him.

This murder was a personal and political calamity. Everybody knew that Benoît XI had decided to excommunicate him in order to punish Philip the Fair for his attempt to force out Boniface VIII. Had this excommunication come to pass, it would have deeply injured Nogaret, who was an extremely religious man, and cast a long shadow over his future political career. In other words he had better reasons than anyone for instigating this poisoning. As the hours slipped by before dawn, his concern for the future of the kingdom eclipsed any fears he might have about his own.

Nogaret and Plaisians were not yet prepared. They had begun spinning their web, advancing their pawns across the papal chessboard. They had counted on a few years of relative respite during Benoît's pontificate, which they hoped would be brief. Not as brief as this, however.

It was barely four o'clock in the morning when, sleep resolutely refusing to come, he decided to rise from his bed and pray before getting down to some work.

Francesco de Leone, known as Capella for reasons of his espionage mission, was already busy checking registers when Nogaret opened the door to his office. The Counsellor hesitated between feeling irritation at not being able to enjoy a few hours of solitude, and contentment at having engaged such a diligent secretary. The latter prevailed – perhaps because he felt the need to engage in pleasant conversation.

'You are an early riser, Francesco.'

'No, it is the work, my Lord, it seems to pile up overnight as if by magic.'

The reply elicited a weak smile from Nogaret, who nodded: 'It often seems so.'

'My Lord . . .' Francesco paused with consummate skill. 'What are we to think of the appalling demise of our Pope?'

'Who do you mean by "we"? "We" the State, or "we" you and I?'

'Are not "you" and "the State" one and the same?'

The flattery was too subtle for Nogaret to perceive. On the contrary, the remark pleased him to the point of lifting his troubled mood a little. He responded with an already lighter sigh:

'Not now, not any more. You see, Francesco, I do not know what to think. Naturally, the threat of being excommunicated worried me, even though I understood that it was Benoît's way of affirming his authority over that of the kingdom of France.' Suddenly it seemed essential to Guillaume de Nogaret to be clear on one point – perhaps because he realised that the man he had just taken into his employ possessed a keen intellect and deserved to be treated as his equal. 'You should know that I swear before God I played no part in the attempt on Boniface's life at Anagni. I went there to give him a summons to appear before the next ecumenical council. I was in the wrong place at the wrong time. We had a strong chance of removing that unworthy Pope by means of a religious tribunal. Any intervention by force was therefore superfluous.'

Leone studied him in silence for a moment then declared in a slow and sincere voice:

'I believe you, my Lord.'

He was certain that this powerful man was speaking the truth, he who recognised a lie as plainly as the nose on his own face.

Nogaret was filled with a disproportionate sense of relief, and it surprised him. After all, Francesco Capella was a mere secretary and the nephew of one of the most predatory usurers of the Place de Paris; what did it matter to him what the man thought? He went on:

'In answer to your question . . . This premature death could turn out to be an untimely setback. We are unprepared to take action behind the scenes, unless we can delay the election of a new pope.'

'How would you achieve that?'

'By relying on man's basest instincts, which the vast majority of our cardinals have not been spared. Namely cupidity, envy, jealousy and a thirst for power.'

Francesco estimated he had discovered enough for one day, and was afraid of rousing Nogaret's suspicions with more questions. He changed the subject:

'I have been checking the register of court accounts while I waited for you, and . . .'

Leone made a play of pausing awkwardly.

'And what? Come on, speak up, Francesco.'

'Well . . . Monsieur de Marigny's accounts are . . . how should I put it? Well . . . Large sums of money have been credited to him without any mention of what they have been used for.'

'There are three Marignys: the King's Head Chamberlain, Enguerran, who is well placed in court and close to the Queen, Joan of Navarre; his brother Jean, Bishop of Beauvais, and Philippe, the King's clerk and Bishop of Cambrai. To which do you refer?'

'To the latter in particular. As for Charles de Valois,* he is a bottomless pit!'

Nogaret, frowning at this remark, explained:

'The King's only brother is beyond reproach. Our sovereign is at times blinded by the affection he feels for him. That is the way it is and we have no choice but to accept it. His Royal Highness Charles is very generous with other people's money. We must tolerate it while deftly alerting our sovereign.'

Leone was surprised that Nogaret did not demand details of expenditure carried out in Philippe de Marigny's name. He continued bluntly:

'Monsieur de Marigny, Philippe, spent ten thousand pounds

of Treasury money in less than six months. That is no small sum! His letters of withdrawal were drafted by Monsieur Enguerran and countersigned by the King and there is nowhere any mention of how the money was to be used.'

'If the King countersigned them then it is no concern of ours,' retorted the Counsellor drily.

Leone blinked deferentially by way of assent and returned to his work.

What had this money the King approved been destined for? The withdrawals had begun six months ago – some time before Benoît XI's death. Moreover, Nogaret had been obliged to call upon Giotto Capella to raise the necessary funds in order to manipulate the next papal election. The money granted to Philippe de Marigny must have been meant for some other mission, secret enough to warrant it being unaccounted for in the Treasury register. Guillaume de Nogaret's brusque response was proof that he knew about it.

Nearly an hour passed. Leone did not glance up from his work. The task the King's Counsellor had given him, though tedious, was undemanding and his mind was occupied elsewhere. Soon, he sensed. Soon he would have completed his mission in this place. But Arnaud de Viancourt, the prior of the commandery at Cyprus, need not know straight away. Under the guise of continuing his investigation Francesco could stay in France in order to reach the end of his own quest. And then what? Then the world would no longer be what it was now. There would be an end to hypocrisy, scheming and guile. The idols would fall . . . He must first reach the commandery at Arville, the property of the Knights Templar. They would be reluctant to offer their help to a Knight Hospitaller, at least the sort of help Leone badly needed.

Guillaume de Nogaret cleared his throat. The Knight looked up from the rows of figures he had been examining since his arrival.

'Let us rest for a moment, Francesco. Your uncle told the truth, you speak French admirably well.'

'There is no merit in it, my Lord. My mother was French.' Leone quickly changed the subject. 'Your task would indeed appear to be vexing you.'

'My head is spinning from these marriage contracts. Every contingency must be covered, even – above all – the unforeseeable.'

'What marriage is this, if I may be so bold as to ask?'

'It is no great mystery. His Royal Highness Philippe, Comte de Poitou and our King's second son, is to wed Madame Jeanne de Bourgogne, daughter of Othon IV, Comte de Bourgogne, and of Comtesse Mahaut d'Artois. The county of Artois is a permanently troublesome area. And that of Burgundy – well! In brief, allowance must be made for every eventuality: deaths, births, marriages, annulments, sterility . . . I tell you, my head is spinning.'

Sensing that Monsieur de Nogaret regretted his earlier ill temper, the Knight gave him a look of commiseration and waited for what would come next. It did not take long.

'It is so gloomy within these cheerless walls of the Louvre citadel. Do you not yearn for the Rome light and the splendour of the papal palace?'

'The early-morning light in Rome . . . is an utter marvel.'

Leone's enchanted smile faded. 'Naturally, I long for it . . . But I do not miss the years I spent in Boniface's service.'

The Counsellor tried to feign indifference and began smoothing down his quill pen. The man was a useless liar and dissembler, thought Leone, and berated himself; he must be careful not to take a liking to Nogaret. Nogaret was the enemy and he should not forget it. Nogaret tried, rather unsuccessfully, to pretend no more than polite interest.

'Is that so? And yet, though it was an honorary function, it was not without material benefits.'

'Indeed.'

Leone was brilliant at feigning discretion, drawing the Counsellor out even further.

'Now it is I who fear being too bold, Francesco. However, I am greatly satisfied with your work and I believe this to be the start of a long and fruitful association. It is therefore my . . . fatherly concern that makes me suspect there was some other reason for your departure than this . . . lady.'

Leone stared at him wide-eyed, as though stunned by the man's perceptiveness.

'Indeed . . .' he repeated.

'I would not wish to . . .'

'My Lord . . . if a king considers your honour and devotion worthy of his friendship, it would be madness for a humble clerk such as I not to put my trust in you. It is simply that . . . it is such a difficult thing to confide. For we are speaking in confidence, are we not?'

'You have my word,' Nogaret assured him with complete sincerity.

If what the secretary revealed proved important he could always divulge his confidences without naming his source – thus keeping his promise.

'Well, you see, my Seigneur de Nogaret, there were so many falsehoods, conspiracies, undesirable connections under Boniface's reign. The papacy was not enough for him, he wanted to be emperor.'

Nogaret was convinced of the truth of this, largely because the loathing he felt for the deceased Pope blinded him at times. All the same, hearing it from the mouth of a chamberlain, and moreover an Italian, who had served Boniface for years, was a great comfort to him.

'Did it offend you?'

'It did . . . though I fear my reasons will displease you.'

'If it is the case then I shall tell you and we will avoid any future exchanges of ideas. Pray continue.'

'The kingdom of souls, the defence of our faith and the purity of our devotion to God – all these things, in my view, come under the domain of the Holy Father's authority and wisdom. On the other hand, the construction, administration and protection of the State are the responsibility of the king or emperor. Boniface refused to accept this.'

Nogaret was growing increasingly pleased at having taken on Giotto Capella's nephew. He agreed:

'We share your feelings. But you spoke, too, of undesirable connections and conspiracies . . .'

'Oh yes . . .'

Nogaret champed at the bit, waiting for the other man to continue, not rushing him for fear he might close up. Francesco de Leone, meanwhile, was desperately trying to think up some convincing lie. For a lie to be convincing it must be simple, rooted in reality and, above all, pleasing to the listener.

'The Bishop of Pamiers, Bernard Saisset* . . . exiled by King Philip after he plotted against him . . .'

'Yes? What about him?'

'Saisset lacked finesse. He was reckless and easily manipulated.'

Nogaret froze with astonishment:

'Do you mean to say that Boniface was behind Saisset's mutiny against the King, and not the other way round, as we have always supposed?'

'Just so. I was present at one of the Pope's meetings with the Bishop. Saisset was a puppet. All that was necessary in order for him to charge was a red rag.'

'Gentle Jesus,' murmured Nogaret.

A few moments of silence elapsed before the Counsellor continued:

'And . . . these rumours that reached my ears . . .'

Francesco waited. He knew what Nogaret was referring to, but the question was a delicate one, and the man opposite him weighed each word before uttering it, for the accusation was serious:

'These . . . how should I say . . . shocking rumours about Boniface, or one of his acolytes, resorting to witchcraft in order to reinforce his power?'

This slanderous rumour had indeed circulated. Leone had never given it any credence. He had encountered many fake witches and bogus magicians, in many different countries and cultures, and none had succeeded in demonstrating powers that stood up under the scrutiny of logic and science. On the other hand, he knew the origin of this evil rumour that had cast a further slur on the previous Pope's character. He wondered briefly whether the best approach would not be to agree whole-heartedly with the Counsellor. The man's intelligence in theoretical matters was keen, but he was naive where the occult universe was concerned. Leone's instinct, as well as the necessity of convincing Nogaret of his absolute sincerity in order to gain his friendship, dissuaded him:

'Frankly, I never witnessed such things nor had any reason to suspect them. May I let you into a secret?'

'Naturally, it will be safe with me.'

'I replaced in His Holy Father's service a certain Gachelin Humeau. He was . . . how may I describe him in the simplest terms? Let us say that he had a very peculiar notion of the meaning of duty, honour and gratitude. Humeau was a parasite, a sneak thief, a spy who enjoyed unearthing people's secrets and selling them to the highest bidder. He was caught red-handed stealing manuscripts from the Pope's private library. His fall from grace was swift and justly deserved. Gachelin Humeau disappeared, but not before avenging himself in the way he knew best by slandering Boniface and his cardinals.'

The story was partly true, though the actual events had taken place not four but five years before.

Gachelin Humeau had decided to supplement the remuneration he received in his position as chamberlain by purloining, sometimes to order, diverse objects of value – above all, rare manuscripts of whose existence nobody but the Pope and his cardinals knew. A discreet inventory of the library's contents revealed that fifteen books were missing, five of which, it turned out, were unique copies. The works whose loss was immeasurable included a parchment written in Archimedes'* hand, which Humeau claimed contained astonishing advances in mathematics, a terrifying work on necromancy, the mere mention of which caused Humeau to cross himself, and a treatise on astronomy with the rather undistinguished title *Vallombroso's Theory*. The thief maintained that the contents of this last book if they became known would shake the entire universe to its foundations. Gachelin Humeau escaped arrest – fearing, and rightly so, that the Inquisition would force him to confess where he had hidden his priceless and redoubtable booty. He had then traded them in the utmost secrecy for a not inconsiderable sum that allowed him to envisage a future free from care. One of his customers had been none other than the Knight Francesco de Leone himself, who had ordered two works, for which he paid a small fortune. And it was thus he discovered where to resume his quest. The manuscripts, with their alarming and wonderful revelations, were now in a safe place. Before vanishing forever, Humeau had wished to spread his venom, further tarnishing the Pope's reputation.

Nogaret took in the words of his secretary before declaring:

'I am grateful for your honesty, Francesco. It is entirely appropriate and, rest assured, I appreciate it.'

Nogaret, because he believed his secretary had taken him into his confidence, felt relieved to be able to do the same. The position of King's Counsellor was a lonely, hazardous one. It warmed his heart to have found in this young man seated before him an unexpected friend.

Francesco de Leone immersed himself once more in the tedious inventories. Nogaret would be attending the King's Council that afternoon. This would provide him with a few hours in which to discover some clue as to the identity of the French cardinals whom the Counsellor was trying to persuade or buy.

For the past few days Leone had been acutely aware that time was running short. Evil, dark forces were at work, toiling relentlessly. He had never doubted their tenacity or savagery but now their imminence was growing apparent. The Darkness was approaching to engulf the emerging Light. The Darkness would resort to any weapon or artifice, however base, in order to perpetuate the shadows it fed upon.

He needed to reach the Templar commandery at Arville as soon as possible. He was not so foolish as to believe that he would discover the key to the Light within its walls, but he knew that concealed within those foundations and flagstones was the instrument necessary to forge it.

ENSCONCED in the little office the Inquisition had provided him with, Nicolas Florin was radiant. Recalling his anxiety at leaving Carcassonne, he felt annoyed at his 'girlish fright', as he called it. He realised now that even the young Dominican Bartolomeo, whom he thought he might be a little sorry to leave behind, bored him to death with all his timidity. How predictable the little friar was! Nicolas had wanted to see whether he could seduce him. It had proved so easy that he had instantly wearied of his victory. Seduction was a weapon and, as with any weapon, it was advisable to test its reliability and effectiveness on a variety of targets. In spite of his habit, Bartolomeo was easy to penetrate, he put up little resistance. A none too intelligent, awkward virgin summed him up to perfection. Undeserving prey for Nicolas. It is true that, in Carcassonne, Nicolas had not been spoiled for choice. He had been surrounded by sententious old fogies, monks embalmed in their dignity and their ridiculous doctrinaire squabbling. What did he care whether Francesco Bernadone – who after a life of poverty and devotion to Christ would take the name of Francis of Assisi – had emptied his father's warehouses in order to pay for the restoration of San Damiano? His father had ended by disinheriting him – a fact Nicolas considered wholly appropriate. As for the endless controversy over whether Saint Martin of Tours had offered all or only half his coat to a beggar whom he identified as the Saviour – he was sick to death of hearing about it. Of course this pedantic quibbling had but one aim: to separate the advocates of the poverty of Christ and his disciples, and consequently of the Church, from their virulent opponents who were legion. Nicolas could not have cared less. If he had been born to riches he would have laboured to protect his wealth and would never have been tempted by religion. He was poor but his Inquisitor's robes and position would help him to make this poverty provisional.

An image flashed through his mind. His mother enamoured of her only son. She had been so clever at delivering the off-spring of Madame d'Espagne's ladies-in-waiting, and yet so foolish. What had become of her after he left? What did it matter? And his father, that timid scholar and lover of pretty historiated vignettes[35] and initial letters[36] ornamented with tracery,[37] his fingers stained with brightly coloured inks and powdered gold. He would mix cuttlefish and oak gall with egg white and powdered clove,[38] failing to remember that the Comte for whom he was ruining his eyesight preferred war and women's bellies to manuscripts. Lackeys! That was all they both were. Nicolas's perfect features, as well as his talent for duplicity, had earned him the favours of many ladies and a few lords. His intelligence would soon place him high above them all. No one could stop him and he would no longer need to grovel to anyone. Even the great lords of the realm trembled before the Inquisition. Only one master, the Pope, and he was far away.

The power of terror. He already enjoyed it and would exploit it to the full.

The tidy recompense torture brought – the death he could mete out as he saw fit. It was so easy to accuse someone of heresy or possession. So easy to force someone to confess to crimes he, Nicolas, had invented. There was no need even for an executioner, he dispensed with them and completed the job himself. A few moments in the interrogation chamber with him. Nothing more. Nicolas had confirmed it again and again. If the accused was wealthy an agreement could be reached. If not, he died, and his terror, his pain were compensation for Nicolas. In both cases he won. The thought made him sigh with pleasure.

What a perfect model, that Robert le Bougre. A tidal wave of screams, blood, strewn viscera, crushed feet, put-out eyes, torn flesh. Fifty deaths in a few months – victims of his brief stays at Châlons-sur-Marne, Péronne, Douai and Lille. The great pyre of Saint-Aimé: a hundred and eighty-three 'pure', or so they claimed, Cathars burnt to cinders in a few hours.

Poor tiresome Bartolomeo. He would never experience greatness – even less the joy it procures.

He must now devote himself to the matter of Agnès de Souarcy, recently brought before him together with a first handsome payment. He would receive the second after her disgrace. Why not her death? But the Baron who had sought his services had insisted the young widow must not die, either on the rack or at the stake. And as far as torture was concerned he was to be as restrained as possible; the more 'benevolent' nature of the abuse inflicted on women compared to men made this possible.[39] This was all Nicolas needed in order to understand that he was dealing with an incestuous lover seeking retribution – one, moreover, who had been spurned.

A woman, a lady, how pleasurable. How stirring they were when they squirmed with terror! Especially this one, whom he had heard tell was ravishingly beautiful.

What a disappointment! No matter. After all, he had been handsomely rewarded. Some other brainless victim would serve to vent his frustration. There was no lack of people falsely accused.

The evidence the Baron had provided as justification for an inquisitorial examination was a little unclear and so Nicolas had decided to furnish his own. Heresy was the most suitable charge. He knew all the necessary ruses for these trials. None of the accused, even those who were innocent as new-born lambs, escaped his clutches.

He stretched his arms out contentedly and fell back in his chair, closing his eyes, and then, sensing another presence, instinctively opened them again.

The figure, wrapped in a brown cloak of coarse wool with a cowl drawn over its eyes, was standing motionless in front of him. He had heard no one enter his study. Nicolas's good humour was eclipsed by a sudden rage. Who dared to enter unannounced? Who had the gall to disregard his importance and his position in this way?

He rose, and was about to scold the intruder when a gloved hand emerged from a sleeve and handed him a small scroll of paper.

He was overcome by a series of conflicting emotions as he

read the contents: astonishment, fear, avidity and finally intense joy.

The figure waited in silence.

'What am I to think of this?' murmured Nicolas, his voice trembling with delight.

A deep voice, disguised by the thick cowl concealing the face, said tersely:

'She must die. Three hundred pounds in exchange for a life, it is more than enough.'

Nicolas was tempted by the idea of a little blackmail in order to raise the fee:

'Only . . .'

'Three hundred pounds or your life, decide quickly.'

The coldness in the voice of the person standing before him convinced him the threat was real.

'Madame de Souarcy will die.'

'You are a sensible man. You will stay at Clairets Abbey during the period of grace. Thus you will be closer to your new . . . toy. No order is rich or powerful enough to oppose the actions of a Grand Inquisitor and the good nuns will do as they are told. Thus you will find yourself only a few leagues away from your prey, the sweet Agnès.'

Château d'Authon-du-Perche, July 1304

THE news of Apolline de Larnay's death during childbirth did not surprise Artus d'Authon, although he was more affected by it than he had imagined he would be. Death was already visible in the grey woman's eyes when he last saw her. And in her belly. The new-born baby, another girl, had outlived her mother by only a few hours. No one expected their loss to upset the feudal Baron unduly.

The death of this creature, whom he had once despised, stirred in him a strange sadness, the sadness of senseless waste.

He surprised himself contemplating Apolline's life. She was one of those women who live only through their desire to be loved by the one they love. Eudes was neither her beloved nor had he ever loved her. And so she had remained locked inside herself, observing the passing of the years, emerging only on rare occasions – as when he had visited her two weeks before.

What on earth was the matter with him? Why did everything seem so painful to him of late? After the devastation caused by the death of his son, he had managed to make a life for himself that was relatively dull yet almost devoid of pain. True, he had never been one of those cheerful light-hearted fellows who are well liked in society. And yet since Gauzelin's death nothing had come near to hurting him. So what was happening to him now? Why did Madame Apolline's unjust end affect him so much? Countless women died in childbirth. He had discovered in himself recently an edginess and sensitivity he was unaware he possessed.

That woman . . . A smile appeared on his lips for the first time that bleak day, which had been heralded by one equally gloomy. He urged himself to think clearly – it would save time. He admitted that he had not stopped thinking about her since he left Souarcy. He was visited by images of her at night or in the middle of a meeting with his tenant farmers or during a hunt – causing him to miss his mark. When he calculated the difference between their ages he was shocked to discover that he was nearly twenty years her senior, and yet her deceased husband had been more than thirty years older than her. And besides, a man's age was of little consequence since his role was to provide for, honour and protect in exchange for love, obedience and a fecundity that would last his lifetime. Yes, but she was a widow, and the status of a widowed noblewoman with a child was without question one of the most favourable any lady could enjoy. If she possessed no fortune of her own at least she would enjoy a dower, since it was unthinkable that a woman who had fulfilled her duties as both wife and mother could be left to fend for herself. Without a father or husband such a woman became mistress of her own destiny. This fortuitous status explained why many a noblewomen or burgher had no wish to remarry. Did Agnès de Souarcy subscribe to this way of thinking? He had no way of knowing. And anyway, who was to say she found him attractive or even simply agreeable?

After he had finished posing these troubling and

unanswerable questions a black mood replaced the nervousness that was preventing him from finding any peace.

He brought his fist down on the table, almost upsetting the ink pot in the shape of a ship's hull.

A strumpet was what he needed. Attractive and glad to accept the money he offered her. A girl who would provoke no interest in him. A moment of paid pleasure, meaningless and unmemorable. He had already grown tired of the idea before taking it any further. He did not want a girl.

The announcement of Monge de Brineux interrupted his troubled thoughts.

'We have made some progress regarding the fifth and last victim.'

'Have you determined his identity?'

'Not as yet. However, he must have died a terrible death.'

'How so?'

'He almost certainly died from internal bleeding.'

'What proof have you?'

'The inside of his mouth was full of very fine cuts.[40] In my opinion the victim was given food containing crushed glass. By the time he realised, it was too late. The poor devil bled to death internally.'

'It is a method they use to kill wild animals in some countries. A truly terrible way to die. What of the other victims? Have you made any progress?'

'It is very slow. I sought the advice of a medical theologian at the Sorbonne.'

'And?'

'An awful lot of science and very little assistance.'

'I see. And what was his opinion?'

'Only that the victims died violently.'

'An inspired conclusion! He has solved the mystery for us!' said Artus sardonically. 'You would have done as well to seek the advice of my doctor, Joseph.'

'The problem with those people is that they never leave their amphitheatres, and they keep as far away as possible from their patients, or the corpses they are entrusted with, for fear of being contaminated. They are content to learn by rote and trot out what others discovered over a thousand years ago. They can quote Latin at you until your head is spinning, but if it is treatment you want for a boil or a corn on your foot . . .'

'We shall reach the bottom of this, Brineux, I assure you.'

'Yes, but when? How? At least four of the victims were friars. One was an emissary of our Holy Father Benoît XI who has just died, poisoned. This affair, which might have remained a local act of villainy, is taking on the proportions of a political incident. We must make progress, and quickly.'

For several days now Artus had feared this. The last thing the delicate situation between the French monarchy and the papacy needed was a papal emissary discovered burnt to death without any trace of fire.

Clairets Abbey, Perche, July 1304

ÉLEUSIE de Beaufort listened calmly to the young Dominican who had been announced earlier. The Extern Sister, Jeanne d'Amblin, her usually beaming face wearing an ominous expression of solemnity, had brought him to her study.

In common with her, Jeanne d'Amblin, Yolande de Fleury, Annelette Beaupré, the apothecary nun, and, in particular, Hedwige du Thilay, the treasurer nun,[41] whose uncle by marriage had perished in the slaughter at Carcassonne, were sufficiently intelligent women to be able to articulate, on occasion and in veiled terms, their disapproval of Rome's chosen methods for defending the purity of the faith. Doubtless others shared their reservations – Adélaïde or even Blanche de Blinot during her moments of lucidity – but they were more reticent. Éleusie found herself regretting, however, that the majority of her girls did not.

Indeed, despite her unquestioning faith and her obedience, the alarming evolution of the Inquisition upset the Abbess. Saving the souls of those who have strayed so that they might rejoin God's flock was of the utmost importance, and yet it remained inconceivable to her that friars should resort to torture and death in the name of Christ's love and tolerance. Naturally, they had no blood on their hands since those condemned were surrendered to the secular authorities for them to carry out the death sentence; but this expedient hypocrisy did not reassure her, especially now that a certain number of Grand Inquisitors presided over the torture sessions.

She recalled the courageous, nearly century-old warning Hilaire de Poitiers had given upon meeting Auxence de Milan:

I ask you who would call yourselves bishops: how did the Apostles ensure the purity of the Gospels? What powers did they depend upon in order to spread Christ's teachings? . . . Alas, today . . . the Church uses imprisonment and exile to force people to believe what once they believed in the face of imprisonment and exile.

Even so, these Dominicans and Franciscans had full powers and could exercise them over everybody, and that included her.

How handsome and radiant he was, this Brother Nicolas Florin. The ease with which he had requested that the convent extend him its hospitality for a month pointed to an order beneath the polite formalities. Strangely, no sooner had he entered her study than the Abbess had been seized by an almost uncontrollable feeling of revulsion. This had surprised her – she who was, always so distrustful of instinctive responses. And yet there was something about this young man although she could not put her finger on what it was, which alarmed her.

'You are compiling information for an inquiry, you say?'

'That is correct, Abbess. I would normally be accompanied by two brothers, but the urgency . . .'

'I do not believe I can recall a single case of heresy in Perche, my son.'

'And what of sorcery and demonic possession, for I assume you must have had your share of succubi and incubi?'

'Who has not?'

He gave her an angelic smile, agreeing in a soft pained voice:

'A sad but true admission. Doubtless you understand that I cannot reveal to you the identity of the person I am investigating. You also know that our methods are wholly compassionate and just. I will duly inform the person concerned of their month's grace. If within this time they do not denounce themselves their interrogation will commence. If, on the other hand, they confess to their sins they will almost certainly be pardoned and their identity kept a secret in order to spare them the condemnation of their . . . neighbours.'

He clasped his beautiful long hands together and prayed that Agnès would maintain her innocence. If what he had heard about her was true there was every chance that she would. And, if not, then he was prepared. He would simply claim that she had retracted her confession, relapsed heretics being considered the worst kind. None escaped the flames. Agnès de Souarcy's word counted for nothing against that of a Grand Inquisitor. The feudal Baron who merely wished to terrorise and disgrace his half-sister was in for a nasty surprise. Nicolas felt drunk on his own duplicity. He was powerful enough now to challenge and overrule the orders of a baron.

'It requires at least two witnesses to bring an accusation,' Éleusie de Beaufort insisted.

'Oh, I would not even be here if I did not have more than

that. There again, as you know, our aim is above all to protect. And so our witnesses and their depositions remain a secret. We wish to spare them any possible reprisals.'

A dark-haired angel, his face tilted slightly towards his shoulder, his brow illuminated by an almost unearthly glow that reminded Éleusie of the light that shone through the mullioned windows in the abbey's Notre-Dame church. The long eyelashes curling towards the brow veiled with a bluish transparency the bottomless gaze, the gaze of death.

A mask. Raw red beneath the pale skin eaten away by vermin. Festering flesh, strips of greenish skin, viscous foul-smelling fluids. Liquefied cheeks, hollowed eye-sockets, rotting gums. Reddish carapaces, a mass of legs, hungry mouths and tenacious claws burrowing into flesh. The stench of rotting carcasses. A piercing shriek lifted the empty thorax and the rib cage gnawed by unforgiving teeth. A rat scuttled out, its snout red with blood.

The beast was upon them.

Éleusie de Beaufort gripped the edge of her great desk with both hands, suppressing the scream she felt rising in her throat. A voice spoke to her from far away:

'Is anything the matter, Abbess?'

'A dizzy spell, nothing more,' she managed to reply before adding, 'You are welcome, my son. Pray excuse me for a few moments. It must be the heat . . .'

He took his leave at once, and Éleusie remained standing alone in the middle of the vast study whose edges were beginning to recede.

They had come back. The infernal visions. There was nowhere she could seek protection from them now.

Manoir de Souarcy-en-Perche, July 1304

H E was so young and handsome, so radiant, that Agnès foolishly thought he must be benevolent.

When Adeline had come to announce in a stammering voice the arrival of a lord monk from Alençon who was waiting for her in the great hall, dressed in a beige cloak and a black robe, she had known immediately. She had paused briefly: it was too late to turn back now.

He was standing waiting, his hands clasped around his big wooden crucifix.

'Monsieur?'

'Brother Nicolas . . . I am attached to the headquarters of the Inquisition at Alençon.'

She raised her eyebrows, feigning surprise, struggling to calm her pounding heart. He smiled at her and it occurred to her that he had the most moving smile she had ever seen. Something resembling sadness seemed to well up in the Dominican's eyes, and he murmured in a pained voice:

'It has reached our ears, Madame my sister in Christ, that you once sheltered a heretic rather than surrender her to our justice. It has reached our ears that you brought up her posthumous son under circumstances that suggest the work of a demon.'

'You must be referring to a lady's maid by the name of

Sybille who served me briefly before dying of weakness during childbirth. It was a deadly cold winter that year and claimed many lives.'

'Indeed, Madame. Everything points to her having been an escaped heretic.'

'Nonsense. They are the rumours of a jealous woman and I can even provide you with the name of your informant. I am a pious Christian . . .'

He interrupted her with an elegant gesture of his hand.

'As your chaplain, Brother Bernard, would confirm?'

'The Abbess of Clairets as well as the Extern Sister, Jeanne d'Amblin, who is a frequent visitor here, would swear it before God.'

After a few days and some clever questioning at the abbey, Nicolas had arrived at the same conclusion. He had also resolved to put aside the charge of carnal relations with a man of God. He would use it only as a last resort. He moved on:

'We have not yet arrived at the trial stage, still less at the verdict. This is the time of grace, my sister.' He closed his eyes and his angelic face stiffened with pain. 'Confess. Confess and repent, Madame, for the Church is good and just and watches over you. The Church will pardon you. Nobody will know I have been here and you will have washed your soul of all its impurities.'

The Church would pardon her, but she would be handed over to the secular authorities who would confiscate her dower, her daughter and Clément. She hesitated, doubting her ability to withstand an inquisitorial interrogation, and decided to try to gain a little time.

'My brother . . . I know nothing about the atrocious crimes of which I stand accused. However, your robes and your office inspire me with trust. Have I let myself be deceived? Am I guilty of having been too trusting? I must search my soul for the answer. Be that as it may, Clément was brought up to respect and love the Holy Church and has no knowledge of the deplorable error of his mother's ways . . . if such they were.'

Replacing his crucifix in the inside pocket of his surcoat, he walked towards her, arms outstretched, a satisfied smile on his lips.

A mask . . . Raw red . . . eaten away by vermin . . . Reddish carapaces, a mass of legs, hungry mouths and tenacious claws burrowing into flesh. The stench of rotting carcasses . . . the rib cage gnawed by unforgiving teeth . . . A rat, its snout red with blood.

The image was so real it made Agnès gasp. Where did they come from, these excruciating visions of death and suffering? The beast was before her. She stepped back.

Nicolas paused a few paces from Agnès, attempting to penetrate the mystery of the pretty face that suddenly looked so distraught. He had the fleeting impression that he had experienced this scene before, though he was unable to recall the precise circumstances. A feeling he had believed himself rid of forever made his throat go dry: fear. He stifled it and leapt at the chance to turn Agnès de Souarcy's strange reaction to his advantage.

'Have you strayed so far down the road to perdition that you fear the embrace of a man of God?'

'No,' she breathed in an almost inaudible voice.

This man was a personification of Evil. He loved Evil. She was certain of it, though she did not know how. And yet for the last few moments, since that horrific vision, she was no longer alone. A powerful shade was fighting beside her. More than one. She was filled with a strength she thought she had lost. She let herself be guided, replying boldly:

'No . . . I am taken aback by your assertion. Did Sybille deceive me? Did she take advantage of my kindness, my naivety? What a terrible thought. I am afraid that if Clément were to learn the awful truth about his mother it would destroy him,' she dissimulated with an ease imparted to her by the good shades.

They, too, compelled her with open arms towards this diabolical angel and made her clasp the shoulders of this man who repelled her in a gesture of love and trust.

He had not come here for her confession – he wanted her life, whispered the shades to Agnès, whose mind was now humming with voices that were not her own. Was one of them Clémence? Agnès could not tell.

As she relaxed her embrace the eyes staring back at her had become veiled with a kind of anger. The struggle threatened to be more prolonged than he had envisaged. If she confessed before the inquisitorial court that the lady's maid had been a heretic but insisted that her error had been made in good faith, the judges would be predisposed to leniency. She would be let off with a mere pilgrimage or, at worst, a few novenas. He could bid farewell to the Baron's hundred pounds – which he had had no intention of returning following the death of his half-sister, as well as the three hundred pledged to him by the mysterious messenger. He could say goodbye to his pleasure.

Then the anguish Nicolas had contrived to suppress returned, striking him with full force; his life was in danger should he fail. The cloaked figure had the power to show no mercy. Whereas before he had merely despised his future victim – his toy – now he was beginning to detest her.

No sooner had he left than Agnès slumped to her knees. She begged the voices to come back, for they had grown silent since the Inquisitor's departure.

Was she losing her mind? She prayed for what seemed like hours. She was in the grip of a sort of delirium. At that very moment, she would have given anything for the voices to live in her again, to soothe her.

'My angel,' she sobbed quietly.

A sigh, like a caress, inside her head.

Clément found Agnès huddled on the stone floor in the main hall. A moment of sheer panic. He rushed to her side as it struck him she might be dead. She was sleeping. The child stroked the thick plaits coiled round his mistress's head and beseeched her:

'Madame! Pray wake up, Madame. What is the matter? Why . . .'

'Hush! He was here, and it was Evil who embraced me. You must leave here immediately, Clément.' Sensing a mounting protest, she added in a firm voice, 'It is an order and I will not accept any argument.' Softening all of a sudden, she continued, still seated on the floor, 'You must do as I say out of love for me. The inquisitorial procedure has begun.'

Clément's eyes grew wide with fright and he trembled:

'My God . . .'

'Hush and listen to me. Something extraordinary has occurred. Something so extraordinary that I hesitate to share it with you for I myself am so bewildered that I can barely gather my thoughts.'

'What was it, Madame?'

'A presence, or rather several presences . . . It is very difficult to describe. The realisation that I was being helped by some kind of benevolent force.'

'By God?'

'No. But whatever they might be they inspired me with a feeling of confidence, a strength that tells me I am able to defeat this evil being, this Inquisitor named Nicolas Florin. He is . . . a personification of the worst, Clément. How can I explain it to you? Eudes is wicked but this man is evil. You must disappear, for while you have been my strength all these years, now you are my biggest weakness. You know as well as I. If that man manages to persuade the superstitious fools he will appoint as judges that you are an incubus, your youth will be no protection, on the contrary. And if he finds out that we have concealed your true sex the outcome will be even worse. His judgement will be implacable in their eyes for you are the child of a heretic. And then they will believe anything that monster tells them. You must leave, Clément. For my sake.'

'What about Mathilde?'

'I shall ask the Abbess of Clairets to take her in for a while.'

'But I can . . .' he tried to argue.

'I beg you, Clément! You can help me by leaving. Go quickly.'

'Would it really be helping you, Madame? Are you not just trying to protect me?'

'I am trying to protect us all.'

'But where will I go, Madame?'

Her immediate response was a despairing smile:

'Of course nobody will rush to our aid. The only person I could think of approaching for protection is Artus d'Authon and I do not know whether he will grant it to me on your behalf. If he refuses for fear of the consequences, flee, it does not matter where. Swear to me on your soul. Swear!'

He paused then yielded before her insistence:

'I swear.'

She clasped the child to her, and he buried his face in her rosemary-scented, silky hair. A terrible grief made him want to burst into tears, to cling on to his lady. He felt as if all his strength were being sucked out of him. Without her he was lost, without her he knew not which way to turn. For her he could do anything, of that he was certain. But the huge void that grew even as she spoke paralysed his body and crushed his spirit.

'Thank you, my sweet child. I shall write a letter for you to give the Comte. If he should refuse to hide you . . . I have saved some gold coins, not many but enough for you to reach a port and sail to England – the only country that has not yielded to the temptation of the Inquisition. Go and saddle a horse and fetch some supplies and join me in my chamber.'

When she released him from her embrace, he felt he was dying there at her feet.

Did she sense it? She whispered in his ear:

'I am not afraid any more, Clément. I will prevail – for your sake and mine, for everyone's sake, and for the sake of the good shades. Never forget that you are always with me even though we are apart. Never forget that I am guided by love and when love fights it overcomes all. Never forget.'

'I will not forget, Madame. I love you so.'

'Prove it to me by not coming back until I have defeated this creature of darkness.'

In a few short years Clément would have grown into a young woman. The deception that had allowed Agnès to keep her by her side would be too difficult to maintain. What would be Clément's, Clémence's, reaction when she discovered the whole truth about her birth? The weighty secret shared by three women, two of whom were now dead.

In a few short years . . . if God allowed them both to live.

As she watched the child leave, Agnès was surprised by how much he had grown in a few months. His breeches reached halfway up his legs and his heels were sticking out over the backs of his clogs. She felt absurdly cross with herself for not having noticed it before. Suddenly it seemed vital to her to remedy the situation before his departure – as though such a simple gesture were a clear link to the future, as though it were proof they would soon be reunited.

And what if she was deluding herself? What if she was unable to survive an interrogation, to defeat that beautiful infernal creature? What if she never saw Clément again? What if she perished? What if Comte Artus was merely a pleasant façade concealing a coward? What if he sent Clément away or, worse still, delivered him into the hands of the Inquisition?

Stop! Stop this instant!

A month would pass, a month of grace. She had time to reflect, to prepare her defence, to think of other solutions. Clément had already helped her to do so one evening when he came back from one of his mysterious night-time forays.

A courage she had not expected to feel since the shades grew silent returned. She was no longer alone, even though she had chosen to send Clément away. She had not been lying to him. He was at this moment her greatest weakness. She felt capable of resisting anything except a threat to his young life. Now he was gone, out of harm's way, she could confront them. A strange thought occurred to her, a thought which up until a few days before she would never have had. She would show no mercy. Eudes had woven the web that was closing in on her. If she survived this ordeal she would make him pay, ruthlessly. The time for forgiveness, for moderation was over.

She went to the kitchens and calmly ordered Adeline to find some clothes that would fit Clément and to pack a bundle of food for him, without satisfying the girl's silent curiosity.

Château d'Authon-du-Perche, August 1304

TORRENTIAL rain had threatened to ruin the harvest, which took place later in Perche than in Beauce. Everybody had pitched in, working night and day to beat the storms.

Artus had galvanised his troop of peasants and serfs, riding from one farm to another, scolding some, praising others. They had watched him roll up the sleeves of his fine linen tunic, pacify two enormous Perche horses harnessed to a cart and drive them to collect the harvested wheat. The women had marvelled at his physical strength and the men admired him for not shying away from such ignoble and punishing work. He had shared their meals of cider, coarse bread and bacon, and, like them, had collapsed onto the haystacks for an hour's rest and sworn like a soldier that 'this accursed weather won't get the better of me, by God!' They had worked for two whole days and nights without stopping.

Artus d'Authon had returned worn out, soaked to the skin, covered in grime and stinking. Before collapsing fully dressed onto the bed he had felt comforted by the fact that since morning he had hardly thought about her at all.

He slept through the night and most of the next day. When he awoke, Ronan, who had served his father, had drawn him a hot bath and was waiting armed with brush, soap and bath sheets.

'Those hay fleas have eaten you alive, my Lord,' observed the old man.

'In which case they must all be dead,' Artus joked. 'Careful, you evil tormentor, my eyes aren't dirty so don't put soap in them!'

'Forgive me, my Lord, you're covered in grime and, well, it's very stubborn grime.'

'It is the real sort, the sort that comes from the earth. I am hungry, Ronan, very hungry. Are you planning to torture me much longer with this brush?'

'There's still your hair to do, my Lord. I was leaving the best until last. A young boy arrived last night. He seemed exhausted.'

'Who?'

'His name is Clément, and he claims he had the honour of meeting you at his mistress's house.'

Artus d'Authon rose suddenly to his feet, causing a wave of soapy grey water to spill over the sides of the huge tub and soak the floorboards. He cried, almost shouted:

'What did you do with him? Is he still here?'

'Your hair, my Lord, your hair! I shall tell you the rest if you sit down quietly in the tub and let me clean that . . . stuff on your head.'

Ronan had witnessed worse, first with the late Comte d'Authon and then with Artus, whom he had known since he was born.

'Don't speak to me like a nanny,' grumbled the Comte.

'Why not since that's what I am?'

'I was afraid you would say that.'

Artus adored Ronan. He embodied Artus's living memories – the most wonderful and most dreadful. He was the only one who had braved his master's murderous rage following the death of little Gauzelin. Without saying a word he had doggedly carried on taking Artus's supper up to his chamber, despite his master's threats if he continued. The only time Artus had ever begged for God's forgiveness was on account of Ronan, on account of the slap he had given his faithful servant that had sent him crashing to the floor. Ronan had picked himself up, the imprint of Artus's fingers reddening on his cheek. He had stared at the Comte, a terrible sadness in his eyes, and said:

'Until the morning, then, my Lord. I hope the night is kind to you.'

The following day an even more haggard-looking Artus had apologised, his head bowed in obediance. Ronan, his eyes brimming with tears, had walked over and embraced Artus for the first time since he was a child:

'My poor boy, my poor boy, it is a terrible injustice . . . I beg you during this dreadful ordeal not to forget your goodness and generosity of spirit, for if you do then death will have triumphed on all fronts.'

It was no doubt thanks to that slap that Artus's rage had abated. He had continued along the path of life.

'Quick, tell me, what did you do with him?' Artus repeated, wincing as Ronan scrubbed his head hard enough to take the skin off.

'I put him in one of the outbuildings and gave him some food, a blanket and a straw mattress until I could find out what you wanted to do with him. One of the farm hands saw to his horse. The boy has a letter. He showed me the roll of parchment, but refused to give it to me. It is addressed to you and no one else. His story sounded true enough. I hope I did not act naively regarding the boy.'

'No. You did well. Gently does it – it's my hair, not a horse's mane.'

'It could easily be mistaken for one, my Lord.'

'So what about this Clément? What story was this?'

'His mistress ordered him to come here to you.' Ronan sighed before continuing, 'The boy's terrified, and I think I am right in saying that he did not wish to leave her side, only she commanded it. He is waiting for you.'

'Have you done with that brush yet? There we are. I'm as shiny as a new gold coin!'

'Talking of gold coins . . .'

Ronan paused. His voice had a strange catch in it as he continued:

'He asked me how much the meal I gave him last night would cost. He explained that he had seven gold coins – his mistress's entire fortune, which she entrusted to him when he left. He said he did not wish to squander what she had worked so hard to save, and would prefer to eat only a little bread and soup. I had great difficulty trying to convince him that I was not an inn keeper and that he was your guest.'

Artus closed his eyes, pretending they were stinging from the soap. The heart he had believed lifeless skipped a beat. He was overwhelmed by a sweet pain raging in his breast. His life was so empty of love it felt as if he were discovering it anew: the boundless love Clément had for his lady, the love she felt for the brave boy, his own love for Agnès. Seven gold coins. The whole of her tiny fortune – barely the price of a handsome coat with a fur trim.

'Yes, yes, I've finished,' Ronan informed him. 'And yes, the boy is fed and rested and waiting for you, my Lord.'

Artus stepped out of his bath and, hopping about impatiently, allowed Ronan to dry him.

Artus walked up and down, hunched forward, his hands clasped behind his back. The large blue-green eyes followed his every movement. Clément had explained the situation in a few words. The Inquisition, Mabile's supposed revelations, the Dominican's visit, the time of grace dwindling like the grains of sand in an hourglass. He had sobbed when he related Agnès's fear that he would be arrested and tortured, and how she had made him swear on his soul to go away and not come back, to flee, leaving her to face the Inquisition alone. And then he had had to stop, for his tears drowned out his words – and he was so afraid for her.

The Comte d'Authon walked over to his desk again and read Agnès's letter for the tenth time.

Monsieur,

Believe me when I tell you I regret the anguish I am about to cause you. Believe me also when I say that I am your humble and loyal under-vassal and that your decision will be mine.

I find myself at present in a dangerous and very delicate situation. It is my destiny to confront it and I am prepared — at least I hope I am. God will be my guide.

This is not the motive of my appeal, but I am indeed appealing to you. You know Clément. He has served me faithfully and is very dear to my heart. He is a pure and loyal soul and as such deserves protection.

When I understood that I must send him away for his own safety, is it not curious that only your name should come to my mind?

If you decide after hearing the boy that you cannot accept Clément into your household, I beg you, with all due obedience and respect, to let him go and to inform no one. I have given him seven gold coins, all that I possess. He should be able to survive for some time on that sum. I would be eternally grateful to you.

I am guilty of none of the monstrosities of which I stand accused and Clément even less so. If I am right in thinking I know the origin of this plot that threatens my life, I have a vague feeling that it is no longer in the hands of its perpetrator.

Whatever the case, Monsieur, rest assured that the memory of your visit to Souarcy is the most agreeable one I have had since I was widowed. In truth, and if I may be so bold, I avow that I have not experienced such pleasant moments since death took Madame Clémence from me — may she rest in everlasting peace.

May God protect you, and may He protect Clément.

Your very sincere and obedient vassal,

Agnès de Souarcy.

The Comte was plunged into a maelstrom of conflicting emotions that prevented him from speaking to this oddly slender boy, who seemed so young, standing before him, his head held high, his gaze steady even as he trembled with fear.

But why had she not sought his protection herself? He could have intervened, made this Inquisitor withdraw his accusations. Admittedly they wielded great power, but it did not extend to angering the King of France, and for her Artus was prepared to lower himself to request the King to intervene. For her. Philip would have understood. He was a great king and a man of honour and of his word when the affairs of state were not in the balance. And, moreover, he was not overly fond of the Church or of the Inquisition, even if he used them as his needs dictated.

This woman bowled him over, exasperated him, humbled him, moved him in a way nobody else ever had. Her courage was equalled only by her reckless blindness.

Did she really believe she could fight a Grand Inquisitor alone? With what weapons?

No, she was not blind. She was as Monge had described her – a lynx. She was using guile, protecting her young, exposing her throat in order to distract her enemy momentarily.

Did she really believe she could turn on him, bury her teeth in his accursed flesh? She could not stand up to them. They had full powers and enjoyed complete immunity since each absolved the other of his sins whatever they might be.

What if she knew this? What if it was deliberate suicide? He was enough of a huntsman to know that female lynxes were capable of it, and when this happened he would stop the chase and let the animal go. Once, one had turned after fleeing a few paces and gazed at him with her yellow eyes before vanishing like a ghost into the thicket. Artus had been struck by the mysterious certainty that the animal had been acknowledging, perhaps even thanking him.

The predator Clément had described would never retract his claws and release his prey. Agnès stood no chance against him.

His fist struck the table and he cried out:

'No!'

Clément did not flinch.

'We must find a way out,' mumbled Artus. 'But how? We have no pope. Any petition, even from the King himself, would be lost in the Vatican's maze of officialdom, each in turn giving the excuse of there being no pontiff as a justification for doing nothing.'

Clément waited, motionless, expecting he knew not what from this man – a miracle perhaps. He suggested:

'Was not the King's brother, Monsieur Charles de Valois, awarded the county of Alençon last year?'

'Yes, he was.'

'The headquarters of the Inquisition to which Nicolas Florin is attached are at Alençon,' insisted the child.

'If I thought that an intervention by the royal family might help us, I would choose Philip, not our good Charles, who is not known for his political finesse. My boy . . . Comte d'Alençon or no, Charles can do nothing. The Inquisition takes orders from no one but the Pope.'

'And we have no pope,' repeated Clément.

His voice was quaking, and he bit his lip to stop himself from continuing, but Artus must have read his thoughts and bellowed:

'No! Cast that idea from your mind! She is not lost! I am not done thinking about it yet. Leave me now. I need peace in order to reflect and your deafening silence prevents me.'

Clément left without a sound.

Reflect.

The realisation he had just come to while he was speaking to the young boy with the blue-green eyes stunned him by its simplicity, its intensity. He would do anything to save her. It was accompanied by his increasing lucidity, cynicism even, as regards almost the entire religious apparatus. Faith was quickly set aside when power and money came into play. Artus knew that some Inquisitors could be bought, and this one was no exception to the rule since Eudes had clearly paid him for his services. All he needed to do, then, was to offer a higher price.

He would leave for Alençon the next day.

Aᴿᵀᵁˢ was stunned by the young man's perfect beauty. The image Agnès and Clément had painted of him was by no means exaggerated. The Inquisitor's unctuousness was so predictable that under any other circumstances he might have found it amusing.

'Your visit is an honour for me, Monsieur, lowly monk that I am.'

'A lowly monk! You judge yourself too harshly, Monsieur.'

Nicolas resented this noble who put him at a secular level, denuding him of his religious aura. All the more so, since his polite phrase had permitted the Comte not to return the honour. He did not doubt that the Comte's choice of words had been deliberate.

During the journey there, Artus had mulled over the best way to tackle the Inquisitor. Should he broach his subject gradually or go straight to the point? His deep uneasiness, and the fact that he wanted above all to avoid giving the other man the impression he was unsure of himself, made him choose the second strategy.

'I understand you recently went to notify a lady – a friend of mine – of her time of grace, did you not?'

'Madame de Souarcy?'

Artus nodded. He sensed the Inquisitor's uncertainty. Nicolas cursed that fool Larnay who had assured him that the Comte d'Authon would not intervene in favour of the lady. He recalled the words, and the warning, of the figure in the dark cloak and quickly calmed down. What could the Comte do in the face of such power, even if he did enjoy the friendship of the King? He replied in a soft voice:

'I was unaware that Madame de Souarcy was a friend of yours, Monsieur.'

It occurred to Artus that had Agnès not opened his eyes to Nicolas Florin through Clément, he would almost certainly have considered him above suspicion. After all, if evil were not so deeply seductive, how did it win over so many adepts?

'She is.' Artus paused then continued, 'I do not doubt that you are a man of faith . . .'

A pair of blinking eyes responded.

'. . . and intelligence. The motive for Monsieur de Larnay's anger at his half-sister is not one with which a pious man of honour would wish to be associated. It is of a personal nature and . . . how should I say . . . reprehensible in the extreme.'

'What are you trying to tell me?' said the offended Florin, amused at his own duplicity.

'He failed to mention that aspect to you, and the true nature of his resentment.'

'Indeed!' agreed Nicolas, who had understood perfectly that Eudes was not motivated by religious zeal and the defence of the purity of the faith.

'In short, he has made you waste your precious time,' continued Artus, 'for which I insist on compensating you. Nobody is aware yet that an inquiry has been instigated against Madame de Souarcy. Therefore you may call a halt to it.'

Nicolas was enjoying himself greatly. Power. Power was finally his – the power to slap down the Comte, to send him packing. The power to be his superior. He gave a clumsy show of wounded indignation in order to make it clear to the other man that he was mocking him.

'Monsieur . . . I hardly dare believe that you are offering me money in order to . . . Do you imagine that I would have been to see Madame de Souarcy had I not been convinced of the legitimacy of her half-brother's suspicions concerning her? I am indeed a man of God. I have given Him my labour and my life.'

'How much?'

'Monsieur, I must ask you to leave here at once and never return. You have offended both me and the Church. Out of respect for your reputation I bid you, let it rest.'

Artus understood the implicit threat and, while it did not unduly alarm him, something else made him feel far more uneasy. What hidden power was protecting Nicolas Florin, making him feel so unassailable that he could allow himself the luxury of mocking a lord? Certainly not that cipher Eudes de Larnay.

He recalled Agnès's suspicion: something far darker and more fearsome was at work behind these accusations against her.

On the road back to Authon, Artus came to a decision.

If necessary Nicolas Florin would die – an inconspicuous death that would have all the appearance of being an accident. He was clear in his mind that the annihilation of harmful vermin did not constitute a crime. His mouth set in a grimace. All the more so as he would afterwards turn the vermin's weapons against Agnès's enemies. He would loudly proclaim that God's judgement had intervened. That God had punished Nicolas for his inclemency and injustice. In His infinite wisdom and His magnificent goodness He had spared the innocent Agnès. While most people now had reservations regarding divine intervention, which had never once been proven during the many trials by ordeal,[42] none would dare contradict him.

Artus relaxed and Ogier shook his mane in harmony with his master's changed mood.

If necessary he was prepared. Though he hoped a reversal of fortune would spare him from having to bloody his hands outside the field of honourable combat.

Louvre Palace, Paris, August 1304

T HE candlelight cast eerie shadows on the ugly walls of the office cluttered with registers. Monsieur de Nogaret certainly had an austere notion of comfort. There was little in the way of wall hangings to protect the occupants from the cold and damp. In fact there was only one that covered the large stones behind Nogaret's work table. Francesco de Leone kicked himself for not having thought of it before. Taking advantage of the absences of the King's Counsellor, he had searched for hours, finding nothing of any interest. And then, the previous evening, as he was preparing to go to bed after the meagre supper Giotto Capella had had sent up to him, an image flashed through his mind of a pack of dogs on a dark-blue background, their flanks hollow from exertion, their open mouths high-lighted with red stitching.

He lifted the tapestry. Flush with the stone was a small metal plate. A padlocked safe set in the wall. Leone studied it. He had opened enough prison doors and safes considered foolproof by their inventors for this lock not to present any great difficulty. He pulled a fine metal rod out of his breeches and skilfully opened it within seconds. Even if his intrusion were discovered, which he doubted, he would be gone within a few hours, and Capella would have to deal with Nogaret's men. Inside the tiny space were scrolls of parchment and a bag bulging with what must have been gold pieces. A slim notebook bound in black calfskin caught his attention. The pages were covered in the Counsellor's narrow, hurried script. Francesco skimmed through it. The State secrets it contained, if divulged, would cause repercussions throughout the whole of Christendom. And so the holy crusade against the Albigensians had been a pretext to remove Raymond VI of Toulouse, recover the Languedoc and allow the lords of the North to carve out the southern fiefs as they wished. And so despite the bitter defeat at Courtrai the previous year, King Philip's army was preparing for battle again in a few days' time in Flanders. He felt a painful wrench in his heart when he came across the rows of figures spread over several pages: an estimate of the fortunes of the Templars and the Order of the Hospitallers. So it was true: their suppression was planned. The Templars, who were wealthier, as well as more vulnerable, would be the first to go. Then it would be the turn of the Hospitallers.

There was a sound of footsteps close by. Francesco replaced the tapestry and unsheathed his dagger. They approached the door then died away along the corridor. He must hurry.

Underneath the rows of figures were a few brief comments dotted with questions marks:

Exemption from taxes granted to Templars? Will hopefully increase anger and resentment on the part of the populace.

Association with heretics or demons? Secret dealings with the infidel? Sodomy? Perjury, blasphemy or idolatry? Human sacrifice, sacrifice of children?

So the prior, Arnaud de Viancourt, had been right; exemption from taxes had only been granted to the Templars so as to precipitate their downfall. As for the rest, what did it mean? Were these authentic suspicions, or a list of imaginary and interchangeable charges for King Philip to make use of when the time came to justify an inquiry and a trial? The fate of the two great military orders was sealed. Arnaud de Viancourt and the Grand-Master had been right. When would sentence be passed?

Leone struggled with the anger and grief choking him and read on.

There were other sets of figures – a detailed inventory right down to the payment of a few pennies to spies in service, which accounted for some of Monsieur Philippe de Marigny's expenditure of Treasury money. Thus he learnt that Squire Thierry had received a hundred pennies for examining the contents of a cardinal's letters, and a launderer by the name of Ninon eighty for inspecting a prelate's bed linen in order to ascertain whether the man was ill before approaching him. Monsieur de Nogaret was a meticulous and prudent man. Finally he came across two names underlined in a list including four others that had been crossed out: Renaud de Cherlieu, Cardinal of Troyes, and Bertrand de Got, Archbishop of Bordeaux.

The Knight replaced the notebook and closed the padlock.

He regretted not having more time to peruse the other documents. What did it matter in the end? Only one kingdom mattered to him, that of God. Men would continue to tear each other apart over stupidities blown out of all proportion. Soon the truth would be clear for all to see, and nobody would be able to pretend that it wasn't there any more simply by closing their eyes.

Francesco de Leone left the Louvre. The night was fortuitously dark. The stench in the streets, intensified by the seasonal heat, did not bother him any more than the odour emanating from the mass of humanity crowded into hovels.

He had a few minutes left in which to compose a coded letter to Arnaud de Viancourt. He must then deliver it to a priest friend at the Église Saint-Germain-l'Auxerrois who would make sure it reached Cyprus. The content was to the point and would make little sense to the uninitiated.

Dearest Cousin,

My research into angelology is proceeding at a slower pace than I had anticipated and than you had hoped, despite the inestimable help provided by the writings of Augustine – above all the remarkable City of God. *The second order[43] of Dominations, Virtues and Powers is extremely difficult to comprehend in its entirety and no less so the third order of Principalities, Archangels and Angels. Nevertheless, I persevere in earnest and hope that in my next missive I shall be able to inform you of important advances in my work.*

Your humble and indebted Guillaume.

Arnaud de Viancourt would understand from this that Leone had discovered the names of six French prelates who enjoyed the King of France's backing, but that he needed more time to unearth the identity of those most likely to be elected pope. The Knight did not mention the catastrophic discovery of the planned demise of the Templar and Hospitaller orders. He must reflect more on the best form of counter attack.

He left the little church[44] that stood near the Seine less than an hour later. The horse he had left with an ostler was waiting for him, together with his meagre baggage.

South to Perche, the commandery at Arville and Clairets Abbey. South to the Sign.

Clairets Abbey, Perche, August 1304

THE tall figure scaled the walled enclosure around the abbey, placing its feet in the crevices as though it knew exactly where the mortar was worn away between the rough stones. It crept quietly along Notre-Dame church and made directly for the long building containing the Abbess's chambers and the nuns' dormitories.

Éleusie de Beaufort woke up with a start. She had had difficulty sleeping since the arrival of that creature she so feared and detested, and since the hallucination that had revealed to her his true nature. Nicolas Florin was, without doubt, an emanation of the Dark Forces. The Abbess had just drifted into sleep, although troubled by impenetrable nightmares, when a repetitive scratching at the window of her study, next to her bedchamber, had wrenched her back to consciousness. She pulled herself out of bed and walked unsteadily into the adjoining room. She paused, fearful. Who was that man out on the stone ledge? How had he contrived to be there? She saw him raise his hand and pull back his cowl to reveal his face.

'Jesus be praised . . .'

She hurried to open the window. The figure hopped nimbly into the room and took her in its arms.

'Aunt, how happy I am to see you again at last! Shall we go next door? Let me take a better look at you.'

'Francesco, you scared me out of my wits! I hope nobody saw you. The majority of my girls are not strictly cloistered.'

Her delight at seeing him and embracing him was so great she cried out:

'What joy! You seem to have grown even taller. Oh! I have so many things to tell you, so many dreadful things, so many riddles I hardly know where to begin.'

'The night is still young, aunt.'

'My God . . . The emissary they found burnt to death but with no trace of any fire, my vanished letter, the Pope's death by poisoning, Agnès de Souarcy the object of an inquisitorial inquiry, falsely accused by someone, we suppose, for she is certainly innocent, the visions that have returned and are driving me mad, the Inquisitor, Nicolas Florin, who as he speaks to me changes into a repulsive flesh-eating insect. He has installed himself here in the abbey. You must on no account let him or any of my nuns see you. Little Mathilde de Souarcy is here and her uncle insists on taking her.' She let out a dry sob that caught in her throat, causing her to cough. 'Oh Francesco, Francesco, I thought I would never see you again and that all was lost. My nephew, my dear sweet nephew.'

A look of contentment flashed across Éleusie's pretty face, and she observed:

'You look more and more like your mother, my sister. Did you know she was the prettiest of us all? Pious, charming Claire. Her name could not have suited her more.'

Francesco had grown tense at the mention of another name.

He led the Abbess into her bedchamber. The study windows overlooked the courtyard and they risked being seen.

'You say Agnès de Souarcy is threatened with an inquisitorial inquiry?'

'That evil man Florin refused to divulge her name when he arrived. It was Madame de Souarcy herself who confirmed it to me over two weeks ago now, when she came to implore me to look after her daughter. Our guest mistress, Thibaude de Gartempe, has taken the girl under her wing, but Mathilde is proving unruly.'

'What more did Madame de Souarcy tell you?'

Éleusie sat down on the edge of her bed and clasped her hands together. She was shivering. A deadly cold coursed through her veins despite the heat of the past few days. She saw in it a sign of her impending demise. But this coming end did not worry her, for there was no end. She was more afraid of not having the time to help her nephew.

'She said very little. She was aware the Inquisitor was staying with us and was concerned lest she compromise my situation in relation to him. Nicolas Florin's foul odour pollutes the air and suffocates us – well, some of us anyway. Jeanne, our Extern Sister, has never been so long about her rounds and spends as little time in the abbey as possible. Annelette Beaupré, our apothecary nun, no longer leaves her herbarium, and gentle Adélaïde stays close to her pots and spit as if her life depended on it. As for my good Blanche, the silent reveries her age permits grow longer every day. There are plenty of others who let themselves be taken in by the perfect façade of that insidious creature. Indeed, he is so beautiful, so refined and so devout that

I even wonder sometimes whether I am not losing my mind in suspecting the worst of him. He has the face of an angel. I dare not confide in my friends for fear of placing them in an awkward position. And besides, most of those whom I sense are on my side have no doubt found the right solution in fleeing. However, some of my girls surprise and worry me. Berthe de Marchiennes, our cellarer . . . I knew I should have got rid of her when I first arrived at Clairets. As for Emma de Pathus, the schoolmistress, her brother is a Dominican monk and an Inquisitor at Toulouse. I do not trust one inch these alleged purists who have never experienced doubt.'

Éleusie sighed, her eyes gazing off into he knew not what space before continuing:

'I shall not list all those of whom I am unsure: Thibaude de Gartempe and even the delightful Yolande de Fleury . . . Did it take this creature coming into our midst for me to discover that I knew some of them only as a smile and a face? I am just beginning to reach an understanding of what lies in their hearts.'

She was straying from the point, but Francesco sensed her relief at being able to confide these secrets and waited.

She started suddenly, exclaiming:

'I have forgotten my duties as your second mother. Are you hungry?'

For a split second the Knight felt the immense burden he had been carrying for so long lighten. A wave of infinitesimal memories, warm and pleasant, washed over him from his Éleusie years, as he referred to them. The years that followed the horror.

Éleusie, sweet Éleusie, and her husband Henri de Beaufort had taken him in after the death of his father and the massacre of his mother and sister at Acre. Éleusie had brought him up with love and care, in place of Claire, whose memory she evoked daily in order that the child keep the image of his mother alive. Éleusie, who with her ceaseless love had contrived to soothe a little the terrible pain of the child he still was. He had clung to her and it was she no doubt who had saved him from developing a desire for vengeance. He owed her his soul. He owed her more than his life, and how good it felt to owe her so much.

'I am famished, for I have eaten nothing since I left Paris last night. But my stomach can wait. Speak to me of Agnès de Souarcy and the deaths of these messengers.'

Éleusie related what Agnès had told her and what she thought she had understood from her silences, and went on to tell of Eudes de Larnay and his destructive passion, Mathilde, Sybille and her heretical past, the repulsive role played by Mabile, and, above all, Clément and his devotion to his mistress, before concluding:

'As for the messengers, I received only one. As I explained to the Chief Bailiff, Monge de Brineux, the others never came to the abbey. Do you suppose they were on their way to see me when they encountered their killer? The thought torments me. For if so, then what became of the missives they were relaying from Benoît to me? Did they fall into the hands of our enemies? Is there some connection between their contents and the Pope's recent poisoning? What were their contents? Now that they have murdered our dear Holy Father we have no way of knowing. Day and night my mind is assailed by questions I am unable to find the answers to.'

Daylight was tentatively beginning to push back the darkness when they entered the secret library. They had both agreed on this hiding place, where he would be out of sight of the Inquisitor and the nuns and able to consult the rare manuscripts he had purchased from that crook, Gachelin Humeau.

Éleusie de Beaufort took advantage of the pre-dawn lull to go down to the kitchens and fetch some food for her nephew.

She then took an hour's sleep, free from nightmares, awakening just before lauds. The peace she felt filled her with wonder, like a sign. Death could come, she had fulfilled her duty. Francesco had returned.

What must be would be.

The light was fading when Leone awoke. He stretched and groaned, his body sore from the hardness of the flagstones, which was barely attenuated by the two hangings he had laid one on top of the other to form a mattress.

He was surprised to find a water jar and a wooden basin beside him. His aunt had attended to his toilet before going about her various tasks.

Leone immediately spotted the Knight Eustache de Rioux's distinguished notebook on top of some heavy volumes that filled one of the shelves. Eustache, his godfather in the order, who had guided his first steps as a Knight. Eustache, one of the seven Hospitallers who survived the siege of Acre.

A series of the kind of coincidences that only occur during the most terrible events had placed in the Knight de Rioux's hands the revelations which he had consigned to those pages. During the massive assault on the Temple Keep, Eustache, already twice wounded, sensed that all was lost and the slaughter was about to commence. He was ready to die in combat to defend the 'lambs', as he called them, and his faith. Death meant nothing to him since he had already sacrificed his life when he joined the Order of the Hospitallers. Enemy soldiers killing one another, whether they were friars or not, was for him part of the cycle of life. But not all these women and children ... If he managed to save even a handful of them, then his life would not have been in vain; he offered it willingly in exchange for theirs. Accompanied by two Knights of the Order of the Templars, he had made one more attempt to break out, leading a flock of panic-stricken women and children into the tunnels that came out near the beaches – near to where the Frankish ships were anchored off the coast, unable to reach harbour due to rough seas. By then the Temple Keep, a veritable fortress made up of five towers and considered impregnable because it had resisted longer than the New Tower of Madame de Blois, had begun to collapse and a mass of rocks as high as a man had fallen, blocking all the exits. Eustache de Rioux had tried hopelessly to calm the twenty-odd women and thirty-odd children who had followed him. His warnings and prayers were drowned out by the cries of the children clinging to their mothers' skirts, and by the women's sobbing and occasional outbursts of hysteria. In every crowd there is always one man or woman who believes they know best, and whose incompetence and stupidity is matched only by their self-assurance. They are the ones who drive the herd over the cliff's edge to their death below. And that is what happened. Eustache de Rioux would never forget the tall, skinny woman whose name he never knew. She had exhorted the women to surrender, insisting they should trust the infidel soldiers to spare their lives. He had shouted at her, almost struck her. They had without exception followed her, dragging their children behind them. Eustache, beside himself with rage at the stupid woman, had refused to escort them back to the slaughter. In contrast, the two Knights Templar had gone after them, despite the certain knowledge that none of their little flock would escape. As if proof were needed, the older of the two had turned towards Eustache and handed him a notebook stained with his own blood, which he had been carrying under his surcoat next to his skin. In a hopeless but brave voice he had murmured:

'My brother . . . the end is near. My whole life's research is contained within these pages. I owe much of it to the tireless efforts of a few other Templars. It was born of an encounter in the souks of Jerusalem with a Bedouin from whom I purchased a roll of papyrus written in Aramaic. It did not take me long to realise that I had in my possession one of the holiest texts in the whole of civilisation. I kept it hidden in a safe place – at one of our commanderies. A series of other events ensued, events so incredible they could not have been simple coincidences. They convinced me that I, that we, were not suffering from a delusion or some other form of insanity. Time is running out. This quest far outweighs me and must not be allowed to perish here with me. You are a man of God, of war and of honour.

You will know what to do with it. My life has been directed by a higher force and I believe I was meant to give you this notebook on this day in this place and that none of it has been fortuitous. Live, my friend, I beg you. Live for the love of God and continue the sublime quest. Pray for those of us who are about to die.'

They had disappeared around a bend in the collapsed tunnel. The battle raged above. Cries mingled with the whistle of stones launched from catapults and the clash of blades and arrows raining down.

In the now deserted passage, Eustache collapsed to the damp earth floor, sobbing like a baby and clutching the thick notebook of worn leather. Why was he not up there with the others, fighting destiny alongside them? Why was he not sacrificing his life in a lost battle?

The Knight of Light and Grace Eustache de Rioux had survived and returned to Cyprus. As soon as he arrived on the island refuge, overwhelmed by the scope and complexity of the quest, Rioux had sought the man who must take up the burdensome torch with him and continue bearing it after him. A very young man, still almost an adolescent, had crossed his path by a curious route. Curious because from its very inception it was the tradition in the novice's family for the men to join the Order of the Templars. It was almost inevitable, therefore, that he would do likewise. And yet he had requested to join the Hospitallers. When Eustache asked him why this was, the young man had been at a loss to reply. Of course, he argued, the element of caring for the poor and sick had influenced him, but if he were to be honest his choice had been guided by an intuition. Rioux had seen in this the sign that they should continue their path together.

They had copied out the notebook belonging to the Knight Templar who had died at Acre, and in an attempt to unlock its secrets had scoured the libraries of the world to try to penetrate its many mysteries. Some of these had gradually revealed themselves, though the majority had remained stubbornly hidden.

The Knight Eustache de Rioux had spent the last seven years of his life regretting by turns having not followed his two brothers and believing that the notebook was destined to be saved, and that some mysterious divine intervention had meant him to take possession of it. He was to suffer until the very end, like some ordeal, the burden of his life being spared at Acre.

When finally Rioux died in the Cypriot citadel, Leone had vowed to him that he would continue their quest to find the Light and would keep it secret until at last the Light burst forth.

Despite Leone's tireless efforts, at times he felt he had barely made any progress since his godfather's death. Except perhaps in the matter of the runes, which a Viking he ran into in Constantinople had explained to him.

Eustache and he had mistakenly thought they were Aramaic. They were not. The alphabet was known as futhark, and the Scandinavians had almost certainly adapted it from the Etruscan. These ancient letters gradually transcended their own meaning to become symbols, divinations. One evening, many years before, at a stall serving refreshing drinks made from the leaves of the chai tree, Leone had placed the strange cross upon a table before a merchant seafarer. The smile had vanished from the Viking's face. He had shaken his head and pursed his lips.

Leone had urged him to speak and offered him money. The man had refused, muttering:

'No good. Witchcraft. Forbidden.'

'I need to understand the meaning of these symbols, pray, help me.'

'I not know all. That one Freya's cross.'

'Freya?'

'Freya twin sister Frey. Woman-god.'

'A goddess?'

The man had nodded and continued:

'She woman-god beauty and love . . . love of flesh. She woman-god of war, like Tyr, he man-god. She lead warriors. Twin brother Frey. Other man-god, riches, fertility, land. Freya's cross to know if we win war.'

The sailor had but one desire: to leave the stall as quickly as possible. Leone had held him back by his sleeve and insisted:

'But what do the other symbols mean?'

'Not know. All forbidden.'

He had pulled away brusquely and disappeared into the colourful maze of the grand bazaar.

It had taken Leone more than a year to unravel the mystery of the almonds. He had had to wait for another of those unlikely coincidences, those improbable encounters the Knight Templar had evoked in the tunnel under Acre.

That morning, Francesco de Leone had been leaving on a mission to see Henri II of Lusignan. The hopes they had entertained of forcing the King of Cyprus to permit them to reinforce their numbers on the island had once again been dashed. He was approached by a small young girl dressed in rags, with long curly brown hair so tangled it resembled a clump of straw. Her head bowed, she silently held out a small grubby palm. Smiling, he placed a few small coins there – nothing much, enough to buy a little bread and cheese. Finally, when she looked up at him with her pale amber, almost yellow, eyes, Leone was astonished. The expression in them was so profound, so old for one of her years that he wondered whether she might not indeed be older than she looked. In a strikingly deep voice, she said to him:

'You are a good man. That is as it should be. I have been looking for you. I am told you possess a paper cross whose meaning you do not understand. I can help you.'

For a brief moment the Knight imagined he must be dreaming. How could this little beggar girl, one of many on the island, know about the mystery and address him as though she were a thousand-year-old woman? How could a Cypriot child decipher symbols belonging to an ancient alphabet known only to a handful of Vikings?

She led him, or, more precisely, he followed her, a few alleyways further along. She sat cross-legged on the floor behind a hut made of mud and straw. He did likewise.

Once again she held out her hand in silence. He took from his surcoat the piece of folded parchment he carried with him always. The small girl had spread it out on the ground and, hunched over, studied it.

A long moment passed before she looked up at him with her yellow eyes:

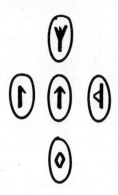

'Everything is written in this cross, brother. It is Freya's cross, but you already knew this. It is used to predict the outcome of a battle. And this is a battle. The left-hand branch signifies what is, what you inherit. It is Lagu, water. Water is inert yet sensitive and intuitive. Lagu is upright on your cross. You are lost, reality seems insurmountable to you. Listen to your soul and to your dreams. Long journeys are imminent. Keep in mind that you have been chosen, that you are a mere tool.'

Leone had taken a breath but the little girl had stopped him in a firm voice:

'Do not speak. It is pointless to ask me any questions. I am telling you what you must know. The rest will come from you. The right-hand branch signifies the obstacles you must overcome. It is negative. This sign is Thorn. Thorn is the warrior god of thunder and rain. He is strong and free of all immorality. But the rune is reversed. Beware of anger and revenge – they would spell doom for you. Do not trust advice, it will mostly mislead you. Your enemies are powerful and hidden. They hide behind the beauty of angels and have been hatching their plot for a long time, for a very long time. The top branch symbolises the help that will be given to you and which you must accept.' She paused for a moment before continuing, 'Are you aware, brother, that this is not one man's quest. It is an unbreakable chain. The rune Eolh is upright . . .'

The young girl's face broke into a beautiful smile and she said in a soft voice:

'I am glad. Eolh offers the most powerful protection you could enjoy. It is magical and so unpredictable that you will not recognise it when it appears. Do not fear being swayed by influences you do not understand. The lowest branch signifies what will happen in the near future. It is Ing and is reversed. Ing is the god of fertility and all its cycles. A task is nearing its end . . . yet the outcome is not favourable to you. You have failed. You have made a mistake and must go back to the beginning . . .'

She had stared at him with her cat-like eyes before asking:

'What mistake have you made, brother? When? Where? You must find out very soon, time is running short. It has been running short for centuries.' She lifted her hand to silence the questions the Knight was burning to ask. 'Be quiet. I know nothing of the nature of the mistake, only that if you do not correct it very soon, the quest will reach an impasse. Nor do I know anything about the nature of the quest. I am, like you, a mere tool and my work will soon be done. Yours might never be. Ing reversed, then, means the period is unfavourable. Step back a little. Allow yourself time to repair the errors of judgement, whether yours or your predecessor's. The rune at the middle of the cross signifies the future outcome. Tyr upright. Tyr is the sacred lance, the just war. It stands for courage, honour and sacrifice. As a guarantee, Tyr left his hand in the mouth of the wolf Fenrir who threatened the world with destruction. The struggle will be long and fierce but crowned with victory. You will need to be loyal, just and, at times, merciless. Keep in mind that pity, like all else, must be merited. Do not waste it on those who show none. I do not know whether you will be present at this victory or whether it is reserved for the one who comes after you. The struggle is already more than a thousand years old. It has been hiding in the shadows for over twelve hundred years.'

For the past few minutes, Leone had by turns been reassured by this reading of the runes and worried that he understood even less than he had before his meeting with the little beggar girl. He had stammered:

'I implore you, speak to me of this struggle!'

'Did you not hear what I said? I know nothing. I have revealed all I know. My task was to interpret this cross.'

'Who entrusted you with it?' Leone had roared, his panic gaining the upper hand.

All of a sudden, the young girl's yellow gaze had fixed on a point behind him and he had turned his head. There had been nothing but a hill planted with olive groves, no menacing shadow. When he had turned back she had vanished, and only the imprint of her ragged dress on the dusty earth and the few coins he had given her proved he had not been dreaming.

He spent a whole week vainly searching for the girl in alleyways, peering inside stalls or churches, without ever glimpsing her frail figure.

*

Through a dogged effort Francesco de Leone had gradually understood the mistake they had all made from the very initiation of the chain, as the Cypriot beggar girl had referred to it. The two birth charts in the Templar Knight's notebook were false. The equatoire used to interpret them was an aberration derived from an obsolete astronomical theory.

The mathematician monk from an Italian monastery – the Vallombroso Monastery[45] – had discovered this truth and, fearing the consequences, hastened to conceal it. He had died soon afterwards in a crypt, having mysteriously fallen and cracked his skull open against a pillar. His notebook was never found. Until the day that the thief, Humeau, catering to the demands of his purchasers, had drawn up a small inventory of books in the Pope's private library. Leone had approached him as a buyer, bidding against another anonymous customer. Gachelin Humeau played the two off against each other, coaxing, using delaying tactics and, above all, pushing up the price. Which one should he sell to? He procrastinated. He wanted to please everybody, but after all business was business. With a movement so swift as to barely give the man time to blink, Leone had pulled his dagger, grabbed the scoundrel by the throat and, pressing the sharp blade against his neck, had announced in a clear, calm voice:

'How much for your life? Quick, name a price and then add it to the offer I just made. Is the other bid still higher?'

These were not empty threats and Humeau knew it. He had begrudgingly handed over the stolen work – for an exorbitant sum nonetheless.

Do not waste your pity on those who show none, the little girl had warned.

Leone was stupefied upon reading the treatise. There were other distant and invisible planets, whose existence had been proven by these calculations. Two giant stars,[46] named by their discoverer *GE1* and *GE2*, and an asteroid that was certainly smaller than the Moon but massive[47] nonetheless, which he had denominated *As*. A further shocking revelation affirmed that the Earth was not fixed at the centre of the firmament but turned around the Sun.

For weeks on end the Knight had busied himself with painstaking and complex calculations. He had been obliged to go back to the positions of the planets in the signs and houses of the zodiac in order to discover the dates of birth of two people, or two events, whose star charts were almost identical. His deductions were still incomplete, for he lacked the necessary data to calculate *GE2*'s revolutions. However, he had reached a new stage in his clarifications that had allowed him to discover one date: the first decan of Capricorn, 25 December. Christmas Day. Agnès de Souarcy's birthday.

Ing, the rune indicating error, had been overcome. Leone was waiting for a sign that would allow him to complete his astral charts, and, more importantly, to understand their vital meaning. He was also waiting for his 'powerful, hidden' enemies to show themselves. He could sense them unseen in the shadows, ready to strike. They had already dealt one deadly blow, and Benoît XI had been felled by it, of that Leone was certain.

*

He walked over to one of the book cabinets and gave it a sharp push. The high shelves slid along invisible rails, revealing a flagstone that was wider and lighter than the others. A niche had been hollowed out below. There was the Vallombroso manuscript, carefully wrapped in a piece of linen coated in beeswax to protect it from damp and insects. Underneath was a second volume he had glanced through only once, the acid saliva of nausea rising up his gorge. He had purchased it from Humeau with the intention of destroying it, and then something had dissuaded him. It was a work of necromancy written by a certain Justus and filled with loathsome instructions whose aim was not to communicate with the dead, but to torment them, to enslave them, turning them into servants of the living. Leone felt a ripple of disgust each time he saw the cover, and yet he kept putting off the moment when he would consign it to the flames, reducing it to mere ashes.

He re-read the Vallombroso treatise on astronomy for the thousandth time, and for the thousandth time studied the annotations Eustache and he had written in the large notebook. It was then that a tiny detail caught his attention. He walked over to the wall where the high arrow slits afforded a little more light and took a closer look.

What was the faint smudge of ink that resembled a finger mark?

Behind him a rustling sound, elegant and feminine, made his heart skip a beat. No, it was not the unknown woman in the church from his dream, it was his aunt. He swivelled round.

'You made me jump, aunt. Have you consulted this notebook in my absence?'

'You know perfectly well how uneasy I feel about those hieroglyphs.'

'They are not hieroglyphs, they are secret runes.'

'They are forbidden by the Church.'

'Like many things.'

'Are you blaspheming, my nephew?'

'Blasphemy exists only against God, and I would rather die than allow it. What do you think would befall us if our quest became known?'

'I do not know . . . The purity of it would convince them and make them rejoice.'

'Do you really think so?'

'Why this sarcasm, nephew?'

He looked at her for a moment, bowing his head before replying:

'Do you really believe that those who wield such power and wealth would gladly let it slip through their fingers?'

'I still have hopes that the Light will impose itself of its own accord, Francesco.'

'How I envy you.'

'Benoît died on account of this Light, Francesco. And many more before him,' she reminded him in a sad voice.

'You are right. Forgive me, aunt.'

'You know I am incapable of being cross with you, my dear.'

He paused for a moment before enquiring:

'Are you absolutely certain that Madame de Souarcy was born on 25 December?'

She stifled a chuckle before replying:

'Do you think me an old fool, my sweet boy? I have told you

repeatedly that she was born on Christmas Day. It is a significant enough date, despite its pagan origins,[48] for it to be remarked upon and remembered . . . I came to make sure you have everything you need. I must leave you now – there are many things that require my attention. I shall see you presently, nephew.'

'Farewell, aunt.'

The Abbess gone, Leone trawled through the many notes he and Eustache had scribbled on the notebook's pages. All of a sudden his blood ran cold and for a moment he felt so dizzy he nearly lost his balance.

Somebody had torn out the last but one page of the notebook!

A moment of sheer panic made his mind go blank. Somebody had consulted the notebook. But who? He was certain his aunt was telling the truth when she said she had not looked at it during his absence. Who then? One of the other nuns? Nobody else knew of the library's existence.

He had been mistaken. Ing, the rune signifying error, was not pointing to the erroneous astral charts, but to his unforgivable stupidity.

The last two deceptively blank pages contained the calculations and diagrams – the most secret notes of all.

Did the thief know this?

Since Nicolas Florin's arrival, Éleusie de Beaufort had tried her best to perform her usual tasks in the belief that her diligence would be a comfort to her girls. Were it not for this wish to carry on as though nothing in their lives had changed, she would have remained in her chambers despising her cowardice.

She was on her way to the steam room, walking unhurriedly, when her attention was caught by two figures standing side by side. Without really knowing why, the Abbess flattened herself against the wall behind one of the pillars holding up the vaulted ceiling, and watched the scene taking place twenty yards away. Her heart was pounding and she pressed her hand against her mouth, convinced that her quickened breathing could be heard at the other end of the abbey.

Florin. Florin was leaning over and whispering something to one of the sisters. The Inquisitor's back obscured the listener's identity. A few seconds passed, which seemed to her like an eternity. At last the two figures separated and the Inquisitor promptly disappeared down the right-hand corridor leading to the relics' chamber.

The person to whom he had been speaking remained motionless for a moment, and then appeared to make up her mind, turning towards the gardens.

It was Emma de Pathus, the schoolmistress.

Hôtel d'Estouville, Rue de la Harpe, Paris, August 1304

Esquive d'Estouville put down the phoenix she had started embroidering many months before. The piece of linen cloth was fraying in places and covered in poor stitching that was coming loose. Needlework had always bored her, but it gave her the appearance of composure.

The young woman let out a sigh and her charming face became tense with frustration. It was such a long wait, and she was so eager to join her beautiful archangel, her Hospitaller. Her frustration was mixed with a curious happiness. To suffer a little each day for the one who would suffer so much. He did not know it yet and it was better that way.

When would she see him again, when would she permit herself to see him?

Esquive's lady's maid knocked at the door of the little room in the townhouse where she spent most of her time, when she was not handling weapons.

The maid was carrying a sumptuous cream-coloured dress over her arm.

'It's ready, Madame. I thought you'd want to see it straight away.'

'You were right, Hermione. Let us look at this marvel I have been waiting for three weeks to see.'

Hermione approached her, avoiding as always the young Comtesse's gaze, which made her so uneasy — those huge amber, almost yellow, eyes. The eyes of a little wild cat.

Clairets Abbey, Perche, September 1304

THE bell for prime had sounded, but he would not be there. Nicolas Florin was in too much of a good mood to risk ruining it by inflicting a service upon himself. Thirty-one days, thirty-one days exactly. Thank God she had neither confessed to nor atoned for her sins. She was all his and nothing, no one, could save her now.

The armed escort had arrived the evening before and was just waiting for a sign from him. Agnès de Souarcy would be escorted in a few hours by carriage to the headquarters of the Inquisition at Alençon. Once inside its walls no one would hear her supplications or her screams, however loud.

He stretched with contentment as he lay on his bed trying to envisage Comte Artus's confusion. Soon, everybody would dread the new Inquisitor's power.

A momentary doubt clouded his optimism. The Abbess seemed to him changed of late, as though some unexpected certainty had all of a sudden allayed her fears. What of it! She might be an Abbess but she was only another female.

He gave a satisfied laugh. His female was so pretty, the one he had been coveting for a whole month now. He imagined her receiving him later, wringing her hands, wiping away her tears, her face pale and distraught with fear. Even though she had no idea to what extent her terror was justified.

A wave of voluptuousness washed over him, leaving him breathless with joy.

He would play for a long time, for a very long time. He closed his eyes as an explosion of pleasure wrenched his belly.

Manoir de Souarcy-en-Perche, September 1304

AGNÈS read one last time Clément's brief message, which Comte Artus had ordered his men-at-arms to bring, before casting it reluctantly into the hearth. She so wished she could have kept it with her.

The young woman had not been mistaken and Clément had taken great care with his words in case the missive fell into the wrong hands.

> *My dear Madame,*
>
> *I miss you so. I grow more anxious by the day. The Comte is very good to me and has allowed me access to his wonderful library. His doctor, a Jew from Bologna, who is not only a physic but a great scholar, is teaching me, among other things, about medicine.*
>
> *I am very worried, Madame. Since you will not allow me to come to you, I beg you to take the greatest care of yourself, in every possible way.*
>
> *Your life is mine.*
>
> *Your Clément.*

The Comte had also scribbled a few cryptic lines, intended only to be understood by the addressee.

Everything is being done to try to frustrate this dreadful deception. Everything. Take heart, Madame, you are dear to us.

Your respectful, Artus, Comte d'Authon.

Adeline burst into the great hall without troubling to knock. She was weeping and stammering:

'He's here . . . He's here, the black monk, the evil one.'

And she fled, as though her life, too, were in danger.

'Madame?'

'I was waiting for you, Monsieur.'

Agnès turned to face him, her back to the hearth. Florin's good mood faltered. She was not weeping. Nor was she wringing her hands in dread.

'I am ready. You may take me.'

'Have you nothing . . .'

She interrupted him sharply:

'I have nothing to confess. I have not sinned and I intend to prove it. Let us go, Monsieur, it is a long way to Alençon.'

APPENDIX I
HISTORICAL REFERENCES

Abu-Bakr-Mohammed-ibn-Zakariya al-Raʒi, 865–932, known as Rhazes. Philosopher, alchemist, mathematician and prodigious Persian physician to whom we owe, amongst other things, the discovery and the first description of allergy-based asthma and hay fever. He demonstrated the connection of the latter with certain flowers. He is considered to be the forefather of experimental medicine and successfully performed cataract operations.

Anagni, the Outrage at, September 1303. Pope Boniface VIII, who challenged the authority of Philip IV (the Fair), was 'detained' in Anagni. Guillaume de Nogaret happened to be in Anagni; he had come to ask the Pope to convoke a general council in Lyon. The origin of the conflict between Pope and King was the tithe that Philip was trying to impose on the French clergy to support his war effort against the English. (Some historians think, on the other hand, that Guillaume de Nogaret orchestrated the sequestration of Boniface on the orders of Philip the Fair, with the aid of the Colonna brothers, who entertained a personal hatred for the sovereign pontiff.)

Archimedes, 287–212 BC. Greek mathematical genius and inventor to whom we owe very many mathematical advances, including the famous hydrostatic principle, which is named after him. He also gave the first precise definition of the number pi, and set himself up to be the advocate of experimentation and demonstration. Archimedes is credited with being the author of several inventions, including the catapult, the Archimedes screw, the pulley and the cog.

A palimpsest was recently auctioned at Christie's for US$2 million. It recounted the progress made by Archimedes in getting to grips with infinity. The document, which had been overwritten with the copy of a religious text, also contained the first crucial steps towards differential calculus, a branch of mathematics that had to be re-invented after the Renaissance. It is rumoured that Bill Gates was the successful bidder for the document, which has been donated to the Walters Art Museum in Baltimore, where it has been subjected to sophisticated analysis.

Ballads of Marie de France. Twelve ballads popularly attributed to a certain Marie, originally from France but living at the English court. Some historians believe she was a daughter of Louis VII or of the Comte de Meulan. The ballads were written before 1167 and Marie's fables around 1180. Marie de France was also the author of a novel *Le Purgatoire de Saint-Patrice.*

Benoît XI, Pope, Nicolas Boccasini, 1240–1304. Relatively little is known about him. Product of a very poor background, Boccasini, a Dominican, remained humble throughout his life. One of the few anecdotes about him demonstrates this: when his mother paid him a visit after his election, she made herself look pretty for her son. He gently explained that her outfit was too ostentatious and that he preferred women to be simply dressed. Known for his conciliatory temperament, Boccasini, who had been Bishop of Ostia, tried to mediate in the disagreements between the Church and Philip the Fair, but he showed his disapproval of Guillaume de Nogaret and the Colonna brothers. He died after eight months of the pontificate, on 7 July 1304, poisoned by figs or dates.

Boniface VIII, Pope, Benedetto Caetani, *c.* 1235–1303. Cardinal and legate in France, then pope. He was a passionate defender of pontifical theocracy, which was opposed to the new authority of the State. He was openly hostile to Philip the Fair from 1296 onwards and the affair continued even after his death – France attempted to try him posthumously.

Carcassonne. In August 1303, when Philip the Fair paid a visit to the town, its population rebelled against the Inquisition, encouraged by the campaign of Bernard Délicieux, a Franciscan who was passionately opposed to the Dominicans and their Inquisition. He even took part in a plot to stir up the Languedoc against Philip. He was arrested several times and ended his days in prison in 1320.

Catharism. From *katharoi*, meaning 'the pure ones' in Greek. The Cathar movement originated in Bulgaria towards the end of the tenth century and spread as a result of the preachings of a priest named Bogomile. Viewed as heretics, the Cathars were pursued by the Inquisition. Very broadly Catharism was a form of Dualism. It contrasted irreversible Evil (matter, the world) with God and Goodness (perfection). Catharism condemned society, the family, the clergy, but also the Eucharist and the communion of saints. Although not definitive on the point, the first Cathars denied that Christ was human, seeing him as an angel sent to earth. Catharism was defined by an extreme purity, which encompassed, along with sexual abstinence, a ban on meat-eating, and was particularly appealing to the well-off and the cultivated who were suffering from spiritual malaise. From 1200 onwards the Catholic Church struggled to suppress the Cathars, after having condemned them in 1119 in Toulouse. The 'crusades' against the Albigensians followed. Simon de Montfort led the 'crusaders' from 1209 to 1215. This bloody war, taken up by the Inquisition, did not end until the surrender of the last strongholds of the Cathars, notably Montségur in 1244. The Cathar Church was never to recover from that, despite the attraction its ideal of purity exercised on the mendicant orders. Catharism died out around 1270.

Clairets Abbey, Orne. Situated on the edge of Clairets Forest, in the parish of Masle, the abbey was built by a charter issued in July 1204 by Geoffroy III, Comte du Perche, and his wife, Mathilde of Brunswick, sister of Emperor Otto IV. The abbey's construction took seven years and finished in 1212. Its consecration was co-signed by the commander of the Knights Templar, Guillaume d'Arville, about whom little is known. The abbey is only open to Bernardine nuns of the Cistercian order, who have the right to all forms of seigneurial justice.

Galen, Claudius, 131–210, a Greek born in Asia Minor, was one of the greatest scientists of antiquity. He became chief physician to the gladiator school in Pergamum, and allegedly made use of 'volunteers' to perfect his knowledge of surgery. He served as physician to Marcus Aurelius and treated the Emperor's two sons, Commodus and Sextus. Amongst other discoveries, Galen described how the nervous system works and its role in muscular activity, and the circulation of blood through veins and arteries. His most important discovery was that arteries carry blood and not air, as had previously been believed. He also demonstrated that it is the brain that controls the voice.

The Hospitallers of Saint John of Jerusalem were recognised by Pope Pascal III in 1113. Unlike the other soldier orders, the original function of the Hospitallers was charitable. It was only later that they assumed a military function. After the Siege of Acre in 1291, the Hospitallers withdrew to Cyprus and then Rhodes, and finally Malta. The order was governed by a Grand-Master, elected by the general chapter made up of dignitaries. The chapter was subdivided into provinces, governed in their turn by priors. Unlike the Templars and in spite of their great wealth, the Hospitallers always enjoyed a very favourable reputation, no doubt because of their charitable works, which they never abandoned and because of the humility of their members.

The Knights Templar. The order was created in 1118 in Jerusalem by the knight Hugues de Payns and other knights from Champagne and Burgundy. The order was officially endorsed by the Church at the Council of Troyes in 1128, having been championed by Bernard of Clairvaux. The order was led by a Grand-Master, whose authority was backed up by dignitaries. The order owned considerable assets (3,450 chateaux, fortresses and houses in 1257). With its system of transferring money to the Holy Lands, the order acted in the thirteenth century as one of Christianity's principal bankers. After the Siege of Acre in 1291 – which was in the end fatal to the order – the Templars almost all withdrew to the West. Public opinion turned against them and they were regarded as indolent profiteers. Various expressions of the period bear witness to this. For example, 'Going to the Temple' was a euphemism for going to a brothel. When the Grand-Master, Jacques de Molay, refused to merge the Templars with the Hospitallers, the Templars were arrested on 13 October 1307. An investigation followed, confessions were obtained (in the case of Jacques de Molay, some historians believe, with the use of torture), followed by retractions. Clément V, who feared Philip the Fair for various unrelated reasons, passed a decree suppressing the order on 22 March 1312. Jacques de Molay again stood by the retraction of his confession and on 18 March 1314 was burnt at the stake along with other Templars. It is generally agreed that the seizure of the Templars' assets and their redistribution to the Hospitallers cost Philip the Fair more money than it gained him.

The Medieval Inquisition. It is important to distinguish the Medieval Inquisition from the Spanish Inquisition. The repression and intolerance of the latter were incomparably more violent than anything known in France. Under the leadership of

Tomas de Torquemada alone, there were more than two thousand deaths recorded in Spain.

The Medieval Inquisition was at first enforced by the bishops. Pope Innocent III (1160–1216) set out the regulations for the inquisitorial procedure in the papal bull *Vergentis in senium* of 1199. The aim was not to eliminate individuals – as was proved by the Fourth Council of the Lateran, called by Innocent III a year before his death, which emphasised that it was forbidden to inflict the Ordeal on dissidents. (The Ordeal or 'judgement of God' was a trial by fire, water or the sword to test whether an accused person was a heretic or not.) What the Pope was aiming for was the eradication of heresies that threatened the foundation of the Church by promoting, amongst other things, the poverty of Christ as a model way to live – a model that was obviously rarely followed if the vast wealth earned by most of the monasteries from land tax is anything to go by. Later the Inquisition was enforced by the Pope, starting with Gregory IX, who conferred inquisitorial powers on the Dominicans in 1232 and, in a lesser way, on the Franciscans. Gregory's motives in reinforcing the powers of the Inquisition and placing them under his sole control were entirely political. He was ensuring that on no account would Emperor Frederick II be able to control the Inquisition for reasons that had nothing to do with spirituality. It was Innocent IV who took the ultimate step in authorising recourse to torture in his papal bull *Ad extirpanda* of 15 May 1252. Witches as well as heretics were then hunted down by the Inquisition.

The real impact of the Inquisition has been exaggerated. There were relatively few Inquisitors to cover the whole territory of the kingdom of France and they would have had little effect had they not received the help of powerful lay people and benefited from numerous denunciations. But thanks to their ability to excuse each other for their faults, certain Inquisitors were guilty of terrifying atrocities that sometimes provoked riots and scandalised many prelates.

In March 2000, roughly eight centuries after the beginnings of the Inquisition, Pope John Paul II asked God's pardon for the crimes and horrors committed in its name.

Mendicant Convents. They were founded sometime between the twelfth and thirteenth centuries and were distinguished by their refusal to own land in common, promoting the return to evangelical poverty. They very quickly attracted a significant level of patronage, which led to a rivalry with the secular clergy, who considered that they had lost several of their regular donors to the mendicant orders. This conflict led to the suppression of many of the mendicant orders in 1274 (by the Second Council of Lyon); only the Carmelites, the Hermits of Saint Augustine, the Dominicans and the Franciscans were officially recognised by the Council. The Celestines joined the mendicant orders in 1294.

Nogaret, Guillaume de, c. 1270–1313. Nogaret was a professor of civil law and taught at Montpellier before joining Philip the Fair's Council in 1295. His responsibilities rapidly grew more widespread. He involved himself, at first more or less clandestinely, in the great religious debates that were shaking France, for example the trial of Bernard Saisset. Nogaret progressively emerged from the shadows and played a pivotal role in the campaign against the Knights Templar and the King's struggle with Pope Boniface VIII. Nogaret was of unshakeable faith and great intelligence. He would go on to become the King's Chancellor, and although he was displaced for a while by Enguerran de Marigny, he took up the seal again in 1311.

Philip the Fair, 1268–1314. The son of Philip III (known as Philip the Bold) and Isabelle of Aragon. With his consort Joan of Navarre, he had three sons who would all become kings of France – Louis X (Louis the Stubborn), Philip V (Philip the Tall) and Charles IV (Charles the Fair). He also had one daughter Isabelle whom he married to Edward II of England. Philip was brave and an excellent war leader, but he also had the reputation of being inflexible and harsh. It is now generally agreed, however, that perhaps that reputation has been overstated, since contemporary accounts relate that Philip the Fair was manipulated by his advisers who flattered him whilst mocking him behind his back.

Philip the Fair is best known for the major role he played in the suppression of the Knights Templar, but he was above all a reforming king whose objective was to free the politics of the French kingdom from papal interference.

Robert le Bougre, also known as Robert the Small, was possibly Bulgarian in origin. He originally embraced Catharism and acceded to the highest rank and became an expert in that faith. But he later converted to Catholicism and became a Dominican monk. Gregory IX (1227–1241) valued him for his extraordinary ability to expose heretics. He seemed capable of trapping even the most skilled at concealment. In 1235 he was appointed Inquisitor General of Charité-sur-Loire, after his predecessor Conrad de Marbourg was assassinated, and was then responsible for cruel mistreatment and horrifying torture. The Archbishops of Sens and Rheims, amongst others, scandalised by the accounts that were reaching their ears, protested against Robert's behaviour. After the first written report on the methods used by Robert, he was stripped of his powers in 1234. Yet he returned to favour in August of the following year, and immediately took up his 'amusements' again. It was not until 1241 that he was definitively removed from power and imprisoned for life.

Roman de la Rose. A long allegorical poem written by two authors in two stages. Guillaume de Lorris started writing in around 1230 the love song of a courtier. However, the part written by Jean de Meung between 1270 and 1280 is much more ironic, not to say cynical and misogynistic, with some barely disguised licentiousness. Jean de Meung did not hold back from attacking the mendicant orders by creating the character of a monk, named 'The Pretender'.

Saisset, Bernard, ?–1311. The first Bishop of Pamiers. Very unwisely, he tried to challenge the legitimacy of Philip the Fair's claim to the French throne, going as far as to hatch a plot to install the Comte de Foix as sovereign in Languedoc. Saisset refused to appear at his trial before the King, preferring to rely on the support of Boniface VIII to save him. In the end Philip the Fair exiled Saisset, who died in Rome.

Valois, Charles de, 1270–1325. Philip the Fair's only full brother. The King showed Charles a somewhat blind affection all his life and conferred on him missions that were probably beyond his capabilities. Charles de Valois, who was father, son, brother, brother-in-law, uncle and son-in-law to kings and queens, dreamt all his life of his own crown, which he never obtained.

Villeneuve, Arnaud de, or Arnoldus de Villanova, *c.* 1230–1311, born in Montpellier. Probably one of the most prestigious scientists of the thirteenth and fourteenth centuries. Raised in Spain by Dominican monks, he became a doctor, astrologer, alchemist and lawyer of very determined character who sparked controversy and did not hesitate to launch attacks on the mendicant orders. He only escaped the clutches of the Inquisition because he cured Boniface VIII, who pardoned him for his 'errors'. He remained the Pope's doctor until his death, then became doctor to Benoit XI, and then Clément V, all the while working on secret missions for the King of Aragon.

APPENDIX II
GLOSSARY

Liturgical Hours

Aside from Mass – which was not strictly part of them – ritualised prayers, as set out in the sixth century by the Regulation of Saint Benoît, were to be said several times a day. They regulated the rhythm of the day. Monks and nuns were not permitted to dine before nightfall, that is until after vespers. This strict routine of prayers was largely adhered to until the eleventh century, when it was reduced to enable monks and nuns to devote more time to reading and manual labour.

Matins: at 2.30 am or 3 am.

Lauds: just before dawn, between 5 am and 6 am.

Prime: around 7.30 am, the first prayers of the day, as soon as possible after sunrise and just before Mass.

Terce: around 9 am.

Sext: around midday

None: between 2 pm and 3 pm in the afternoon.

Vespers: at the end of the afternoon, at roughly 4.30 pm or 5 pm, at sunset.

Compline: after Vespers, the last prayers of the day, sometime between 6 pm and 8 pm.

Measurements

It is quite hard to translate measurements into their modern-day equivalents, as the definitions varied from region to region.

League: about two and a half miles.

Ell: about 45 inches in Paris, 37 inches in Arras.

Foot: as today.

APPENDIX III
NOTES

[1] Jesus, we adore you.

[2] The age of consent was thirteen for girls and fourteen for boys.

[3] The customary usufruct of the deceased husband's properties awarded to widows. In the Paris region this was half of the husband's properties and in Normandy a third.

[4] Meat was not eaten on Wednesdays, Fridays, Saturdays, feast days, or during Lent.

[5] The dynastic name of Plantagenet was a nickname given to one of Edward's ancestors, Geoffroy, Comte d'Anjou, who transformed his lands into moors, planting, among other things, broom (Fr. *genêts*) in order to be able to hunt.

[6] Water closet.

[7] Practice of offering female children to convents.

[8] The origin of the words 'saccharose' (the chemical name for sugar) and 'saccharine'.

[9] Traditional word denoting beehives.

[10] It was believed up until the end of the seventeenth century that the swarms surrounded a king and not a queen bee.

[11] The Knights of Justice and Grace belonged to the Order of the Hospitallers of Saint John of Jerusalem.* A Knight of Justice must boast at least eight quarters of nobility in France and Italy and sixteen in Germany. The title Knight of Grace was bestowed on merit alone.

[12] Friars were obliged to carry this when they travelled. Any friar unable to provide this pass when asked for it by a commander was summarily arrested and judged by the order.

[13] Whosoever washes himself in the divine blood purifies his sins and acquires a beauty resembling that of the angels.

[14] Unlike physics, surgeons, who were most often barbers, were looked down upon.

[15] 12 June 1218.

[16] The production of paper made of flax or hemp, although an invention of the Chinese, remained in the hands of the Muslims. In that capacity Christendom rejected it until the Italians invented a new method of fabrication towards the middle of the thirteenth century.

[17] A non-cloistered nun responsible for the abbey's relations with the outside world.

[18] A nun who answered directly to the Abbess and the prioress. Her function was to take care of the abbey's provisions and food stocks. She was authorised to buy and sell land and she collected tolls. She also took care of the barns, the mills, the breweries, the fish ponds and so on.

[19] Place where visitors were received.

[20] So be it. Have pity on us. Dreaded day when the universe will be reduced to ashes.

[21] 'But immediately after the tribulation of those days the sun shall be darkened, and the moon shall not give her light, and the stars shall fall from heaven, and the powers of the heavens shall be shaken' (Matthew 24: 29).

[22] The nun responsible for educating children and novices was the only one authorised to raise a hand to them or mete out punishment.

[23] A sort of short, sleeveless jacket with a buttoned neck, often richly ornamented, which men of stature wore over their short tunics.

[24] And thus appeared the sign of the Son of Man.

[25] Metal refiners whose job it was to beat bars into sheets before selling them on to manufacturers.

[26] Grey-squirrel fur was prized at the time. Two thousand of the small rodents were needed to line one man's coat.

[27] The sexual taboo between blood relations extended even to godparents.

[28] Fine woollen or linen-and-wool garment worn over the chemise.

[29] Probably a forerunner of the hurdy-gurdy.

[30] Wind instrument akin to bagpipes.

[31] Mellow-sounding string instrument.

[32] Uranus, Neptune and Pluto were discovered later.

[33] An apparatus for determining the positions of the planets in the system described by the Greek astronomer Ptolemy (second century BC). This fixed system, which was completely erroneous, was favoured by the Church and as such would remain in force during seventeen centuries.

[34] Guy Faucoi 'le Gros' (in English 'Guy Foulques the Fat'), Pope Clément IV (late twelfth century–1268). A former soldier and jurist.

[35] Inserts depicting a scene often in bold colours.

[36] Large initial letters at the beginning of each chapter or paragraph usually decorated with interlacing.

[37] Stylised decorative ornaments of intertwined leaves and vegetation.

[38] Pigments and binding agents used in the making of inks.

[39] Men were subjected above all to the *strappado* (which consisted in causing the condemned man on the end of a rope to fall repeatedly with all his weight), water and fire; women were generally whipped.

[40] Neither autopsy nor dissection was practised, for religious reasons. Medicine was therefore based on the works of Hippocrates and Galen, professor of anatomy, and to a lesser extent those of Avicenna. Dissections began to be practised at the University of Montpellier in 1340.

[41] Nun charged with keeping the accounts of the abbey's revenues, with overseeing and paying the farrier, entertainers and vets.

[42] Divine Justice. Ordeals of fire and water or verbal duels before a court (the latter unrelated to duels of honour that became widespread during the eleventh century) intended to prove innocence or guilt. Fell largely into disuse by the fifteenth century.

[43] The universe of angels contained three hierarchies.

[44] Built on top of a sixth-century baptistery, Saint-Germain-l'Auxerrois dates back to the twelfth and thirteenth centuries. Of modest size during that era, it would later be enlarged.

[45] Monastery where Galileo studied before going to Pisa to take up medicine.

[46] Uranus and Neptune.

[47] Pluto.

[48] 25 December was originally a feast day of pagans and saturnal plurimillenarians who celebrated the winter solstice. The Church decided around AD 336 to celebrate it as Christ's birthday.

COMING IN MARCH 2009

THE *SECOND* AGNES DE SOUARCY CHRONICLE

THE BREATH OF THE ROSE

Andrea H. Japp

1304. Agnes de Souarcy is in the hands of the Inquisition, accused of demonic acts and harbouring a heretic. Can her allies save Agnes from Nicolas Florin, the Grand Inquisitor?

Meanwhile at Clairets Abbey, the nuns are being poisoned one by one. Is the murderer trying to gain access to the abbey's secret library of manuscripts? Can her allies save Agnes from Nicolas Florin, the Grand Inquisitor?

Drama and mystery combine in this gripping sequel to The Season of the Beast

GALLIC BOOKS

May 2009

978-1-906040-21-5

THE SUN KING RISES

Yves Jégo and Denis Lépée

1661 is a year of destiny for France and its young king, Louis XIV.

Cardinal Mazarin, the prime minister who has governed throughout the king's early years, lies dying. As a fierce power struggle develops to succeed him, a religious brotherhood, guardian of a centuries-old secret, also sees its chance to influence events.

Gabriel de Pontbriand, a young actor, becomes unwittingly involved when documents stolen from Mazarin's palace fall into his hands. The coded papers will alter Gabriel's life forever, and their explosive contents have the power to change the course of history for France and Louis XIV.

Fact and fiction combine in a fast-moving story of intrigue, conspiracy and love set in seventeenth-century France.

'. . . has all the life, spirit and momentum of the best historical novels'
Le Figaro

'The heroes of the book are the stars of the era: Molière, La Fontaine, Colbert . . . a book to savour'
Paris Match

'A suspense-filled mystery, a cross between the Three Musketeers and the Da Vinci Code'
Europe 1

GALLIC BOOKS
978-1-906040-02-4
£7.99

The First Nicolas Le Floch investigation

THE CHÂTELET APPRENTICE

Jean-François Parot
Translated by Michael Glencross

France 1761. Beyond the glittering court of Louis XV and the Marquise de Pompadour at Versailles, lies Paris, a capital in the grip of crime and immorality . . .

A police officer disappears and Nicolas Le Floch, a young recruit to the force, is instructed to find him. When unidentified human remains suddenly come to light, he seems to have a murder investigation on his hands. As the city descends into Carnival debauchery, Le Floch will need all his skill, courage and integrity to unravel a mystery which threatens to implicate the highest in the land.

'A terrific debut . . . brilliantly evokes the casual brutality of life in eighteenth-century France' *Sunday Times*

'Jean-François Parot's evocation of eighteenth-century Paris is richly imagined and full of fascinating historical snippets . . .'
Mail on Sunday

'Has all the twists, turns and surprises the genre demands'
Independent of Sunday

'An engaging murder mystery that picks away at the delicate power balance between king, police and state.' *Financial Times*

GALLIC BOOKS
Paperback
978-1-906040-06-2
£7.99

The Second Nicolas Le Floch Investigation

THE MAN WITH THE LEAD STOMACH

Jean-François Parot

An unusual death during an evening at the Opera reveals something sinister at the heart of the French court . . .

October 1761 finds the newly-promoted Commissioner Le Floch on duty at a Royal performance of Rameau's latest work. Events take a dramatic turn and Nicolas is soon embarked on his second major investigation when the body of a prominent courtier's son is found. The initial evidence points to suicide, but Le Floch's instincts tell him he is dealing with murder of the most gruesome kind.

'. . . the superb Parisian detail and atmosphere . . . truly beguile'
The Times

Gallic Books
Paperback £11.99
978-1-906040-07-9

THE OFFICER'S PREY

A Grande Armée murder featuring Captain Quentin Margont

Armand Cabasson

June 1812. Napoleon begins his invasion of Russia leading to the largest army Europe has ever seen.

But amongst the troops of the Grande Armée is a savage murderer whose bloodlust is not satisfied in battle.

When an innocent Polish woman is brutally stabbed, Captain Quentin Margont of the 84th regiment is put in charge of a secret investigation to unmask the perpetrator. Armed with the sole fact that the killer is an officer, Margont knows that he faces a near-impossible task and the greatest challenge to his military career.

'Combines the suspense of a thriller with the compelling narrative of a war epic' *Le Parisian*

'Cabasson skilfully weaves an intriguing mystery into a rich historical background' *Mail on Sunday*

'. . . an enthralling and unromantic account of Napoleonic war seen from a soldier's perspective' *The Morning Star*

'. . . vivid portrayal of the Grande Armée . . .' *Literary Review*

'Cabasson's atmospheric novel makes a splendid war epic . . .' *The Sunday Telegraph*

GALLIC BOOKS
Paperback
978-1-906040-03-1
£7.99

WOLF HUNT

A Grande Armée murder featuring Captain Quentin Margont

Armand Cabasson

May 1809. The forces of Napoleon's Grande Armée are in
Austria. For young Lieutenant Lukas Relmyer it is hard to
return to the place where he and fellow orphan, Franz were
kidnapped four years earlier. Franz was brutally murdered and
Lukas has vowed to avenge his death.

When the body of another orphan is found on the battlefield,
Captain Quentin Margont and Lukas join forces to track down
the wolf who is prowling once more in the forests of Apern . . .

Winner of The Napoleon Foundation's fiction award 2005

GALLIC BOOKS

978-1-906040-08-6

£7.99